Shortlisted for the Kate O'Brien Award

'A finely observed Irish debut'

Guardian

'Beautifully observed... thrillingly unravels into family secrets and tragedy'

Grazia

'Exquisitely captured... beautifully paced, confident and insightful'

Daily Mail

'This delicately studied tale of an Irish family's turmoil shows how pain can unite us'

Sunday Times Ireland

'Hugely accomplished... makes for a compelling portrait of a woman losing her grip on reality and a perceptive study of enduring grief'

The Herald

'Dramatizes the way death rips through families, destabilizing the fragile structures keeping them in place'

Times Literary Supplement

'Here is a sprightliness and deftness of touch... interspersed with wry and dark humour'

The Bookseller

'Triumphs in its balanced portrayal of family dynamics... gleefully, excruciatingly, uncomfortable'

Irish Independent

'A quite brilliant look at family dynamics and the secrets that fuel dissent'

Irish Examiner

'Sarah Gilmartin is a natural writer: she gives us terrific, complex characters and strong themes, in prose that is fluent and charged with insight'

Anne Enright, Booker Prize-winning author of *The Gathering*

'I loved her clean, forensic writing. Gilmartin is clearly a writer to watch'

Clare Chambers, author of
Women's Prize-longlisted *Small Pleasures*

'Astutely captures the claustrophobia of Irish families – disappointments, rivalry and the need to make everyone happy'

Sinéad Gleeson, author of *Constellations*

'The search is off… Here is an expert writer. Taut, compelling, Enright-esque'

Meg Mason, author of *Sorrow and Bliss*

'Sarah Gilmartin's depiction of an Irish family across the decades leaves the reader in no doubt how complicated love can be. A brilliant debut'

John Boyne, bestselling author of *The Heart's Invisible Furies*

'One of the best Irish debuts I've read this year. A novel of family – full of warmth, insight, tragedy and, ultimately, how to survive it all'

Rick O'Shea

SARAH GILMARTIN is a critic who reviews fiction for the *Irish Times*. She is co-editor of the anthology *Stinging Fly Stories* and has an MFA from University College Dublin. She won Best Playwright at the inaugural Short+Sweet Dublin festival. Her short stories have been published in *The Dublin Review*, *The Tangerine* and *New Irish Writing*. Her story 'The Wife' won the 2020 Máirtín Crawford Award at Belfast Book Festival.

Dinner Party

Sarah Gilmartin

Pushkin Press
71–75 Shelton Street
London WC2H 9JQ

First published by Pushkin Press in 2021
This edition published 2022

1 3 5 7 9 8 6 4 2

ISBN 13: 978-1-91159-058-3

Designed and typeset by Tetragon, London
Printed in the United States of America
www.pushkinpress.com

People eat their dinner, just eat their dinner, and all the while their happiness is taking form, or their lives are falling apart.

ANTON CHEKHOV

DUBLIN

Halloween 2018

WHEN THE GLEESON TWINS were eleven years old, they ran away from home one afternoon. They made it as far as the old mill on the outskirts of town before their mother's red Jeep pulled up beside them in the rough. The girls got into the back without a word. They didn't look at each other, just knew somehow to accept defeat, because most things in life were to be accepted. Later that night, Elaine had woken Kate up, her cold fingers prodding Kate's shoulder across the divide of their single beds. In the soft darkness of the room, Elaine had announced that one day soon they would get off the farm. They would, in fact, get off the island of Ireland entirely and be free to do whatever they wanted in some unknown country with no family ties at all. Kate, who was used to keeping her ideas to herself, especially in the middle of the night when she wanted to go back to sleep, didn't point out that if the twins were together, they would always have family wherever they went. Instead she'd squinted at Elaine, pulled the duvet over her shoulder and rolled in to face her side of the wall.

Every year on her sister's anniversary, Kate thought of that night with useless, superstitious longing. If only she could change it. If only she had said yes, for once. What parts of her she would give to have another chance. Her arms, her legs, her rickety bones. But no—enough—this game helped no one. As the bus back to Raheny stalled in the morning traffic, she tried to focus on the day ahead. She shifted closer to the window, away from her seatmate and his sandwich. With a cool swipe of her hand,

9

she cleared the condensation and looked down at the street, the chalky pavement of College Green and all the people rushing by.

Today was the sixteenth anniversary of her sister's death. An incredible number, but you couldn't argue with numbers—they had no give. This evening the family, or some of the family, were coming to her apartment for dinner. Kate had the day off work to prepare, the recipes laid out on the counter at home, the final few things she needed in the lime green grocery bag at her feet. It wasn't even half eleven. Everything was going to be fine.

At the turn for the Northside quays, the bus missed the lights. A woman in front of Kate said to the person next to her, 'There's so much traffic we're going backwards.' The seatmate agreed and the conversation went relentlessly round, each of them talking over the other, saying the same things, until Kate felt that she might never get off the bus. The windows had fogged again and the vents at her feet piped sour heat up to her face. She popped a button on her coat, elbowing the man beside her by mistake. 'Sorry,' she said. He ignored her and leaned forward for another bite of his breakfast bap. The yolk split, smearing the ketchup like pus into blood. Kate moved as far away from him as she could, which was not very far at all. Her right ear started to ring, a kind of static fuzzing inside her head. Across the aisle, a toddler screamed, his sharp little cries sucking the light right out of the sky.

At Fairview they stopped for more passengers. A group of teenage boys stomped up the stairs, all jerky limbs and stale smoke. The tallest one pulled on a *Scream* mask and lurched at some girls by the stairwell. Kate closed her eyes, drowning out the shrieks. She ran through the evening's recipes in her head, visualizing the photo of the Baked Alaska, the sheen of the meringue, the torched golden tips.

A loud hiccup broke her concentration. The man had finished his bap. Instantly, the teenagers took up the challenge, their frog chorus bouncing hiccups and burps around the deck. The noise, the way they seemed to liquify and fill the space—graffitied satchels, bum fluff, trainers with scraggly laces. Some unknown floor gave way inside her. Reaching for her shopping, her hand touched the man's rucksack and she stood up too quickly, her thigh striking the frame of the seat. 'Excuse me,' she said. 'I'm sorry.' The man made room for her to get out. At the bottom of the stairs, a standing passenger stared at her with dense curiosity. Two women in the disabled bay nudged each other. Kate moved past them, pressed the red button on the side panel and bit into a hangnail while she waited for the Coast Road stop.

Home, finally, she dropped the bags on the couch and kneaded her thigh. The apartment was cold, but she left her coat on a chair all the same, glad to be free of it. Incense from the morning's mass was still on her jumper, woody and cloying. She'd tried to light a candle after the service but the slot snatched her euro without a flicker. Looking over her preparations now, she wondered if it had been a sign. The four settings on the dining table, immaculate last night, seemed cramped and showy in the daylight. The gold-rimmed china her mother had given her for her thirtieth was meant for a grander room. But no, she was being ridiculous—it was just her family coming for dinner. Her two brothers and her sister-in-law, that was it. Peter, the eldest, on his own from Carlow, then Ray and Liz, who could be all over each other or not speaking to each other, depending on the day. They were her family, and she had made them dinner before. They were not hard people to please. And yet. The feeling returned, stronger than before: she could so easily have cancelled. She could have stayed in and drunk a bottle of wine. Three bottles of wine. She could have taken the Luas to Ray's house in Ranelagh and gone trick-or-treating with Liz and the girls. She could have gone home to Cranavon and sat up with Peter and Mammy until the early hours, like she'd done for other anniversaries. Instead Kate had invited them all for dinner, though if you pressed her, she couldn't say exactly when this had happened. Things had been strange for a while now. Life was blurry; each morning the sun rose in a muslin veil. The small stuff was more to the centre, somehow, taking up all the space, blunting her capacities.

In the kitchen, she unloaded her shopping and folded the bag into the bag of bags. She lined up her spoils on the island. Truffle oil from the Arno valley, elastic bands, a pre-carved pumpkin, hand cream, cereal, juniper berries for Liz's G&Ts. She left the pumpkin and cream to one side and put everything else away. On the counter, the recipes in their clear plastic sleeves were shining in the morning sun. Kate looked out the picture window and thought of her sister.

Between the chopping and the mincing and the rolling and the baking, the hours passed quickly. Her last job was to pipe meringue over the ice cream and slot the dessert into the freezer. When she'd finished the spikes, she stood back to admire her creation. She was proud of it, a mad-looking thing like a jester's hat. All at once, the evening stretched in front of her, full of possibility. She opened the window over the sink as wide as it would go and the fresh, salty wind came across the room. Outside the light was low in the sky, a strip of pale blue between two bands of cloud. 'Everything is OK,' she said out loud to no one.

At ten to seven, she rushed into the bedroom and took off the silk dress that had seemed like such a good idea earlier in the week. The olive green did nothing for her complexion, her mother was right. Kate's eyes were the wrong kind of brown, different to Elaine's—their amber warmth, the dark limbal rings around the iris. Non-identical twins. *Fraternal twins*, their mother used to say. If Kate had been able to salvage something of her sister's, it would have been her eyes. These were the kind of terrible thoughts she'd been having for years. There was no one you could tell. The only person who would get it—who would, in fact, have been thrilled to hear it—was dead.

After ransacking the wardrobe, Kate put on her black wrap dress and reapplied concealer over the crusty patch beside her lip, leaving a haw mark as she leaned closer to the mirror. The doorbell gave a jerky ring. She took one last look at her reflection and told herself to move.

At the hall table, she stopped and lit the tea lights in the pumpkin before opening the door.

'Hello! Hello! Hi! How *are* you?'

Everyone spoke at once, then stopped at the same time, and there was a moment, a split second, where Kate thought she might quickly close the door in their faces without them noticing. But no. Her brothers were right there, standing like little-and-large bodyguards on either side of Liz.

'Kate?' said Ray, as if he didn't know her.

Liz looked beyond her into the apartment. She'd had her hair done, the blonde ends feathery.

'You look gorgeous, Liz,' Kate said, ushering them into the hall. 'I love the hur.'

'Sullivan! I'll book you in. You won't know yourself.' Liz left a moist kiss on Kate's cheek.

Ray said, 'Only a thousand euro a go. Extra for the grey bits.' He patted his own hair, which was mostly black and stiff with gel. They all laughed, a trifle too loudly and for too long. The pumpkin light seemed to grow in thin, lambent fingers up the wall.

Kate complimented Liz's blouse only to discover that it was a dress, an all-in-one designed to look like separates.

'Well, now,' said Peter. 'Imagine that.' He was taking an age to undo his wax jacket and Kate wished he would hurry up.

Liz gave a twirl, a flash of silver in the hallway.

'All looks the same to me,' said Ray.

'You're such a gentleman, Raymond.' Liz backhanded his chest. 'I married him for his manners.'

Kate felt like she was holding them to account in the hallway. 'Come in, won't you, come in.'

'I'll take that for you, Liz.' Peter hung up their coats. 'And you, Ray.'

'No!'

They all looked at Ray. His heavy-lidded eyes held some secret or joke, impossible to say which.

'What are you like?' said Liz.

'Sorry.' He pulled the navy sports jacket so that it strained against his shoulders. 'Sorry, I'm a bit cold.'

As they moved down the hall, a saxophone solo came from the living room.

'Is that jazz I hear?' Peter sucked his cheeks in—the sharp bone structure of the Gleeson men, a face that suited the extra flesh of ageing.

'I think so,' Kate said. 'Random playlist.'

'Might you know who it is, Peter?' Ray winked, but then Liz cut across Peter's jazz musing and said she was desperate for gin. She gave Kate a bottle of wine wrapped in purple crêpe paper and headed for the kitchen, Ray in tow.

Kate was left alone with Peter who surprised her with a bear hug, squashing the bottle into her ribs.

'Well,' she smiled as he let go. 'Thanks for coming this evening. I know it was—'

He held up a hand and she said no more. She loved his gestures, which were always so considered and morose.

He stopped at the entrance to the kitchen, sniffing the air. 'Beef,' he said. 'I've a nose for meat. It smells delicious, Kate.

Muy bien.' He massaged the jowly bit under his chin and all she could see was their father. Peter and Daddy, walking the fields of her childhood. They would come back in the evenings, stinking of dung and feed, full of the lightness of the outside world.

'Go on,' she said. 'Get yourself a beer. Dinner will be ready in no time.'

When Kate went into the kitchen, Liz was lifting the foil off the parsnips. 'Look at all this,' she said. 'You've put me to shame. My pauper's stroganoff.'

On the counter, a bowl-shaped glass was full of gin, junipers bobbing.

Kate said, 'Your stroganoff is to die for.'

'You think?'

'Totally.'

'Well, your mother loves it anyway,' Liz smiled. 'We had her with us on Sunday again. She gets the bus now, you know. Flies up the motorway.'

'Mammy—on the bus?'

'What's the point in Raymond driving the whole way down just to bring her back? She was fine about it.'

'How are the girls?' said Kate. 'The messers.'

'They'd a party at the crèche this afternoon.' Liz jiggled the ice in her glass. 'One princess, one skeleton pirate. You can guess who.'

'Lainy the pirate,' said Kate. 'Definitely.'

'And Lia beside her like royalty,' Liz laughed. 'Can you picture it?'

'Aw,' said Kate. 'Show us a photo.'

While Liz found her phone, Kate looked into the living room where her brothers were squashed on her two-seater, staring at a blank television. Fair-haired Peter and dark-haired Ray, the difference decreasing with age. She couldn't hear what Peter was saying but it was probably about his new drainage system. He'd called last night and spent nearly half an hour telling her about the trap and the suction and the way gravity wasn't as simple a concept as everyone thought.

'Here, what are you like?' Liz swiped the wine bottle. 'That's not a drink.' She filled Kate's glass, then walked over to the picture window and looked out at the dark. 'So, any word from your man?'

Kate felt her heart quicken. She would kill her brother and his big mouth. 'What man?' she said. Two months on, she could still see Liam's face on their last night together. Tanned, gorgeous, full of shame. *It's over Kate, it's run its course.* All the its had killed her.

'Ray said something about a break-up. I never even knew! You should have brought him over for the stroganoff.'

'It wasn't anything serious,' Kate smiled. 'Anyway, it's finished.'

But Liz was tapping away on her phone now, mercifully uninterested. 'The bloody babysitter is useless. She was watching something called *Demonic* when we left.'

'Well,' said Kate. 'It is Halloween.'

Liz laughed, sweeping the hair off her graceful neck. She turned on her heel and walked into the living room.

Kate took the scallops out of the fridge, the silver bloom on the flesh disappearing when she removed the cling film. The pan hissed on the hob and she quickly dressed the plates with rocket. As she waited for the scallops to caramelize, she tipped half her wine into the sink. Inside she could hear Peter and Liz arguing about childcare, and she waited for Liz's spiel about the twins and her sacrifices and the cost of the crèche. No, she stopped herself, that wasn't fair. She didn't know why she was being so harsh tonight—poor Liz who'd done nothing but compliment her efforts since she'd arrived. Kate placed three fat scallops on each plate and then took one off her own and put it on Peter's.

'This is real china, Raymond.' Liz was examining a side plate as Kate approached the table. 'Did you nick these from herself? I swear I won't tell.'

'Don't touch the good china!' Ray caught Kate's eye and they both laughed.

Liz poked a scallop with her fork. 'What are we eating anyway?'

'Bivalves,' Peter announced. 'You know they make their own shells? The internal organs do the business. They secrete this substance.'

'Fascinating,' Liz said.

'Just scallops,' said Kate, sitting down.

Liz reached for the bread rolls. 'Very fancy.'

'They're delish, Katie.' Ray beamed at her. 'I'm loving the purée.'

'Is that what that is?' Liz peered into it, searching for pond life. 'There's a woody taste.'

'Truffle oil.' Peter shook his head at the ignorance.

'If it isn't Carlow's finest foodie,' Liz said.

They all laughed, even Peter, but Kate felt bad as he reddened and pulled at the collar of his check shirt.

'How are your Spanish classes going, Peter?' she said.

'Oh, muy bien,' he said. 'Muy bien.'

She wondered if that was his repertoire. Well, it had only been a few weeks.

Ray said, 'These are the nicest scallops I've ever had.'

Kate cut through the jellied centre of one. She placed a sliver on her tongue but couldn't taste the delicate flesh through the butter. She looked back at the couch and thought she could smell it on the cushions. 'I used too much butter,' she said.

'Nonsense,' Peter said. 'Good Irish butter. Nothing better for you.' Ray gave him a look over the bread basket. Kate cut another slice, and another, nudging the end of it under the rocket as Liz reached across her for the wine. Her perfume smelled like lilies on the way out and just as Kate had the thought, she noticed that Liz's earrings were flowers too, big silver daisies that covered her lobes, and then, even funnier still, there was another kind of flower, a little pink rose, a logo really, on the breast pocket of her dress. Kate had to get away from the table to stop herself from laughing. She went to the speakers on the mantelpiece, feeling dizzy the closer she got to the music, the track shifting suddenly into a faster chorus. Turned the volume down and up again, wishing she'd left it alone. When she went back to the table, the light felt lower than before—a softer texture to everything, the swish of Liz's hair, the folds in the napkins.

First to finish, Peter left his cutlery in the centre of the plate, shaking his head at the offer of another bread roll. There was a sheen on his forehead and Kate wondered if the room was too hot. Ray still had his jacket on, open now over a crisp white shirt.

'Fair dues, Kate,' said Peter. 'It's a lovely idea to ask us here tonight.'

Liz nodded. 'Away from those bloody trick-or-treaters. I swear, they bus them into the neighbourhood every year.'

'I meant for Elaine.' Peter raised his glass. 'To remember our sister Elaine.'

He gave the toast much louder than necessary and it rang out solemnly.

'To Elaine,' they echoed.

'Mammy should be here with us too,' Peter said. 'We had words this morning, I'll admit it.'

Kate nearly spilled her wine, catching the stem of the glass just in time. She looked across the table at Ray, similarly dumbfounded, though he recovered first, as usual.

'Say that again, Peter, will you?'

'I've said what I wanted to say.'

'That our mother, Bernadette Gleeson, is in the wrong?'

'Don't act the blaggard, Ray.'

'The blaggard!'

'Words were exchanged between Mammy and me,' said Peter. 'But it was not to be. I'll say no more about it.' He closed his eyes for a second, his thick blond lashes confirming the end of the conversation.

Kate wondered how she would have felt if her mother had shown up as a surprise guest. She pictured her sitting at the table in her cream wool two-piece and emerald teardrop earrings, her hair in the rigid platinum bob that was never greasy, not even if she didn't wash it for a week. Her face would be pale with powder, two lightly pinked cheeks offsetting her eyes. She would be immaculate as always and the imaginary effort of it gave Kate a lump in her throat.

'Earth to Kate?' Ray waved a hand in front of her face.

'Sorry,' she said. 'I knew Mammy wouldn't come, but thanks for trying, Peter.' Her mother had never been to the apartment, said it was too far a trip for public transport, which implied that it was Kate's fault for still not knowing how to drive at thirty-two, and in a way, it was. Kate stood to clear the plates. She could smell the sweetness of the meat starting to crisp.

'Peter, you tried.' Ray pursed his lips. 'And look, won't we have a better night without her?'

'Let's not,' Peter said.

Ray said, 'Come on, you of all people.'

'Yes, I'm the one—'

'We have her every Sunday,' Ray said.

'Four children she had.' Peter frowned. 'That's not nothing.'

'She'd have monopolized the evening. It would have been Dinner Party: A Tragedy.' Ray tried to bow in his seat.

Liz laughed. 'Or Halloween Dinner: A Massacre.'

'On tonight of all nights.' Peter grasped his napkin. 'Have ye no heart?'

Ray held up his hands. 'Not another word, I promise.' As Kate set off with the plates, Liz gave a little snort.

Stacking the dishwasher, Kate felt guilty. There was more to her mother than Ray would allow. It would be easier, in fact, if she was a monster. Though he was right that she was insufferable at mealtimes. Kate remembered so many meals at home, years and years of meals, where the food mimicked real food in everything but taste, and nothing got done, not a slab of yellowing butter in a dish, without an explanation of the effort that went into it. And nowadays, although Peter did the cooking, perhaps because he did the cooking, Mammy announced herself in other ways. Ray called it The Noise, her ability to hijack whatever conversation was unfolding—the price of cattle, the Middle East, the various accolades of her own grandchildren—and turn it into some story involving numerous people that none of them knew.

Kate slammed the dishwasher door shut and took a deep breath, five seconds in and out. She reminded herself that her mother was down in Carlow, bothering no one.

The timer pinged for the root vegetables. As she bent for the oven, the red light shone into her eye. Behind her, Ray appeared with the bread basket and some stray cutlery balancing on top. A fork clinked to the floor.

'Whoops, sorry.' Ray almost dropped the basket.

'It's only a fork.' Kate picked it up, wiped a streak from the herringbone tiles.

They came face to face when she stood. The skin on his nose was porous, dozens of tiny black dots.

'Remember what she was like?' he said.

'Not tonight, Ray.'

'OK,' he said. 'Sorry.' He left the cloth in the sink. 'Here, Kate. Are you OK? I mean, this year especially, with your man and all.'

'You know his name.'

'Liam the Shithead.'

Kate smiled in spite of herself. 'You shouldn't have told Liz.'

'She gets all sorts of things out of me.'

'You didn't tell her he was married?'

'Jesus, no.' He lowered his voice. 'Did you hear from the wife again?'

Kate remembered the call from Joanna, the dexterous, violent eloquence of her. 'Once was enough.'

Ray tipped the salad into the bin. 'Well, at least it's done. Over. Those scallops were something else by the way. Did you get enough?'

Kate pretended not to hear. Her brother stooped to help her manoeuvre the Wellington out of the oven. The pastry was golden, just about to flake. The layers held their shape as she lifted it from the tray. It was the best pastry she'd ever made. A feeling of pure bliss came over her at the tiny pastry cow she'd carved onto the top for Peter.

'Wow!' said Ray. 'Will I ring the Michelin crowd?'

'It's kind of pretty, isn't it?'

'Kind of? You're an artist.' Ray moved away as she arranged the plates.

The smell of the meat, salty sweet in its buttery blanket, wafted through the kitchen. Sticking the wooden spoon into the gravy on the hob, she broke the skin that had started to form. The liquid shimmered as the bits dissolved.

'We never see you any more, Katie.' Ray took a beer from the fridge. 'You should come round more. The girls miss you.'

'I'm sorry. I know, I miss them too.'

'How's work going?'

'Anthony's in Frankfurt for the week so I'm just answering phones.'

'Conville Media,' Ray trilled. 'How may I direct your call?'

'Hilarious,' she said. 'It's not all bad. Me and Diya took a two-hour lunch yesterday and no one noticed.'

'Nice.'

'We nearly didn't come back, but I bottled it.'

'Diya's still mad as ever?'

'She's the best.' It was true—their friendship was one of the reasons Kate was still there, languishing away in her marble reception prison.

'Any word on the accounts job?'

'Hmm.' She'd forgotten she'd told him, the night of the stroganoff when he'd been waiting outside the bathroom.

'The one where you'd travel.'

'Didn't get it. They gave it to Francesca. She's been there longer than me.'

But really it was because Kate's boss Anthony had said he couldn't do without her. *A man is nothing without a good PA!* And she'd wanted to say, no, Anthony, a man is nothing when he's dead—bludgeoned into oblivion by a stapler.

She cracked the pastry with the carving knife. The meat was a rosy pink, the juices running off the board. Ray went to the sink to get her a cloth.

'There'll be other jobs,' he said.

'Ah, reception's not that bad. You get to hear the goss, see all the hangovers. I could do a nice sideline in painkillers.'

'But your degree,' he said.

She tapped her temple. 'Still got it.'

'What about—?' He gestured around the kitchen. 'Has Liam said?'

'No.'

'I suppose you can't stay on, not really?'

'I know. I'm looking.' The truth was, Liam had given her a soft deal and she couldn't afford anywhere as nice. 'But the sea, the promenade. I—'

'The promenade?' He eyeballed her. 'You're not back running?'

'No,' she said softly. 'I'm not.'

He looked over at the bin. 'You'll get through this. You just need to focus on the positives. That's all you need.'

Kate hacked into the Wellington, messing up the slices, the duxelles spreading across the board like dirt.

'Careful,' said Ray. 'Watch the poor goat.'

'It's a cow.'

Ray laughed and Kate joined in—it did look more like a goat—but there were tears underneath the laughter, the fizzy pressure of them at her nose. For a moment, she felt her sister's presence in the room. In the warm, warm kitchen, sitting on a stool at the breakfast bar, jumping like a black cat onto the island, her sister, a ghost, dark with love. It was the same every year around the anniversary. You could call it a visit, or you could call it hell.

Kate let go of the counter.

'Do you ever think of her, Ray?'

'Sometimes,' he said. 'But it seems so long ago.'

'You've Liz and the girls.'

'It's mad they're twins too.'

'That's how genes work, you fool.'

'Do you still miss her as much?'

'I—' Kate heard the clack of heels.

Liz landed in, her large, abstracted eyes everywhere at once. 'You pair are having the time of your life in here while I'm out there listening to your man go on about his one true love— sewage. Of all the things to bring up at a dinner party.' She left an empty wine bottle on the counter. 'Is there another in the fridge?'

Kate looked at Liz looking at the mess on the counter.

'I forgot to chill the next one.'

'It's still wine, isn't it?' Liz said. 'And you've ice?'

Kate nodded.

Liz's gilded head was already in the freezer when Kate remembered the dessert, the big surprise.

'You've gone all out, Kate Gleeson!' Liz glanced back at them. 'Is it safe to have meringue in the freezer like that?'

'It's safe.'

Distracted, Kate carved the meat the wrong way, some slices bigger than others, one centimetre, two centimetres, three, impossible to tell now. She couldn't make out the next question, not even when Liz repeated it.

'Are you OK, Katie?' Ray touched her shoulder.

She nodded.

'Come on, Raymond.' Liz tipped ice into a bowl. 'Save me from sewage.'

As Ray shrugged and left her to it, Kate looked at the Wellington getting cold on the counter. She put two slices on their plates and one on her own.

'Look at this feast.' Peter helped set the platter in the centre of the table.

Splashing balsamic over the vegetables, Kate could feel Liz's eyes on her but she kept going, asking Ray about his business as she spooned out the parsnips.

'Did the dry needling bring in clients?'

Ray shook his head. 'The problem is the clinic up the road.'

'The problem is this guy spends his days gossiping,' Liz said.

'I do not.' Ray jigged in his chair.

24

'Tell them what Daniel Hartigan said yesterday.' Liz came in close. 'He's treating the principal of the secondary school. Goodbye waiting list.'

'But the girls are only five,' Kate said.

'Lia is five going on fifteen. Tell them the story, Raymond.'

'Client confidentiality,' he said.

'Go on, you're no fun. And would you take off that jacket for Christ's sake?'

Ray obeyed, draping the jacket over the back of his chair. His shirt made his teeth look unnaturally white. Kate wondered if he'd had them done. Her brother was a long way from Cranavon these days, and it made her both hopeful and sad.

'Come on,' said Liz.

'I can't,' he said. 'No telling tales.'

'Didn't you tell me?' Liz poked Ray in the belly. He smacked her hand away, his thick brows coming together as he tried not to laugh. 'Right,' he said eventually. 'There's this old chapel on the school ground. And one of the fifth years, right.'

'Wait till you hear who her father is.'

'Let's just say he's a well-known TV presenter.'

'Of the *Sunday Night Show!*'

'Jesus, Liz.'

Liz reached over the carrots for the warm Sancerre. 'Wha?'

Between the pair of them, they managed to entertain the table for the duration of the main course. The story had something to keep everyone happy—a fifth-year student selling handjobs in a disused chapel—plus Liz the human footnote to keep things rolling. The playlist had turned to '70s classics at some point, its overlapping, showy melodies matching the bright energy of their back and forth.

'But tell them what she said, Raymond.'

'I'm telling them.'

25

'No, you're not.'

'I am!'

'Tell them the line, won't you? It's the best bit, come on.'

'She said—' Ray convulsed for a second, 'She *said*, with a straight face to Dan Hartigan, that her profits had grown faster in the first quarter than the Tesco case study they were doing in Business.'

Liz howled laughing.

'Well,' said Peter. 'I've heard it all now.'

Kate pushed her pastry to one side. It wasn't often she ate red meat and it was filling. She looked around the table at the sated faces and thought that the evening had been saved, after all. Liz deflaked the remaining slices of Wellington with her sparkly silver fingernails. Peter slumped in the chair, twirling his glass like a connoisseur. 'A mighty feed, Kate,' he smiled. 'You're an excellent cook. You should do it more often. We'd be here in a flash, wouldn't we, lads?'

'Dinner's not over yet,' Ray said. 'Isn't that right, Katie?'

'That's right. Dessert's the best bit.'

'I didn't realize it was a competition,' Liz said. 'You're so… what's the word?' She started to laugh. 'We played this game in work on our last night out where you had to think of the perfect word to describe a person. We should do it now!'

Kate forced a smile.

'Just one word?' Peter frowned. 'You can't sum up a person in one word.'

Kate finished her water, reached for the jug and refilled everyone's glasses, all the ice cubes clinking out.

Peter rolled a leftover piece of gristle between his fingers. 'What did they pick for you, Liz?'

'Innovative.'

There was a giddy kind of silence.

'Fair play,' Peter said.

'Come on. Let's do it for each other.' Liz slugged her wine. 'Each of us in turn. Do me first, I can take it, I promise. And you're not allowed innovative, that's cheating.'

'It's a fine way to start a fight at a dinner party,' Peter said.

'Why?' Ray's brows shot up. 'What are you afraid of, bro?'

Liz started to giggle.

'Peter's right,' Kate said. 'For example, I'd have to pick sap for you, Ray-Ray. Let us never forget the man who cries at dog movies.'

'Who had to wait until the cinema cleared before he could leave,' Peter said, laughing.

Liz hit the side of the table. 'We watched it again at home. Same thing! Lainy said he was a baby.'

'Well, they hadn't changed the bloody ending, had they?' Ray wrinkled his nose and pretended to beg. 'He was so cute. Just like Copernicus.'

Liz topped up the wine glasses, but Kate covered her own and ignored the eye roll. She half rose from the table, hoping that would be the end of the game.

'I've an idea,' said Ray. 'Let's do the word thing for Mammy.'

'No,' said Peter.

'Chicken,' said Liz.

Ray sat forward. 'Go on, Peter, try and capture our mother in a word.'

Peter's folded his arms. 'A lady.'

'That's two words,' Ray said.

'Ladylike.'

Ray doffed an imaginary cap but Peter stayed unsmiling, the stern bulk of him shrinking the table.

'You go, darling.' Ray rubbed Liz's arm.

'Darling?' said Liz.

They all watched her, the non-sibling, the outsider.

'Well, now.' Liz smiled at Peter. 'I need assurance first that it won't leave this table.'

Kate nodded and Peter pointed at her nodding. Liz took up Ray's hand, looked deep into his eyes. 'And what about your assurance—darling?'

Ray grinned. 'Why would a net start a fight between two rackets?'

Liz rounded her fine, full lips that still had a hint of lipstick. 'The best word for your mother is—' She took a dramatic inhale, 'delicate.'

'Yes,' said Peter, who was visibly relieved. 'A fine figure for a woman of age.'

'Sicko!' Ray said. 'Don't let the lads in Griffin's hear you say that.'

Peter folded his serviette, the vein on his temple bulging. He excused himself from the table and asked for directions to the facilities, though he knew well.

'Good,' said Ray. 'I wanted him gone for mine.'

'You're awful.' Liz continued to play with his fingers. 'Go on, so.'

Ray withdrew his hand.

'Go on.'

'Maudlin.' He sat back in the chair, satisfied. 'It's the perfect word, every time we go down. Even at Christmas.' He thought about it. 'Especially at Christmas.'

Liz congratulated him on his choice but Kate thought he was being unfair again. Their mother wasn't always down in the dumps. She was sometimes *delighted* with life, but there was generally a frantic quality to it. Kate supposed it might be a disorder of some sort, if they'd had that kind of thing back in the day. The word came to her unbidden and she blurted it out.

'Undiagnosed.'

It sounded cruel out loud, especially with Liz's high-pitched laughter. 'Perfect!'

'Welcome to the party, Kate Gleeson.' Ray looked over his shoulder and reached into his jacket pocket. 'I've been waiting for the right time for this. You might think it's mad but—quick, before Peter comes back.'

'What?' Liz was typing away on her phone, only half listening.

The door of the living room banged shut.

'That's a fine hand cream you have in the bathroom,' Peter announced.

Ray took his hand out of the jacket and straightened it on the chair back.

Kate went to ask but he shook his head.

'Very unctuous,' said Peter.

'Now *there's* a word,' said Liz. 'It's almost as good as Maria Burke's.' And off she went on the best put-downs from her work party and the fights that had ensued. Whatever was in the jacket was forgotten.

When Kate stood to clear the plates, Liz offered to help, but it was Ray who did the scraping while his wife slumped in her chair and started to play the damn game again. Kate stacked the cutlery to the sound of her own name popping across the table like a ping-pong ball. She drifted into her imagination, and when that failed her, she tuned into the lyrics of the song playing too faintly from the speakers. The day weighed down on her, exhausting, and she wished she could kick them all out now, even Ray.

'Kind.'

'Controlled.'

'Skinny,' Peter said.

Kate could feel Liz's eyes darting over her body. Head, chest, legs, head again, like an elastic snapping each time it landed. She'd been doing it all evening, a kind of slanty, sideways watching, but now it was shameless. Now she had permission.

'Yes, skinny,' Peter said. 'I'm afraid that's the word for it.'

Kate bashed her knee on the table corner. A side plate nearly toppled from the stack.

'You've gone backwards, Kate, have you?' Peter touched her arm as she reached for the last plate, and she froze beside him until he let go.

They all knew—even Liz—that backwards meant third year in Trinity, where the second term had ended with a fractured pelvis and hip, and a bone chip in her sacrum. She'd been hospitalized for three months. They'd said confinement meant her bones would fuse together more quickly, but really it was so that people could monitor her eating. Although she'd agreed to the treatment, deep down she'd known she hadn't been sick enough for such a fuss. (And her mother had agreed. *Silly goose to go running in icy weather.*)

'Kate,' said Ray. 'Is everything OK?'

When she refocused, they were all staring at her. A heat crept up her neck and the plates suddenly felt too heavy. Oh, those mean pinhole eyes, what did they want from her? There was nothing—nothing!—to say. She wished suddenly that her mother was here, for a bit of her liveliness and drama, the wonder of her distraction. Her mother would help her, in that moment she was sure of it.

'Kate?' said Peter.

Afraid she would drop the plates if she didn't go now, she started for the kitchen.

'Can I—'

'You're grand, Ray. I've to do the dessert.'

Liz said, 'Text the Netflixer, Raymond, if you want to be useful.'

Kate reached the sink just in time, leaving the plates down and rubbing her wrist. All around her, the mess she had made. Dirty trays, pink stains on the granite counter, pans steeped in rusty water, a trail of juniper berries across the floor. As Liz's voice came warbling from the living room, Kate stared at the freezer. Her mother's housewarming gift hung from the handle, a tea towel with a frowning woman, the speech bubble protruding from her face like some word-filled growth: *I gave him the skinniest years of my life!* Kate picked up the towel, fingering the sheer material that was so unsuited to drying. She laid it gently on the counter before opening the freezer and taking out the dessert. She stood back to get a better look. Some of the spikes had broken off. She reached out and snapped one of the good ones, then another and another, and two more after that, before lifting the plate again and upending the whole thing into the bin.

When the lid came to a standstill, she realized that the playlist inside had finished, leaving a grim, after-hours echo in the living room. She washed her hands, smoothed her hair and rubbed Vaseline on her lips. She tried to sneak back into the room but the three of them looked at her expectantly.

'Right,' said Liz. 'Where's this masterpiece?'

'Liz.' Ray shook his head.

'What? You know your one will only stay till eleven.'

'It's still rude.'

'I'm afraid I've bad news,' Kate said. 'The freezer door was left open. The Alaska's ruined. I had to dump it.'

'Please don't say that I—'

'Of course not, Liz.' Kate grimaced. 'I checked it before the main and must have forgotten the door.'

Ray sat back in his chair. 'All your hard work, Katie, melted to nothing.'

'That's about the size of it,' Peter confirmed.

'Will anyone have coffee? Tea?' Kate lifted an invisible cup from an invisible saucer, in case they had never heard of the concept. 'More drinks?' Suddenly she wanted them all to stay. The long blue night was waiting for her. Delay, she thought, delay!

But Liz already had her phone out and Kate knew that they would all go soon. She excused herself for a moment, could hear a chair being pushed out as she left. Moments later, Ray hovered behind her at the counter, his hand resting on her shoulder.

'Don't worry about dessert, Katie. We were stuffed. All of us.'

She couldn't turn around.

'What's wrong?'

She couldn't bear the closeness, now.

'Is it Elaine?'

She shook her head, unfair to blame the dead.

'Maybe I can help,' Ray said.

'There's no problem,' she snapped.

'Grand so.'

She gave her brother a hug and walked him to the hallway where Liz was on her phone, talking to the babysitter. Peter already had his cap on.

When they'd left, Kate locked the front door and came back into the kitchen. She worked quickly, rinsing the plates and filling the dishwasher. The room was cool again, the suds soft, soft on her fingers. She hadn't lied to Ray, not really. She could never pin down the problem; it was a shifty kind of thing, something to do with routine. Shopping in the same supermarket, buying the same foods, wearing the same outfit in different colours, or even with things she enjoyed like music or exercise, running the same stretch of beach, having to reach the railing she'd reached the day before—all these arbitrary markers of success or failure that seemed to somehow captivate and imprison her. Diya said it was just the break-up blues making her feel inadequate, but the truth was, it had been going on for years, long before Liam, this impulse to do things to exhaustion. It was extreme living. Or it was living for two. Wringing the sponge, Kate felt the energy leave her body. She sat on a stool and began to count.

Three.

Then five—no four—it was only four.

And a sprout.

Less than ten bites in total, a miracle with all the food. The evening's conversation swirled through her mind, her own words lodging like grit. *I used too much butter. I forgot to chill the next one. Undiagnosed.* Somewhere in the distance was the pop and sputter of fireworks but only the same black sky outside her window. Well, it had been a fine evening, really, but she would not do it again.

In the bathroom, midway through the second cleanse, Kate thought she heard a knock on the door. She washed the froth off her face. Another knock, clearer now, a single, solid thump that sounded like Peter. She went quickly through the living room, scanning for foreign items. Nothing. On the console table in the hallway, the tea lights were out and the pumpkin looked deranged. Oh, what would she do if Peter was back for the chats, with more lessons in drainage, perhaps, or some detail he'd omitted about the characteristics of the soil, or worse again—

But it was Ray's muffled voice that came from the corridor.

'Kate. Katie, it's me.'

'Ray,' she said, forgetting the chain.

Ray smiled sheepishly at her through the gap.

She closed the door and opened it properly. 'What did you forget? Come in.'

'I can't stay. Liz was raging when we doubled back.'

'Right,' said Kate, more confused than ever.

'I brought something for you. For all of us.' His face was a bit pink. He had similar skin to herself, the kind that flashed up feelings to the world.

'Here.' He held out a brown paper bag.

'Ah, Ray,' she said, clueless. 'You shouldn't have?'

'It's not what you think.'

She could see a dark, ridged square through the shiny paper. A cake of some sort, or a slice of a cake.

'Is it dessert?' Her voice seemed loud inside her head. 'Come in, won't you. Do you want to send Liz on?'

'I'd love to.' Ray looked longingly down the corridor. 'There'd be war. But, here—' He pushed the bag into her hands. 'Deco gave it to me this morning after our run, he'd made a batch of them. And I don't know, I thought—'

'A batch of what?'

'Look,' he said. 'I thought it might be fun.'

They stared at each other for a moment, Ray's eyes doleful, a serious green. She looked beyond him to the peeling paint in the corridor. What was he even doing here, tormenting her?

'It's a bit late for dessert.' She crumpled the bag with her fingers. 'And a bit stingy, no offence.'

Ray laughed.

'It's a brownie,' he said.

'For me?'

'Not a regular one, like.'

Did he mean sugar free? She considered the bag again. A supersized one?

'Do you remember that time you visited me in college?'

Kate shook her head.

'In the house in Castletroy with no cooker.'

'Oh,' she said. 'Right.'

34

The house with no cooker, and a hot-press full of weed and mushrooms. Ray had been proud of her for taking the spliff in front of his flatmates and acting as if it was just another cigarette. The next day she'd had sore stomach muscles from laughing. She opened the bag now and sniffed. Not grassy like she expected; sharp, a hint of disinfectant.

'A special brownie,' she said. 'A magic brownie?'

'Exactly.' Ray leaned against the door jamb. 'I thought it could be a laugh after dinner. All of us, like.'

Kate squealed laughing. 'With Liz? With *Peter*?'

'I know, I know. Stupid. I knew it the minute I saw him in his big farmer's coat. Liz might have gone for it.'

'Really?'

Ray shrugged. 'Not with the girls, I suppose. Not now. But you can do it, there's nothing stopping you.'

'On my own?' Kate said. 'Where's the fun in that?'

Ray's phone vibrated in his pocket. It rang off and then began to bleat.

'She'll have the taxi drive off,' he said.

'You could stay. We could?'

'I'd love to.' He seemed to mean it too, but then he answered his phone. 'I'm coming,' he said. 'I'm at the lift.'

When the phone was back in his pocket, he came at Kate, his arms wrapping around her. She rested her chin on his shoulder and squeezed back.

'I'd love to,' he said. 'Just things are a bit—' He wiggled his hand. 'With Liz and me.'

'Oh?'

'Ah, it's nothing. Just work stuff.' He turned to leave. 'Only eat a quarter. Deco said it was laced.'

'Hash?'

Ray shook his head.

35

'Weed?'

'A concoction.' He wagged a finger. 'Only a quarter.'

'All four quarters are going in the bin, Raymond.' Kate waved him down the corridor, watching him break into his familiar strut run.

'Live a little!' The words echoed back and then he was gone.

In the living room, Kate switched on the mood lamp in the corner and sat on the couch with a bottle of beer. There was a dent in the upholstery where Peter had been earlier and she settled into it, capping the beer with the teeth of a novelty shark opener that Liam had brought her back from Sydney. The apartment was full of these token gifts that she couldn't bring herself to part with. Taking a sip of beer, she searched her phone for an album she liked in college, a pre-Liam album. Though they'd only been together two years—only!—she'd struggled since the break-up to remember her life before him. Her interests, her weekends, her friends. Her exes? Yes, there had been others before him. She wasn't some yearling broken in by Liam Carroll. She'd had a past—a life. In college, she'd seen a quick-witted arts student from Armagh, then a lanky jock who'd cheated on her, and after him, the one that hurt, an almost thing with a friend from home, the lovely Conor Doyle who was now *married with children*, a seemingly benign phrase that her mother managed to wield like a knife. In her twenties, Kate had gone out with a banker for a while, and the banker's cousin for a while after that, and she'd had a good time with a Maths teacher, too, until he'd moved to Dubai. But when she looked back on it, these men, these boys, were not really exes, rather brief periods of weakness or respite that all finished in the same way: too much, too much they wanted from her, and then nothing.

Sipping her beer, Kate looked at the greasy paper bag on the coffee table. If only Elaine was alive—the thought landed, as it so often did, and she tried to banish it. Elaine was dead, to begin with. Wallowing only made her sad. Not sad—tiny, vague word that didn't cover any of it—especially not now, years later. But if only her sister hadn't died, maybe they'd both be here, slicing into the brownie, having the time of their lives. *What's it like to lose a twin?* So many people—so many more than you would think—had asked her over the years. She usually said that it was tough. Once, she had said it was like a losing a limb and the person had clutched their arm and said, *how unbearable.*

Kneeling on the rug by the coffee table, Kate took the brownie from the bag. It was a slab of a thing, rectangular in shape, thick as two regular brownies. It was more food than she'd had all evening. There were probably enough calories to keep her going for a week. And what if the drugs made her loopy? Imagine she overdosed on a brownie and her mother found out. Kate had never done anything laced in her life. It sounded filthy and so unlike her. She prodded the top of the cake, the crumbling exterior. Six hundred calories, maybe seven with the depth of it, but she would only eat a quarter, and drugs, anyway, didn't count the same, did they, and—enough! Before she could think again, she scooped a clump into her hand and swallowed, took another clump just to be sure. It was far too sweet, a mousse-like consistency that coated her throat. She felt proud of herself, then immediately anxious. She flicked through old photos on her phone until her mind grew critical. Switching to an electro playlist, she lay back on the couch and closed her eyes.

After half an hour or so, her legs began to tremble. The tingling continued past her thighs into her crotch, and up into her stomach, flitting around her middle. She spread her arms over the top of the couch and leaned her head back. When she opened her eyes, the ceiling was a darker shade of grey—a large bulge in the paintwork above her. She was buzzing all over her body now, hot and cold at the same time. At some point she realized the music had stopped, but she couldn't find her phone. Anything that wasn't attached to her seemed lost and unimportant. Her own hand felt like the hand of a stranger. She pressed it down on her thigh. Then: an image of Liam's face between her legs, his smart, sardonic eyes looking up at her, checking.

Kate jolted forward on the couch. Everything was liquid, fluctuating. She pulled at the criss-cross of her dress, bunching it down as far as her bra. There was wet in the space between her breasts, lodging in the fine hairs that had grown one after the other in secret before recently announcing themselves as a sizeable patch of fur. She had found other patches too, over her hip bones, on the sides of her neck, a downy strip across the small of her back. Kate put a hand up her dress and sought out the patch. Twisting, twisting the strands between her fingers, tighter and tighter. She'd been pretending for months that it was her hormones and she wondered if she could even admit it to herself, now, really admit what was going on. The brownie was giving her the sense that anything was possible. She said the words out loud to no one.

You. Are. No.

She hated the word, the dramatic X, the skeletal shape of it. Yes, she'd had a problem with food in college and she'd gotten help. She'd spent a little time in hospital. A time of blinding whiteness was how she remembered it now, a rare snowy winter, the grounds so clean and beautiful, the white lamp of the nurse's night station, the white whizz of the doctors doing their rounds, their white smiles and gleaming orders. Back then, things had been a little worse than normal, but normal was such an impossible word when it came to food. Normal was bingeing and dieting and cleansing and counting and over and under—and half the world was at it. Really, she had not been sick enough to be hospitalized. To be put in an actual hospital with people who had brain surgery and heart attacks. Though there were days when it felt like she belonged there. Days when she needed to be minded or monitored, when the thought of glistening cheese on a pizza could reduce her to tears, or the idea of sitting still for a whole afternoon brought on a crawly, unclean feeling that made every freckle and bump on her body seem wrong and unsightly. On days like that, she would vow to change her life, to make sure she ate elaborate, healthy meals on a regular basis. But then something would happen to make her see the flaw in the plan, or in herself—or it was all too complicated to think about. And she had not been sick enough, anyway, not one of those lollipop heads her mother liked to talk about, the girls who were a danger to themselves. A disgrace. Even when Kate had been in treatment and done everything they'd asked of her, to the point where they'd discharged her, pleased with her efforts, she knew that she didn't deserve the praise, because she hadn't ever really been sick enough in the first place.

But now, there were signs it was coming back, for months, maybe longer.

Yes?

No. It was not the same thing for an adult in control of her life.

Sedulous. She remembered the word now, hours after she'd needed it for the damn game. Liam's word for her. Liam with his postdoc from Oxford that was so inconsequential she'd only learnt about it from Anthony.

In other news, the ceiling was sliding closer to the couch. She took a long breath, tried to count to five on the exhale. From somewhere, the whistle of a kettle, the skin on her mother's milky tea. Nausea went through her like a wave, a huge, rising wave that appeared in front of her like some sheer metallic cliff, taking her tumbling into the grey hardness of the water, slapping and being slapped, the stinging on her face, her legs gone from under her, then out, out onto the cold, mean carpet.

There were silhouettes behind her eyelids, horribly human, like a faraway crowd cheering or dying. She opened her eyes and found peace for a second in the blank television screen, until it started to throb, black turning to grey then back to black, and there, in the centre of the screen—an outline of a face began to form.

Everything in the room stilled.

Kate's limbs went floppy as a newborn's. She sank into the couch and let it happen.

The face filled out, so like her own, but younger. She knew those eyes, the colour of honey, the dark limbal rings.

Elaine.

Her sister's face was motionless, though the eyes were electrically open, slick with longing.

Kate stared too hard and had to blink. When the blinking stopped, the image was gone. Her heart pounding, she told herself to breathe, in, out—long, gaspy breaths. She kept her eyes on the screen, but it was its ordinary self again, black and stationary.

Some glorious time later, she spotted the bottle of beer. The warm fizz went through her like a medicine and she managed to get off the couch and into the hallway where the pumpkin was flashing purple on the console table. Walking around the apartment in a haze, she checked each room to make sure she was alone, just as she did every night before bed. It didn't usually take so long. Each time she turned on a light, she got sucked into a new world: the butter mountain on the bedspread, the red wine fountain in the shower, the stench of the new tarmac that was only half laid in the spare room. But the men needed their lunch break, of course!—she laughed hysterically at her mistake—and went to lock the door with her pinky.

In the kitchen, the light switch had moved, no longer on the wall. She stood on the threshold, wondering what would happen if she went forward into the darkness. The red digits of the oven clock had vanished, but so too had the oven. It was only a few steps, maybe six or seven, to the fridge. She tiptoed forward, one, two, two and a half, and then forgot where she was going. The extractor fan came on over the cooker, the spotlight a little miracle. Mist gushed from the fan and the soft purr of the motor grew louder and louder until it filled the apartment with its growly breath. This might have lasted thirty seconds, a minute, hours. Who knew? Time, like everything else in her life, had decided to pack it in.

CARLOW

August 1999

K ATE SAT IN FRONT of the grown-up's dressing table with her book in her lap. Her mother was plucking the dead hair out of the hairbrush, a rasping, itchy sound.

'Pick a bobbin.' Her mother nodded at the china bowl near the mirror. She divided Kate's long hair in three and began twisting the strands into a scalp-burning French plait. Without looking, Kate took a go-go from the bowl and left it beside the perfumes.

'You think?' her mother said. 'Not with your dress.'

They were going to the best hotel in the midlands for afternoon tea. Aunt Helen was coming too, but it was their mother's treat.

Kate swapped the yellow one for a pale blue and went back to her book, tracing her finger along the coarse paper until she found the right line. Her mother was talking to no one in particular, as she often did when she was happy, and Kate kept losing track of the story. She read the paragraph again but it made less sense now and she knew she would have to go back to the start of the chapter, later, when the house was quiet.

In the mirror, her mother's green dress shimmered in the sunlight. She owned no in-between clothes, like other mothers did, just dressing gowns or dresses. She would never show up to school in a tracksuit on parents' day. Kate could not, at this moment, remember her in pants. The only way you'd know this was an extra special Sunday was from her necklace. Somehow, the pink pearls at her collarbone made her skin even creamier, her blonde hair blonder. Of the four of them, only Peter was blond and it killed Kate that the colour had been wasted on a boy.

45

'Keep still.' Her mother pulled tighter on the hair—a sneezy tension behind her eyeballs. 'Your scalp has gone greasy,' she said. 'You're overwashing.' She smiled as she bent down to Kate's level and the two of them admired the plait. The room felt stuffy and sleepy, a thin line of light from the midday sun splitting the mirror into uneven panels. Kate smiled at her reflection but quickly closed her mouth at the train tracks, the dull metal clamps like the wire on the chicken coop. She wished she'd been allowed to go for colours.

'Good girl, you're all done.' Her mother patted Kate's arm and left a light, dry kiss on her cheek. 'Your aunt will do her usual, no doubt. She always lands in early.' Her mother studied her own reflection, sucked in her cheeks and plumped the shoulder pads on her dress—two bright green triangular lumps that Kate didn't like. 'The Gleesons love to catch a person out. But we'll be ready for her today, won't we? Off you go. Send in your shadow.'

Kate went to the landing to call her sister. Her mother always spent more time on Elaine. There would be shrieks and giggles and, maybe, those little fits of laughter that Kate picked up too late. They were thirteen years old, too big to be having their hair done like it was their First Communion, but today was a happy day, and why would anyone want to change that?

At the far end of the landing, the door to their bedroom was closed. Even though Kate technically owned half the room, Elaine had been trying to claim the lot all summer. Her sister's stuff (indeed, her sister herself) had no respect for borders. Kate leaned on the banister and shouted her sister's name. Silence. On their door, the hunk in his Levi's wasn't giving anything away. Kate traced her tongue over her braces. If you pressed hard enough, you could get blood. She put her weight on the banister and dangled her feet in the air. Though she was only inches from the carpet, she felt a kind of thrill, right there, between her thighs.

46

At the foot of the stairs, Copernicus was curled up, his silky golden forehead squashed between his paws. He would be four in October and had finally learnt that he was forbidden to go in the bedrooms. When Daddy had brought him home as a surprise, her mother had taken to the bed for a week, which was, in fact, a big mistake because by the time she got up again, Copernicus was a fully fledged member of the family. It was the best example of the power of democracy Kate had ever come across, even better than her history project on the French Revolution which had gotten the silver medal from Mr Byrne.

'Elaine!' Kate touched the carpet with her ankle socks. 'It's your turn.'

Copernicus twitched but didn't wake. Kate wished they could use democracy more often at Cranavon, but getting a pack together was harder than you'd imagine. Unless there was a Labrador to save, people looked out for themselves.

Down below she could hear the squelch of wellies on the kitchen floor and she hoped her father—and it *was* her father, because Peter knew better—would have the sense to tidy up. He was supposed to leave dirty shoes on the plastic honeycomb mat in the utility. How did he not know by now? She looked down the corridor to Ray's box room where the curtains were still drawn even though their mother had been in and out at least five times since breakfast. These days her brother was a narcoleptic who would fail his Leaving Cert if he didn't cop himself on. Men were useless, or they didn't care about consequences, not even when they got older. Ray probably had his headphones on, listening to that depressing wailer music. *Today we escape, we escaaaaaape.* He'd gone around in a mope all summer with them glued to his head, ignoring her, as if they'd never been friends, as if it was her fault they were making him do all honours for the Leaving when Peter had been allowed to do pass.

47

'Kate, tell your sister to come in here—immediately.' A clatter of hangers and she heard her mother curse. There was always some inanimate object in trouble.

Kate kicked the Levi'd crotch. 'Elaine. Hurry up.'

The silence was worrying. She'd probably climbed onto the flat roof of the extension for a cigarette. Their father had been in the fields all morning showing Peter the new barley crop. All he had to do was look up. Reckless, so reckless.

'Kate!' Her mother's voice was like a siren down the hall.

'She's coming, Mammy. One minute.'

Kate walked into the bedroom and saw Elaine sprawled on her unmade bed, face in the peach pillow, hair tied in a messy bun. Her side of the room was like a tip as usual, and she'd another of those goth posters gone up this morning. The men, or women, Kate wasn't sure, had actual blood streaks on their faces.

'Nice poster,' said Kate. 'Classy.'

You could barely see Elaine's wall for all the posters, whereas Kate just had her dog calendar.

'Anything to hide the peach paint,' said Elaine. 'It's like living inside a wound.'

'Yuck,' said Kate. 'Get a move on.'

'I'm sick,' said Elaine.

The radio was too loud. Kate went to the locker and turned it off.

'Cop on,' Elaine said.

She was still in her nightdress, which was actually one of Peter's check shirts. She'd rifled his wardrobe when he was in San Diego, took everything half decent before Kate got a go. Peter would probably take the shirts back now that he was home. He was like their mother in that way, precious about his belongings.

'Get up,' Kate said. 'You don't look a bit sick.'

The twins were never sick, not even when they'd had chickenpox.

Elaine writhed on the bed.

'Seriously, you'll be killed. What's wrong?'

Her sister turned on her side, a little fart breaking air.

'Gross.'

'It was from my vagina,' Elaine smiled. 'They don't smell.'

'Go down to Mammy. She's been waiting ages.'

'What, like four seconds?'

'Seriously.' Kate sat on her own bed, shifted towards the headboard and held her plait out to the side. 'You don't want to ruin today.'

The window was suspiciously open, the floral curtain flapping, bursts of sunshine with each lift. On the back wall, Elaine's rosettes caught the light.

'I don't want to *go* today.' Elaine kicked the duvet down the bed. 'Put on that lacy monstrosity when it's a hundred degrees out there and be all la-di-da, yes sir, no sir, and die of boredom sir, before they even bring the fucking tea.'

Over the summer, her sister had started to say *fucking* as if it was any old word. Only last night their father had sent her to bed without any Kimberleys and here she was, at it again.

'Elaine Gleeson!' Their mother's voice was still, surprisingly, far away.

'What's wrong with you?' Kate looked across the pine locker that separated their beds. 'Aunt Helen's coming. It's always fun.'

'*It's always fun.*' Elaine pushed the duvet onto the floor and got off the bed, her long legs tanned after her summer experiment with the sunflower oil. 'Don't you remember the last time? Mammy complained about her figure the whole way home, and was miserable eating her grapefruit for the rest of the month. It's not worth it.'

49

Their mother had been on some sort of diet for as long as Kate could remember, but a few times a year, there would be some occasion like this where she would *gorge herself*, and they would all be giddy and ridiculous, the envy of onlookers.

'Don't be like that,' said Kate. 'She's all excited.'

'Yeah, today she is. Next weekend she'll have forgotten we ever went and start giving out to me about my jodhpurs being too tight for the show.' Elaine grimaced. 'The last tea was endless. She talked to every single person in the dining room. Yap, yap, yap.' Elaine did a beak with her hand. 'And when we did finally escape, the third years outside the newsagents saw us in our matching dresses. How do you not remember that? The shame.'

It was true, Kate did remember, the way they'd looked like two porcelain doll replicas, but there was no point bringing it up now. 'Get dressed,' she said, pointing at the peach wardrobe by the door.

'Elaine Bernadette Gleeson!'

'Go,' said Kate. 'Just go.'

'Urgh. I hate my middle name.'

'Better than mine.'

'I'd take Maude any day over having a piece of *her* inserted into me.'

Elaine grabbed the new hair straightener off the pine dresser and pounded down the landing. They were the first in their class to have a proper one. Everyone else was still using the iron, the telltale line like a halo around the crown. Their mother had come home from Dublin with the straightener last month for no reason at all. No birthday, no Christmas. And she was the best Mammy in the world then. Elaine had no memory for anything, that was the problem. She was all feeling and no thought.

Kate scooched down the bed and looked at the cover of her book, jet black with a child's drawing of a bird in red. The mockingbird, obviously. They were starting it in second year and she wanted to have it read, had four more weeks to finish it, though she would probably be done by tomorrow. She *inhaled* books, is what her mother told the bridge ladies.

Kate made a fan of the pages and left the book down on the locker. It was no good, the house was too busy today. Or her mind was—all whirly. She decided to go for a walk. On the landing, she checked again for light in Ray's room. Last summer he'd driven her to town most Saturdays in his new Opel while Elaine was at horse riding. They'd jaunted about the place and met his friends by the river, boys who all were in senior school and wore Reebok Classics. But that was last summer, when he still played soccer for Park Ville. She lingered outside his room, listening to his snores. Not only was Ray a narcoleptic now, he was also a big lummox, according to their mother, which was funny because he was small for his age and their father complained that he was useless around the farm.

'You're a big lummox, Ray,' Kate called out and then legged it down the stairs.

In the kitchen, her father was reading the paper and eating digestives from the packet. Elaine's purple tamagotchi was buzzing beside the biscuits.

'Hello, Daddy. How are the bales?' She picked up the tamagotchi and fed it. Her father continued reading, perhaps deafened by the sound of his own teeth.

'HELLO, Daddy.'

'Oh, hello, is it yourself?'

His eyebrows disappeared. A tangle of grey fringe was messy across his forehead. She inched closer to the biscuits. He smelt like engine oil and hay, sweet and sour.

'It is—me, myself and I.'

They smiled at each other.

She took a biscuit. He was in his farm uniform, a beige short-sleeved shirt and trousers bunched into his wellies. There were no streaks on the chequered tiles.

'Watch you don't spoil your tea.' He looked up from the paper. 'That's a fine hairdo you have. Like the king rooster.'

'Shut up, Daddy!'

She patted him on the head like a dog and went out the back door into the sunshine. All the weeds were gone from the tarmac. Since he'd come home, Peter was working harder than ever. A new apple blossom planted near their mother's rose beds, the roof on the cowshed all shiny with clear corrugated panels and the fields re-pestified after Ray had used the wrong nozzle. Peter was like a super farmer robot. Her mother kept telling everyone that America had made a man of him, that it wouldn't be long before he got back together with Hilary Clerkin and settled down for good.

It was too hot to go into the fields in her dress and she stopped at the bench swing at the end of the garden. The plastic seat scalded her bum. She sat down on the grass, checking for mucky bits before she settled. The back of the house was in shade, its cement walls duller than ever. There were drainpipes running in ugly diagonals on both levels and the windows weren't symmetrical like in the front, as if whoever built it had only cared about the view from the road. Visitors were often fooled. The bridge ladies said it was the most charming farmhouse in all of Tullow. They could talk for hours about the wisteria. Kate sometimes imagined interrupting their doubles and trumps and asking them all to come out the back. She would call it a fire drill, in the interest of card safety. But her mother would murder her, of course.

Peter came sideways through the gap in the hedge. He was wearing a plain grey T-shirt, black jeans and a belt with a big silver buckle. For a moment she could see why the girls in school thought he was some kind of movie star. His skin had a soft brown glow after his months away and his sandy blond hair was shaved high at the back in some Californian style known as an uppercut that had nearly given Daddy a stroke.

'All alone, Katie?' He stopped by the swing. 'Where's your other half?'

The movie star vanished with his bogger questions.

Kate pointed to the window of their parents' bedroom.

'In the salon,' said Peter. 'What time are ye off?'

'It's booked for one, but Mammy likes to get there early.' She shielded her face from the sun. 'Here, Peter, do you have any more of those Jelly Bellies from America? You only gave us one packet. I'm not sure if you've noticed but we're actually two separate people.'

'I'm afraid I've no more.'

Kate pulled a tuft of grass.

'If you leave the lawn alone, I might get you some the next time.'

She looked up in surprise, his dark blue eyes round and mysterious.

'What next time?' she said.

'Look at the state of this fella at midday on a Sunday.' Peter pointed at the house.

On the back step, Ray was in his boxers, his squat legs as pasty as Peter's were tanned. Elaine appeared behind him, pushing him off the step. They nearly knocked the begonia pots with their messing.

'Watch the dress!' Elaine ran towards the swing and eventually hid behind Peter. Her hair was in loose curls, half-up half-down, a gunky swipe of their mother's coral lipstick across her mouth.

'That's enough.' Peter blocked Ray. 'You've both been at the Kool-Aid this morning.'

'Wha?' Ray laughed. 'Speak English. You're not off the telly just cos you lived in San Diego.'

Peter coloured. 'Well,' he said. 'Well, now.'

The sun went in behind a cloud and a lovely breeze took up.

Kate patted the ground beside her. 'How did you get those curls?'

Elaine sat in the Buddha pose she'd picked up at pony camp. 'You just need to make her think she had the idea herself.'

'Mammy's no fool,' said Peter.

Ray flattened some daisies with his foot, then flopped on the grass beside them. Peter sat down too. He started talking about the flood control measures in San Diego, a place that Kate pictured exactly like Brittas Bay but with roller-bladers and ice-cream-cookie sandwiches. Elaine unfurled from her Buddha and rested her head in Kate's lap. Her curls would lose their bounce but it was a moment of such strange and unexpected happiness, all her siblings together once more, here in the relative freedom of the back yard, that Kate couldn't bear to have it end. Giving herself up to Peter's hypnotic drone, she took the end of a curl and skimmed it between her fingers.

'Damn.' Ray sat up.

'What?' said Kate, looking at the house.

'I forgot—you'd a call, Peter. Some foreign wan.'

'When was this?'

'Like ten minutes ago. Twenty. I think.'

Peter gave Ray a dig, called him a dope and shot off towards the house.

Kate sighed and got ready to go herself. At Cranavon, there was never peace for long.

Kate was downstairs in the good room, waiting for her mother to redo Elaine's curls. Her stomach gave a strange, dog-like gurgle as she settled on the couch. The brocade cushions were too stiff, no yield to them at all. On the wall above the mahogany bureau, the family photos hung in dull bronze frames. The twins in matching sailor dresses, Ray in his Confirmation suit, Peter's graduation from farming college, the whole family gathered around a weird bed-couch in a photographer's studio. Her father was in the hunting jacket he hated, staring straight and unsmiling at the camera, like a man who'd wandered into the wrong photo.

Occasionally, the wall gallery was repositioned or added to, but the photos on top of the bureau never changed: three separate wedding days in silver rectangular frames. Kate loved the centre one most of all, her mother in puffball white, her face smiling and tilted towards Daddy's. The other photos, both similar in style, were of her grandparents, two quaint-looking couples standing side by side. Her mother's father, Granddad Matheson, was the most handsome of the four, like Frank Sinatra only bigger across the shoulders. In his wife, Kate could just about see Granny as a young woman, the same curious eyes and flat cheeks. Though she only lived in Hackettstown, not even half an hour away, they barely saw her. Once a month, they would call to the house after mass, but never for long. Her mother couldn't stomach Granny's plain cooking, which was perfectly fine to Kate, better even than most of the things she got at home. But her mother always refused a plate; she could barely sit at the table when they were there. She would get up and move things that didn't need to be moved. Or she would open presses and be horrified by the tinned contents inside. It was something to do with her own Daddy dying so young. She was very traumatized by it still. This was a word the twins associated with their mother. A sad, grown-up word that was kind of like an apology.

Granny wasn't lonely, at least, Kate knew that much. She had her bookkeeping business and there were always people coming and going, even on the weekends, cups of tea and shortbread biscuits, heavy glasses of whiskey for the men, the big ledgers with the blue lines and dozens of bills and receipts piled on the Formica table. Mammy hated those receipts more than anything. She would talk about the mess on the zigzag roads back to Cranavon (*That tip*, she'd say, *that tip of a house*), lamenting the way she'd been ignored when she was younger, surrounded by adults with their adult voices. Kate understood that her mother had to wait until she'd a family of her own before she could be heard, but it was a shame she'd forgotten what it was like to be the child.

There was something not quite right about the photos the longer Kate stared, and it wasn't just the reddish tinge of the frames. She got off the couch and fixed the wrinkles in the lace runner beneath them. Then she turned each photo in towards the others, like she'd seen Mammy do. In the third one, Daddy's parents were stern and pale-faced. They had died before Kate was born, though Peter remembered them and he still talked about Nanny Gleeson's vegetable garden that used to have turnips, cauliflowers and even courgettes in it, where now there was just patio squares and Mammy's rotator washing line. Kate and Elaine had played a thousand games of hopscotch on that patio over the years. But you couldn't play hopscotch at thirteen-and-a-half, not even on your own when no one was watching. Kate looked longingly at the window, the Venetian blinds glowing yellow with the sun. Upstairs, her mother went heavy across the landing and seconds later the flurry of leaving began.

They drove up a twisting path through woodland before the ivy-covered mansion came into sight. Their mother had booked a table with a view of the gardens, the grass as bright and smooth as Wimbledon. You could see everyone coming and going, the men in their Sunday suits, the women unsteady on the stones.

An old waiter in a shiny maroon waistcoat called them all *madame* and said *merci bucket* instead of bow-coo as a joke. Kate impressed her aunt by asking for the menu in French. When the waiter left with their order, they went back to people watching. Mammy knew everyone in Leinster and she kept them all entertained with stories that Kate felt privileged to hear.

Despite her earlier complaining, Elaine was similarly agog. They both sat at the table, listening keenly, in their almost matching blue lace dresses—Elaine's an elegant A-line, Kate's criss-cross at the chest. Twin sisters in almost matching dresses with almost matching faces. Fraternal twins, if you wanted to give them their proper name, or *same same but different*, if you listened to the schoolyard taunts. Or there was the family line: *identical from behind*. They both had high foreheads, button noses, big eyes, but then: Elaine's cheekbones, the neatness of her chin beside Kate's wide, flat mouth and the unsightly teeth she'd inherited from her father. No, no—this game was not fun. She pulled herself out of it as the food arrived. The tiered silver cake stand was bulging with scones and crustless sandwiches and tiny glazed pastries.

Kate copied her mother and went through things in the right order: scones, sandwiches, pastries. Her favourite was the mini lemon meringue tart. Over on Elaine's plate, there was now a collection of half-eaten confectionery: a walnut brownie, an eclair, a cocktail fork stuck like a sword into the centre of a coconut macaroon. Her sister was holding up the butter dish, vigorously arguing its merits over the pappy, no-taste cream. Aunt Helen was pretending to be vexed in her generous way that could make light of anything. She looked like Daddy when she smiled, the same soft features and deep-set eyes. Shaking her perm, she dangled the pot of cream over Elaine's plate, tilting it back again just before the drop. The twins started laughing, high on life, on sugar, on the spontaneity of it all. It was nice to be back on the

She seemed exhausted now, perched on her chair, tight-lipped and smiling, her head turning to follow any passing guest.

There was nearly another incident after the final cup of tea when Mammy tucked her stiff bob behind her ear, clearly exposing a pink pearl earring that Aunt Helen failed to notice. Elaine saved the day by saying she wanted them *and* the necklace when Mammy was dead. They had a good laugh about that, and when the joke was over, their aunt duly complimented the exotic colour of the pearls. It was a question of taste and you were either born with it or not. 'What would you like when I'm dead, Kate?' Her mother turned to face her. 'I don't ever want you to die, Mammy,' she said. 'But I'll take the sapphire ring if you're asking.' Everyone laughed again, and it felt wonderful to be the source of the humour instead of a greedy pig. She left the second half of her scone, just in case. She had put far too much jam on it anyway. It was a gummy mess.

The adults spent the rest of the tea talking about death: Mammy's hairdresser's son who'd been decapitated by a steering wheel; the old woman in town with the tumour as big as a baby; the place in Switzerland that you could check into like a hotel and never check out again.

Just as Kate was trying to remember the French word for bill, which was definitely not billet, her mother gave a little squeak. She rose from her chair but sat down again, tucking her bob behind her ears. 'Is that—?' said Aunt Helen. 'The man himself,' her mother replied. 'The luck of it.' From her seat, Kate couldn't see who it was, but she saw the pain on her sister's face. 'Well, now,' her mother said. 'I'll just.' Her fingers clutched at the silk sleeve of her dress, then, smiling, she lifted her arm and waved.

Across the room, there was Principal Clerkin, taller and more ferocious than ever in a dark grey suit. His eyes squinted as he clocked Kate, peering into the secrets of her soul before dismissing her as frivolous. It was not just paranoia. All the girls in her class felt the same. Everyone knew he did not like first years, especially first-year girls. He only asked the boys questions when he came into the classroom. Kate hated his moustache, which she could barely bring herself to look at. Elaine had nailed it, a slug of pubes.

'Please,' Elaine said now, picking up a knife. 'Please don't.'

'If he wants to come over and say hello.' Their mother's hand was up again, flapping like a fish. 'You won't embarrass me,' she smiled.

'I'm going to the toilet,' Elaine said.

'Sit.'

It was more of a hiss than an instruction.

'Isn't this nice?' said Aunt Helen. 'You can both get in his good books before school starts.'

Kate could see him making his way slowly across the dining room, stopping at tables and shaking hands, his wife a few steps behind him in a camisole and tight black pants. At the water jug table, she overtook him and walked towards a group of adults seated at the far end.

'Leather trousers,' Kate's mother said under her breath. 'My God.'

Aunt Helen laughed. 'Watch out—here comes the new millennium.'

Her aunt was right, the new millennium was only five months away, or exactly one hundred and fifty-two days left to convince their father about the firework disco in Rathcrogue House.

'Martin!' Her mother was on her feet, tall and slender as a model in her high heels. She called out again and some of the tables stopped their conversation to stare. In the stillness Kate noticed, for the first time, the pitter-patter against the sash windows and she wondered how long it had been raining.

'Bernadette.' The principal arrived at their table, shook her mother's hand and at the same time managed to manoeuvre her back into her chair. 'I trust you're having a wonderful summer. And that the terrible two are behaving themselves.'

Elaine gave a kind of dead pigeon stare. Kate smiled for both of them but had to look away when she saw the moustache, the ends of it blonder than before, like tie-dye pubes at the corners.

'These two?' her mother laughed. 'Street angels, home devils. But the summer has flown, hasn't it?'

'Indeed. A busy time for a farmer.'

Her mother bit her bottom lip. 'Well, yes,' she said. 'Francis has been working hard. And Peter, of course, back from San Diego in time for the harvest. America has really made a man of him. And how is *my* Hilary?'

Elaine laughed out loud.

The principal gave her a look. 'She's doing well. Got the scholarship exams in Trinity.'

'In Law!'

'Indeed.'

'My word,' said her mother. 'That girl is a credit to you.'

'She's home with us now for a few weeks. Tell Peter to—'

'Tomorrow,' her mother said. 'I'll tell him to call tomorrow.'

Aunt Helen stifled a laugh.

'Excuse my manners.' The principal turned to Aunt Helen. 'Martin Clerkin, Head of Tullow Community. For my sins.'

The adults laughed.

'I don't think we've—'

'She's our aunt.' Elaine cut him off.

Mammy gave her a warning smile.

'Two sets of sisters out for afternoon tea,' he said. 'How lovely. Now, I won't keep you.' He did the roly-poly thing with his hands that he sometimes did in school.

'Oh, we're not related.' Her mother's voice was louder than before. 'This is Francis's sister.'

'Younger sister.' Aunt Helen winked, and Kate said a silent thank you that there was at least one adult behaving normally.

'I'm an only child, sadly,' her mother said now, proving Kate's point. Why was she telling the principal this random information? Even Kate could see he was trying to get away.

'My father,' her mother said. 'Well, I'm sure you know from Hilary.'

'I'm sorry?' The principal looked to her aunt for help.

'Bernadette Gleeson, née Matheson,' her aunt said. 'The Mathesons of Hackettstown.'

The principal said, 'Donald Matheson—of course.'

'I used to watch the big black car collect him every Monday,' her mother said. 'And drop him back to us on Fridays. I'd be there, waiting at the gates. And then—'

'Of course,' the principal said.

'I was only seven years old. Imagine that, girls?' She looked at Elaine first, then Kate. 'I hope you never—'

'Such a tragedy,' he said.

Kate made the mistake of looking at her sister, who had the pained face of someone about to skit herself. She knew exactly what Elaine was thinking. There was no way the principal was getting away now. Their mother was a genius.

'In the prime of his life,' said her mother.

'And the prime of his career.' The principal switched to his assembly voice.

'He was.' Her mother clutched her pearl necklace. 'He'd just signed the Fisheries Act that very morning.'

Across the table, Elaine was pursing her lips and nodding just like Mammy. In front of the principal! Kate didn't know where to look.

'Poor Daddy was a minister for only a year,' her mother said to the principal. 'The driver of the truck had been drinking—did you know that? Within the legal limit, but back then that was whatever you were having yourself, and one for the road too.'

'A disgrace,' the principal agreed.

'He would have been Taoiseach. They all said it. A man who was popular with the people and knew how to carry himself abroad. A true statesman.'

'Indeed.' The principal made another roly-poly. 'He did the state some service—and we know it.'

As they both bowed their heads, Kate could feel the skitters take hold. She knew better than to look at her sister but it was so tempting, just to see, just in case, she might not—oh, but she was. Their eyes locked, a second, maybe two, and Elaine was gone. The laughter burst from her in a loud, high-pitched song that went across the dining room. Kate dug her nails into her palm, but it was no good. Her shoulders had taken on a life of their own, jigging up and down. On the other side of the table, Elaine had given herself over to the hysteria, rocking in her chair like a woman in mourning, an arm clutching her middle, tears streaming down her face. There was nothing for it but to go with her, slide into it and let her sister pull them both out to sea. Everything ached—her cheeks, her tummy, even her lungs—a wonderful, rippling ache that she was powerless to stop. She crossed her legs, afraid that she might wet herself. Somewhere in the background she heard her mother saying her name, only her name and not her sister's, and then her aunt apologizing but giddy herself, not able to fully get the words out.

A firm hand on Kate's shoulder ended it eventually. Like a patient waking from a fever, she gasped for air and went silent. Her mother was staring at her with the kind of deranged look that Copernicus got whenever the vet came to vaccinate the cows.

63

'Girls,' said the principal. 'You won't want to be carrying on like that in September. You're not first years any more. Another year and you'll be in Junior Cert. Indeed.'

'I'm so sorry, Martin.' Their mother glared at Kate. 'I don't know what's come over them.'

'It's all the sugar,' said their aunt. 'I can feel it myself.'

'Well, really, Helen.' Their mother gave a tight smile. 'Don't encourage them.'

'I'm sorry, Principal Clerkin,' Kate said quickly. 'I'm really sorry.'

Once the words were out of her mouth, she felt the giddiness evaporate, their special twin power of invincibility disappear. Across the table, her sister's face had grown cold, inert. The principal nodded at Kate and then everyone looked at Elaine. She murmured an apology, frowning for a finish.

'We'll put it down to midsummer madness.' The principal held out a hand to say goodbye.

'But, Raymond,' her mother said, grasping the hand. 'I wanted to talk to you about Raymond.'

'Oh, yes?'

'What you said last June.'

He took his hand back. 'You'll have to remind me.'

'His abilities. His, what was the word—his *prowess* in the summer exams.'

'Indeed,' the principal smiled. 'He did well in all seven subjects.'

'Eight! He's doing applied maths outside of school.'

'Of course, eight.'

Kate felt the spark of a giggle still in her. When Ray was being lazy around the farm, her father would say, tell Eight Hundred Points to get his bum out of bed.

'Well, Martin, I'm afraid to tell you that he's gone off the rails completely over the summer and gotten it into his head that he wants to do physiotherapy instead of medicine. What I need is a strong man to talk him out of it.'

Kate felt the insult to her father deep inside her. She could see it on her aunt's face too.

'Physiotherapy?' the principal said.

'A glorified masseuse! All those brains.'

'Physiotherapy is high enough points. It's no doddle.'

'It's not medicine.'

'No.'

'But if he has his heart set on physio?' said her aunt.

'You've no children, Helen,' her mother said. 'You don't know what it's like to see their potential and want so much for them.'

Her aunt looked out the window. The rain had stopped and the glistening grass looked fresh and lonely.

'It's just, I care—so much,' her mother said to the principal.

As he droned on about parental guidance, Kate had a longing to give her mother a hug. It was true that she cared about them very much. No one could deny it. Their mother spent her life in the Jeep, bringing them to horse riding, or piano, or grinds after school. And she always had their back against outsiders. Years ago, she'd had a little cheat from senior infants in tears after foul play in an egg-and-spoon race. More recently, she'd made a list of all the dunce teachers in the Community and had somehow managed to keep the twins out of their classes. Kate had often heard adults say that Mammy was a formidable woman, but she was only now beginning to see what they meant. Herself and her siblings had been given so many advantages. She wondered what happened to children with ordinary mothers.

'Perhaps you'll have a word with Raymond?' her mother was saying now. 'I'm sure if he keeps his head he'll get the six hundred for the school. Wouldn't that be nice? To see the Community get national acclaim for their results.'

'Superb,' the principal beamed. 'No better man to do it than Raymond Gleeson. And I'm a big fan of Peter too, of course.' He winked at no one in particular.

Her mother's face was radiant. She looked, to borrow that disgusting phrase of Elaine's, as if she'd creamed herself.

'Tomorrow,' her mother said. 'Peter will call tomorrow.'

The principal told the twins to watch their manners, said good-bye to their aunt and pumped their mother's hand one more time.

Kate sucked in her breath and waited. So much had happened, a whole lifetime of consequences. This could go either way. She tried to nudge Elaine under the table but her sister had moved her leg again.

'Well,' her mother said to their aunt. 'Can you credit it?'

Aunt Helen was still staring at the gardens. 'Sorry?'

'Mark my words—Peter will be back with Hilary before you know it. And Raymond Gleeson, the principal said, is just the man to get six hundred points. Did you hear that, girls? Your brother Raymond.'

'The big lummox?' said Elaine.

Her perfectly straight teeth were all on show. Oh, Elaine, she lived on the edge, and she loved it there too. Her sister took up their mother's water—the only glass that had anything left in it—and downed the drink in one gulp. Kate looked to her aunt for help, but she was no use either, grinning like a monkey at Elaine. They looked like they might high five over the silverware.

'You watch yourself, Elaine Gleeson.' Their mother pointed a finger, the nail varnish the same colour as her pearls. 'Or I'll tell your father about your outburst. You're lucky Principal Clerkin has a sense of humour.'

'That fella?' said their aunt. 'Ah, Bern, he wouldn't know a joke if it kicked him in the bollocks.'

Elaine whooped with laughter.

Her mother tried to hide the smile but it came out, her face radiant once more. She was so beautiful when she was happy. 'You're a disgrace, Helen,' she said. 'But I knew we were right to come to the Mount. No one does tea like the Mount.'

The day, it seemed, had been saved. Kate looked over at her sister to share the moment but could find no way in to her happiness. She remembered, suddenly, the random Saturday last summer when her parents had been fighting and Helen had taken the twins on their own to the cloudy-windowed tea room beside the community hall. A simple fruit scone and a cup of tea, the clear run of the butter as it melted. No excess, none of the agony of choice. Just the three of them having a laugh. It seemed so long ago.

The endless summer gave way to a period of frenzy about the start of a new school year. Second year, no longer the babies of the Community, but proper teenagers who knew the right kind of shoes to buy for the first day back. Elaine had sussed it out from her pony friends—white-soled decks in any colour you liked, except brown. Elaine went for racing-car green and Kate chose navy.

One afternoon when their mother was at her charity ball meeting, they went into her bedroom and modelled their uniforms in her full-length double mirror on the front of the built-in wardrobes. Elaine fixed both their ties to just below the second button, though Kate preferred the knot closer to the top, hiding her neckline. Earlier that summer when she'd fallen asleep in the garden, Ray had connected the bigger freckles together with a red marker. Now he was calling her Join-the-Dot. Kate did up the second button of her blouse. Better to be prissy than freckly any day. After spraying their mother's Shalimar all over their musty jumpers, they turned left and right in the mirrors. They rolled up the waistlines of their tartan skirts, tried the thin tights and the ribbed tights, put on the monstrous navy blazers. 'If we're lucky, they might fit us by sixth year,' said Elaine. She turned up her collar like Elvis and pursed her lips in the mirror.

Next, they held their blouses tight against their chests to see how much bra was showing. Even in side profile, Kate had barely anything. Elaine's were much bigger, practically fourth-year-sized breasts, and Kate couldn't understand what she'd done wrong. 'Yeah, you're way smaller,' Elaine said. 'But there are exercises you can do.' They both froze in the mirror, admiring Elaine's mounds. Maybe it was the cigarettes, Kate thought. Maybe she should take up smoking.

They heard the gravel on the driveway and legged it out of the bedroom.

'What the hell?' said Ray, as they booted past him on the landing. He rubbed his eyes. 'Did I sleep until September?'

Peter came thundering out of his door. 'Where is it?' he said to Ray.

'What?'

'My leather jacket. Is nothing sacred?'

Ray shrugged.

'You know what, Ray?' said Peter. 'I can't wait to see the back of you.'

'Mutual.' Ray pushed past him down the stairs.

Peter was being very optimistic. It would be a long year, Kate could tell, before any of them would see the back of Ray. She felt a prod at her side and saw Elaine eyeballing her. There'd be war if they couldn't sneak the jacket back before Peter copped on.

It wasn't just the breasts. Differences were starting to show up everywhere, differences and distances between them that had never been there before. Elaine no longer liked to go down to the brook at the end of the field and play jump-over. Or she would

68

huff when Kate and Ray put on *The Simpsons*. Or she would get jealous if Daddy brought Kate out on the farm, even though she hated farming herself. Or she would tell Kate she needed the bedroom immediately—*their* bedroom—and Kate would have to wander the house with Copernicus, searching for things to do. Right now she was down in the poky extension behind the kitchen where Peter and Daddy had stuck her piano when it wouldn't fit in the good room. She started to play 'Für Elise', her fingers gliding easily over the keys. Halfway through the piece, she hit the high bit and Copernicus growled and ran out of the room. 'Sorry, doggie,' she said, still playing, racing now to get to the end. She had a sudden flash, some twin synapse firing, that Elaine was up to no good.

On her way to the bedroom, Kate turned sideways on the stairs to let Ray go by. He was in Peter's brand-new Fila hoodie. 'He'll kill you,' she said. Ray put a finger to his lips and then sliced it across his neck.

Kate rapped on the door. 'I'm coming in,' she said, pressing the handle.

'Get out!'

Elaine was hunkered between the beds, sorting something, which was very unlike her. There was a weird smell like a rusted tractor.

'I said—get out.' Elaine threw herself forward on the bed.

Kate went over, pulled at her shoulders. 'What are you doing? What's there?' But she sprang back when she saw: lots of different-sized tampons, their discarded packaging like sweet wrappers on the ground. They looked like woolly bullets, except the last one which was squashed and dirty-looking.

'Gross!' said Kate. 'Use the bathroom.'

'Ray was in there for ages.' Elaine turned, a vicious look across her face. 'Oh, what would you know? Just get out—lemme alone.'

She burst into tears and Kate felt bad, like she'd taken something that didn't belong to her. 'I'm sorry,' she said. 'Do you want a hot-water bottle? *Cosmopolitan* says—'

Elaine flashed her a look so she stopped talking.

'OK,' Elaine said eventually. 'Get me one. But don't let Ray see.'

'Make sure you work the conditioner into the lengths,' Elaine said.

She had her head upside down over the side of the new claw-foot bathtub and her words were muffled by the blanket of thick, wet hair. Kate stood behind her, legs akimbo, trying to get the shampoo out with the spray-hose. There was no point putting in conditioner if there were suds.

'Lots of conditioner,' Elaine said. 'I need to beat Susan Hinchy's shine.'

This was a new thing of hers since they'd started second year, this obsession with winning.

'It's not a competition.' Kate worked her fingers through the tangle at the back.

'I never said it was. I don't care—'

'Shut up and let me do this,' said Kate. 'Before she catches us.' 'Just do a good job.'

It made it worse that Elaine pretended not to be competitive. Of course she was. They couldn't play cards any more for her strops, and her cheating. She'd snuck in a fresh pack from the bridge boards the last time. Ray spotted that she kept getting triple fives. And she was doing it in everyday things too: hair-styles, Creme Egg contests, racing off the bus from school up the driveway. As if Kate would ever want to race her home. It was so annoying. They were still best friends but they were best enemies now too.

Down below, Kate heard the scrape of the fire grate in the television room. She listened for footfall but couldn't pick it up with the water. 'Stop moving.' She started to panic. 'We don't have much time.' They could not get caught tonight. Their mother was already in a mood over Peter and Hilary Clerkin. He was refusing to visit her and no one, not even Mammy, knew why.

'Chill,' said Elaine, which was another new thing of hers. She'd dropped the 'out'. She was too cool for it.

Kate spread the conditioner, not bothering to do the crown. Their mother's documentary on the Nazis would soon be over. Why couldn't she watch soaps all night like other mothers? Why did she think the television was for learning?

'Comb it through,' said Elaine.

'You can do it in the bedroom,' Kate said. 'It's like you want us to get caught.' Their mother had a new policy. They were only allowed to wash their hair once during the week, and Elaine had already wasted her go on Monday. It was the latest in a series of new rules at Cranavon. As if the twins didn't have enough to be getting on with at school. It was like their mother was in competition with Principal Clerkin, and there were no winners, only losers—little loser lemmings who were not, under any circumstance, allowed to question the orders no matter how random they seemed. Only last week she'd forbidden them to wear thermal vests, had taken one from Elaine's drawer and ripped it apart with her fingers. It had been a most magical thing to watch. For a finish, she'd thrown the strips of cloth high in the air and burst out laughing. *The waste, think of the waste!* The twins hadn't known what the hell was going on but like always, their mother's laughter was infectious. The three of them had collapsed onto Elaine's bed for ages, until finally, Daddy came pounding up the stairs and said he was sick of living in a madhouse.

'Give it here.' Elaine snatched the hose. Kate wasn't ready for her and she dropped it on the bathroom tiles. The spray went everywhere, all over her stripy pyjamas.

'Shit,' said Kate. 'Shit, shit.'

Elaine was laughing. She turned off the tap and patted her way like a blind person over to the towels. 'You're so funny when you curse. Like a nun.'

'I am not.'

But then the stiff television room door creaked and they both looked at each other in horror.

'Girls,' their mother's voice was in the hallway. 'Girls, what's going on up there?'

The Saturday of the Halloween midterm had not started well: three plates and the ceramic kitchen clock, the primary casualties of the morning's preparations. In the history of dramatic events at Cranavon, there had been worse. But Kate's heart was still agitated, even though the house was quiet now, only the ghost-creaking on the landing, which Peter said was not a ghost at all but the pipes shrinking and expanding with the weather. Kate took a tissue from the locker and patted her eyes. She'd already made both their beds but was tempted to destroy her own housework, get back under the duvet and start the morning again.

Instead she lay shivering on the covers in her body top and denim shorts. The ceiling was covered in tiny green stars and comets and planets that glowed in the dark when the lights were off. On the carpet between their beds, the offending item—a pink glitter riding crop that Elaine had bought in secret from one of the girls in her camp. Another secret, another little nick. Kate was sure that Elaine's pony friends all had their periods already. She'd crouched on the landing last weekend and listened to her sister squeal and giggle on the old rotary phone down below for nearly a full hour. Some terrible leak for some girl in *jodhpurs* who was now known as Red Riding Hood. Kate didn't even feel sorry for her. At least she was able to leak.

72

This morning had begun like most show mornings, early and high-pitched and full of bustle. Wardrobes banging, hairdryers blasting, the muttering that was not really muttering as it could be heard all over the house. On the morning of the shows, there was, everyone knew it, vast potential for trouble. It was as if their mother couldn't tell the difference between excitement and panic. *High doh*, their father called it, before disappearing into the fields.

Oh, Elaine. Kate could kill her. As if their mother was ever going to let her bring a pink glitter riding crop to a competition where there would be actual photographers from the paper and all the other riders in their serious blacks and creams. Kate reckoned her sister had done it on purpose, after the fight about the jodhpurs. All Mammy had said was that she might want to wear the pair with the side zip, that the darker beige would be more flattering. She hadn't mentioned her thighs at all. That was just Elaine and her feelings again, turning every normal situation into a drama. Well, she had gotten her drama. They all had. Their mother in floods of tears in her royal blue dressing gown, smashing the back wall of the kitchen with one, two, three plates, and it was the last one that did for the clock.

Kate curled up on the duvet and told herself it was OK now. They were both gone, her sister and her mother, tear-stained into the Jeep, and late, crunching down the driveway and bashing over the cattle grid. She hated when her mother drove fast and angry in the car, careening around the bendy back roads into Tullow, giving two fingers to the cars that dared to blow the horn and calling the drivers *piss artists*, which was her new favourite expression. Kate and Elaine had started saying it too, and even Ray occasionally, though he claimed to be nothing like Mammy. *Piss artist.* There was something very catchy about it.

Taking her book, Kate went down to the good room, pushed open the door and felt light-headed as she walked around the

73

staid, polished atmosphere. The bridge boards were in a neat stack on the dining table, ready for Tuesday. She lay on the couch, careful not to disturb the perky gold cushions. In the distance, the harvester hummed. Peter and her father had been out in the fields since daybreak. You had to start early, when there was moisture in the air. Kate had gone to watch the first day, to say goodbye to the spring barley that she'd helped sprinkle, to see the tractor make short work of all that effort and growth. But it was boring after a while—up a field, turn, down a field, turn—and she was getting too big to sit in the cab with her father.

She removed her leather bookmark and read another few pages about the mean old Ewell family before her mind began to drift. It was always going places, like when she was in maths class, or in the night-time when she couldn't sleep, or when the ancient priest said mass on Sundays. He spoke with a stop-start Wexford accent and sounded like a donkey. Once, they'd had to leave mass *before* Communion because Elaine and Mammy couldn't stop sniggering.

The house seemed silent now, kind of dead, without them in it. Not for the first time, Kate wished she'd been allowed to do horse riding. She'd probably have her period already, for one. But she knew it was better for them to form their own identities. Mammy had been saying so for years. And it was important to do what you were good at too, which for Kate was the piano, maybe. She got off the couch and went to straighten the blinds on the window. The tractors had stopped but the silence in the room was heavy with the memory of the humming. Kate was too big and too small for the farm, that was the problem. Her jobs only took an hour, and most of them were over in the morning: feeding the chickens, collecting the eggs, unspooling the green hose to fill up the waterers. Her father wouldn't have minded if she did nothing at all. He didn't expect it of her, or of Elaine.

74

Their mother had set the rules for women before they were even born. It was an old family joke that although she was married to a farmer, she was not a farmer's wife. Elaine had stopped helping around fourth class, but Kate continued on in the hope that they might one day trust her with some of the trickier tasks, the ones that Peter and her father bonded over at dinner times. She would even do the finishing in the sheds out the far fields. But Daddy said the cattle were too fat and greedy this time of year. What would happen if she got squashed? They had four men working full-time, and two of their sons came in for the harvest. They only had sixty acres of tillage anyway. The rest was the damn cows. There was just so little for Kate to do. The outdoor pool in Bagenalstown was too far away for regular trips. They were even a fifteen-minute drive from the nearest teenager, poxy Conor Doyle who only talked to Kate because he fancied Elaine. All their school friends lived in Tullow, or beyond in Carlow town, and though they came over for occasional play dates—she hated that her mother still called them that, as if they were in senior infants—there was always too much faff involved, outfits and cakes and the feeling that she was responsible for people. Because who else would be? Certainly not Elaine, who tried to force her cigarettes on anyone who visited. The real problem was the location of the farm, out here in the back of beyond. Kate wished they lived in town and she could come and go as she pleased. No one would mind what she did. When she grew up, she would marry a man from the city, a businessman who needed to live in a place with more people than cows.

There was a jolly padding across the kitchen floor. She let go of the last blind, rushed to her feet. Too late—Copernicus headbutted the door and bolted across the russet gold carpet.

'No, Copernicus!' He came straight for her and left a warm line of drool on her thigh. 'Bad dog,' she said. His tongue hung out like a melted Wham bar. The kitchen door banged and his ears went into triangles. 'Robbers,' she said, pointing at the door. He cocked his head at her. 'Go get them.' He was gone like a shot. Kate followed after him, checking the carpet as she went.

In the kitchen, her father was at the sink, splashing water on his face. Ray and Peter were in some sort of stand-off at the back door, and she couldn't tell who was blocking who. Ray tried to give Peter a karate chop in the side. He was always picking fights. It was like he'd been born with that jutty face.

'You might use that energy to muck out the barn, son.' Her father turned off the tap and shook his wet hands over the clean sink.

'Be careful, Daddy,' said Kate.

Copernicus had gone to Peter, was trying to sniff his crotch.

'Get that dog out of here,' Ray said. 'He stinks, Katie.'

'He does not,' she said.

Katie, do this. Katie, do that. They never asked Elaine.

'You could do with a shower yourself, brother,' said Peter, waving his hand in front of his nose. 'When's the last time you washed that T-shirt? Is it a tribute to Kurt Cobain, or what?'

Something had happened to Peter in America. It was like he'd brought home a sense of humour with the sachets of Kool-Aid.

'Piss off.' Ray attempted another chop. 'Hilary Clerkin was telling everyone at the Meadowlands last night that you're a loser.'

'Ray—watch your mouth,' her father said. 'And would you get dressed, for the love of God?' He looked at the back wall. 'Where's the clock?'

'It broke,' said Kate.

They all turned to look at her and she felt a mild panic between her ribs.

'The battery?' said Peter.

76

'No,' she said, looking at each of them in turn, hoping one of them might figure it out. They seemed to take up so much space. They were all men now, even Ray. When had that happened?

'Broke, how?' said Ray. 'It took three Saturdays at the clinic to get that clock. It had to be ceramic. I knew she wanted the ceramic.'

Peter went over to the wall and ran his fingers over the copper hook. 'Sturdy,' he said.

Her father looked towards the hall. She followed his gaze, could see the sun bright outside, spilling in the long rectangular windows.

'Well?' Ray demanded.

'It fell,' said Kate.

'I knew that hook wouldn't hold it,' said Ray. 'I told you, Peter.'

'Sturdy.' Peter tapped it again.

Her father went to the fridge, took out the butter and the fancy sliced cheddar that Mammy had discovered in the new supermarket. He left them on the table. 'What happened, Katie?' he said. 'Was there war?' His voice was soft and kind, and she felt like she might cry.

'I didn't hear anything,' said Ray. 'It couldn't have been that bad.'

As if the narcoleptic could be trusted to give a report.

'Yeah, Daddy,' Kate said, 'it was nothing, not really. It was Elaine's fault.'

'The competition,' said Peter. 'The show.'

'Yeah.'

'I see,' said her father.

Kate got the plates from the middle drawer.

'Cheddar and chutney sangers.' Her father sat at the head of the table and opened a button on his shirt.

'Actually,' said Peter. 'I've a new dish to—'

'Hold on a second,' said Ray. 'What about my clock? Eighty-five pounds it cost me in that rip-off pottery place. That's a weekend ticket to Witness *with* camping—and you'd still have change.' He pawed the pale yellow paint on the wall. 'So. What the fuck happened to my clock?'

Her father banged his hand on the table, a fierce loud smack.

'I told you to watch your mouth in this house,' he said to Ray. 'A grades are no substitute for manners.' His fingers turned white as he gripped the table. He saw her watching him and he let go. Ray mumbled something, not an apology she was sure, but he was gone before her father could say another word.

'Go after him,' her father said to Peter. 'He's not going back to bed.'

Peter brushed past her in his rush out the door and she squeezed herself against the counter. She heard them both run up the stairs, taking multiple steps at a time. Left alone with her father, Kate didn't know what to do. She wished he would look at her with his soft hazel eyes and say, *Is it yourself?* Instead he took up the paper and started mashing the pages together in a way that drove her mother mad. She felt frozen to the spot.

'Can you feed that dog, Kate? Stop the blasted whining.'

She only noticed it now, the lonely howl of poor Copernicus by the utility door. It was one of those sounds that you were so used to hearing, you kind of forgot about it. Poor Copernicus. She was very neglectful.

'Sorry, doggie,' she said. 'Who wants his biccies?'

He wagged his tail—long and thick as a kangaroo's, and proof that he wasn't a thoroughbred.

'Go on, Kate,' her father said. He patted the wiry hairs at the back of his head, picked up the paper and frowned at whatever was on the cover. 'Feed that dog.' You couldn't say he was in a bad mood—at Cranavon, that meant something else entirely—but he was gruff with her and she felt aggrieved. What was wrong with him at all? She closed the press drawer a little louder than necessary and went over to the dog, grabbing his studded collar. The little silver bone jangled.

In the utility, Kate dragged the sack of biscuits across the floor and shook just enough into the green plastic bowl. Copernicus would eat a mound if you gave them to him. He had no full button and was getting fat as Christmas. *The waddle on that mongrel,* her mother said. *That mutt.* She pretended not to care about him, but occasionally she would try and detangle the mat of toffee-coloured hair on his underside. He would see her coming with the brush and try to waddle off. Kate patted him on the back now as he hunched over his bowl.

'Good dog,' she said. 'Best dog.'

He snaffled the feed, his teeth grinding the dry biscuits. Crouching beside him, she folded the bag. She knew well what was wrong with her father. He was a laid-back man, *horizontal*, her mother said, but he hated cursing. Useless Ray and his potty mouth. Her father was old-fashioned in that way, more like a granddad than a dad. He was eleven and a half years older than Mammy, which was weird, Kate knew, and she didn't like to talk about it with her school friends whose parents were all the same age. Her father was older. Her father was old. He sometimes used language from another place—motorcar, homestead, gnashers—and he hated swear words above all else, would visibly flinch when her mother used bad language. Elaine reckoned she came up with new ones just to annoy him.

'Are we having lunch, or what?' her father called from the kitchen.

Well, now. How did he expect her to do two things at once? She was not a magician. For a split second, she imagined saying, *make your own sandwich, you piss artist!* It was a ferocious thought.

Kate left the dog feed in the corner beside the dryer and went to the kitchen.

Her father put down the paper. 'Will we have lunch? I'm famished.'

'Is maith an t-anlann an t-ocras,' Kate said.

'Cad?' her father smiled.

He didn't have a word of Irish beyond *cad* and *leithreas*. When her mother was in a good mood, they would say funny things about him to his face and then roar laughing at his bemusement. Kate had taken to Irish easier than Elaine, and she loved it when her mother praised her for a new word or phrase.

'Hunger is the best sauce,' she said.

'Clever clogs.' He did his wiry eyebrows. 'Now, can we ate this tocras, or what?'

'Silly Daddy.' Kate opened the cutlery drawer. 'Do you want the double-decker?'

'Of course.' He smiled and stretched his long legs.

'Forget your old sandwiches,' said Peter, coming back just as she'd put the wooden board and bread knife on the counter. 'I've a surprise for today.' He took a tinfoiled plate from the fridge. She could smell the onions when he passed.

Leaving the plate covered in the middle of the table, he whizzed around Kate, got the mats and cutlery in one swoop and had the table set before she'd brought the four plates from the counter. She followed after him, putting the plates on the sunflower mats.

'Well,' her father said. 'This is something else. The royal treatment.'

Kate took four glasses from the press beside the microwave. She put them on the table but Peter rushed by her again, placed a huge bowl of salad beside the condiments and cleared away three of the glasses.

'Hey,' said Kate.

'Get your brother, Katie,' her father said.

Kate went to the hall and called Ray, who appeared in front of her as she shouted his name.

'I'm not deaf,' he said. His headphones were around his neck but he was dressed at least, a black T-shirt with a collar and a little green alligator on the chest pocket. She looked at his spiky fringe. He was, in fact, suspiciously dressed.

'Are you off to a disco?' she said.

He gave her a soft shove and went into the kitchen.

Peter had left three of Daddy's tall Carlsberg glasses by the mats. There were other strange items on the table: two giant wooden forks in the salad bowl, a glass jug of brown liquid beside some oil, a plate of grated cheese, a tiny bottle of bright orange sauce.

'Sit,' said Peter. 'Everyone, sit.' He smacked his lips together, the way he always did when he was pleased.

Ray sat in the chair farthest from their father. 'What's with the glasses?'

'A Saturday treat,' said Peter, opening the fridge. He brought to the table a large dark bottle that looked like wine but he told them it was beer—Belgian beer.

'What's this codology?' her father said.

'Sorry, Katie,' said Peter. 'I forgot your milk.'

When she came back from the fridge, he had the tinfoil off the plate and was explaining what tamales were to a sceptical-looking Ray.

'You know tacos, right?' Peter rested his hand on his belt buckle.

'Of course we know tacos.' Ray shook his head. 'It's 1999, Peter?'

'So are these things tacos?' Her father took a sip of beer and licked his lips. He hadn't shaved that morning and already there were silvery grey bristles on his top lip.

'Tamales are like tacos,' Peter explained. 'I made them from cornflour but it's a softer dough. And then there's pork and onion and some dried chilli inside.'

'Chilli?' Her father drank more beer.

Kate considered the foreign items. They were a bit like dog bones, with too much meat spilling out the ends, far more than you'd have in a sandwich.

'There's garlic.' Ray leaned into the plate. 'I can smell it.'

'Well, yes,' said Peter. 'Everything has garlic.'

'No garlic,' Ray said. 'Not for me. I've a date.'

Her father put down his drink and gestured for some food.

'Who is it, Ray?' Kate held her plate up for Peter. 'Is it Deirdre Mahony? Is it?'

She had a bet with Elaine. One hundred marshmallow Flumps and a copy of *Smash Hits*.

Ray ignored her and gulped his beer. He let out a disgusting burp at the end of it.

'Cop on,' said Peter. 'We're eating.'

And they were, in fact, all of them, tucking into the delicious dough and soft, stringy meat, even Ray with his no-garlic rule. There was no conversation for the next while, just the moist sound of chewing and swallowing, and the occasional whine from the utility. The food was full of flavour, so different to the kind of dinners her mother put up. Kate would never say this out loud, but it seemed to her that the men in the house, Daddy and Peter at least, were better cooks than the women. Take the special occasion mornings where her father made omelettes, or bacon sandwiches or, her favourite, eggy bread. Or that time her mother had the three-week migraine, and Peter had made the meat and vegetables taste different every night. Kate wished he would cook more often. But their mother controlled the kitchen, that was the problem. Or rather, she controlled the kitchen and, at the same time, did not seem to like the place at all. She was always banging saucepans and cursing at carrots, like a renegade princess who'd inherited a kingdom she'd no interest in. And she was always looking for compliments too, which was especially hard when she made the cauliflower stew dish that tasted like vomit. You could never tell her the truth. She was very sensitive about cooking, which was funny because she didn't seem to care so much about other things. Ironing, for example, or mending clothes. She often made fun of herself as she tossed a blouse or shirt into the bin, needle and thread in after it. *We'll have to go around naked*, she'd say. *I'm no use with my hands.* Mammy took after her father—she was all brain—nothing like her mother.

When Kate finished her tamale, the three of them were still talking about the O'Hanrahan's game.

'Who cares if it was only a point?' she said. 'Newbridge beat them. They lost.'

'But they shouldn't have,' said Peter.

'That's life.' She shrugged and smiled at Daddy.

He gave a hearty laugh like she knew he would.

'Is there any more?' Ray put his fork in the centre of the plate and patted his belly. 'That wasn't bad. For Mexican.'

'All gone,' said Peter.

'What about beer?' Ray said. 'I'd take another beer.'

'You've enough beer,' her father said. 'Have a glass of milk.'

It was a good idea. She poured herself another glass before Ray could get his hands on it. Such a treat to have the carton on the table, to reach out and have it right there when you needed it. She drank the sweet, cold liquid, delicious after the tang of the tamales. Elaine would be raging she'd missed them.

'What are you smiling at, Katie?' Her father was smiling too, tilting his chair backwards.

'Nothing,' she said. 'You're a good cook, Peter. You could open your own restaurant. A tamales restaurant.'

'Oh, there's this place in Mission Beach, you should see it.' Peter's eyes went sparkly. 'Just tamales and tacos, and the line out the door every evening.'

'The line?' Ray looked amused.

'The queue,' said Peter. 'They must make a fortune. Cocktails, tamales and tacos. That's it. They could open three more like it and still get the numbers.'

'Cocktails, is it?' Her father shook his head. 'Might there be another drop of that beer left?' He held up his glass.

'That's the lot, I'm afraid,' Peter said.

'Ring the EU there and see if they'll send us some more.' Daddy and Peter did an identical laugh.

'Have a glass of milk, Daddy,' Ray said, with a sly smile. He stood and collected the plates, left them on the counter, not even close to the sink. A fork dropped to the floor, sending a milky shiver from her belly to her throat.

'Watch it, you,' her father said to Ray. 'You're lucky your brother saved you from a hiding with his fancy tacos.'

'Tamales,' said Kate.

'A hiding!' Ray guffawed. They all laughed. Their father never got physical.

'Just you wait, Eight Hundred Points. One day, when you least expect it.'

It started to rain and her father told Peter they were best to leave the hay until morning. After she'd cleaned up, the four of them sat around the table, eating Kimberleys. Peter and Ray drank espressos made by a tiny silver kettle put directly on the stove. It filled the kitchen with a sharp, nutty smell. Her father had his tea as usual—no milk and two sugars. Ray disappeared into the good room to take a phone call and when he came back he had a face on him, and one of the yellow bridge boards in his hand.

'Mammy will kill you if you've messed up the order,' said Kate.

Ray ignored her. 'Gin rummy,' he said to Peter. 'Four is a good number.'

'I'm game,' Peter said.

'Go on, so,' her father drained his tea, 'but only if Katie promises to take it easy on us.'

She smiled at him, excited now. 'I'll go easy, Daddy.' She put one leg under her and sat forward in the chair.

The rain hit the windows hard and hungry. She felt safe inside. Ray dealt the cards in a clockwise direction, giving them two each to finish.

'We'll have strange cards now,' said Peter.

Kate's seven were all mismatched, only the flimsiest sequence to get going.

'What happened to your date, by the way?' Peter said to Ray.

She flashed Peter a look—could he not see that Ray was back in his old Nirvana T-shirt, that the date was clearly off? Dee Mahony was a known cow around the school.

'You're up,' Ray said to Kate. He burnt the top card and turned over a four. Kate felt a ping of excitement and tried not to show it, but her face must have given her away because her father said, 'We're in trouble already, boys.'

He looked younger when he smiled, like Ray in fact, the same crinkles around their eyes.

'I've nothing,' she said.

'Liar,' said Ray.

They went round another few times, Peter ruining the rhythm each go, staring at his cards as if he could change them with his eyes. Ray was the opposite, firing the cards on the table, and flicking the ones in his hand with his fingernail until her father told him to stop.

'It's distracting the rest of us,' he said. 'I know your game.'

Her father frowned and put down a six, a beautiful, much needed six that Peter spent an agonizing amount of time staring at before plucking it from the pack. Copernicus gave a growl from his mat and Kate knew exactly how he felt. But then Ray, lovely, lovely Ray, put down another six, and that was all it took for her sequence. She waited in steely-eyed concentration for it to go round one more time, praying that Peter hadn't managed it first, but no, it was back to her before she knew it and she laid them proudly down on the table, three-four-five-six and three glorious eights.

'Gin rummy!'

Copernicus was the first to react, a loud bark by the door.

'Good girl,' her father said. 'She's rung rings around us, fellas.'

'Early doors,' said Ray, but he gave her a nod.

'I'm out of practice,' Peter said. 'I didn't play a game all summer.'

'Don't they have cards in San Diego?' Ray dealt again, for her this time. It annoyed her when he did that but she let him away with it this time, still basking in her win. She watched Peter tally the leftover points and write a fine fat zero under her own initial.

They spent the next hour playing cards and telling stories and jokes. In the end, Kate won the gin, though only by the tightest of margins, her father two points behind her. He was magnanimous in defeat, not like other people in the household, and said she had beaten him fair and square. Then he announced that for her grand prize she could—make him another cup of tea. They were all laughing so hard at her reaction that Kate didn't hear the rattle of the cattle grid or the Jeep roll up the driveway.

None of them noticed anything at all until her mother burst into the kitchen, dropped her handbag on the counter and managed to open multiple presses, put on the kettle and run the tap all at the same time. 'And then Nora Jenkins came after me and she kept me an age,' her mother said to the sink. 'I couldn't get away from her. I was running, we were running, weren't we, darling, practically tearing across the car park and she was chasing after us, ranting about her poor, sick father. Nora Jenkins and her sick old father. Well, he's been sick now for decades, dying sick, apparently—and isn't he still miraculously alive? I'm parched. Just parched.' She threw back a glass of water and turned to face the table. Her mad morning hair had been combed and clipped back in her tortoiseshell hairgrip. Her face was free from make-up, gaunt and girlish.

'What's going on here?' Her mother loosened the silk scarf at her neck. 'Is the farm on strike, or what?'

Peter moved to the far chair to give her room but she stayed standing.

'Have you been playing cards all day?'

'No, Mammy,' Kate said. 'Just an hour. A half hour.'

'I see,' she said. 'Isn't that grand?'

Kate knew she was thinking about last weekend, when no one had wanted to play her Old Maid. She had asked just as *The Simpsons* was coming on.

'Well, I can see you're all happy in your card den. I won't disturb you.' She pretended to walk away, but stopped before she got to the door. She glanced back at them. 'Will I bring you some refreshments?'

'We're fine,' said Ray.

As if it had been an actual question! It was all her mother needed. She spun on her heel and lunged at the table.

'Do I look like a skivvy, Raymond? Do I?'

87

Ray flinched. 'No.'

'That's all I am in this house, isn't it?'

'Come on, Bern,' her father said. 'Tell us about the gymkhana. Did she win?'

Her mother folded her arms. 'You only have fun when I'm not here.'

'It was half an hour, Mammy,' Kate said. 'And it wasn't even that good.' She couldn't look at the others now. She felt like Judas Iscariot.

Her mother put a hand to the tanned patch of skin at her collar and looked out the big kitchen window. 'Nothing gets done in this house when I'm away,' she said. 'Nothing.' And she still hadn't noticed her bridge board.

'Rain,' her father said. 'There was rain, Bernadette.'

'Rain?' Her mother tapped the back of a chair and looked at them all individually. There were biscuit crumbs on the table and Kate reached over and gathered them in her hand. It was a relief to have something to clean.

'Marise Murphy was there today,' her mother said to Peter.

'How is she?' he said. 'I saw Phillip last weekend.'

'Oh, she was telling me. What didn't she tell me? She knew more about San Diego than your own mother. The *best* place in the world, she said.'

'You'd love it, Mammy,' said Peter, who didn't really understand sarcasm. 'The beaches, the vibe.'

Her mother humphed, stood back from the table and surveyed the cards. After a painful few seconds, she reached in and picked one up. Kate inhaled. There was a white dot on the tip of her mother's nose, a bit of old skin. The table waited. She turned first towards Kate, to Peter and finally to Ray. Somehow, she always knew. She made him wait a few seconds, and then she pounced, skimming the card at him. It narrowly missed his face. Kate jumped off her chair and picked it up from the floor.

'Are those my bridge boards, Raymond?'

'One deck,' said Ray. 'That's all.'

'That's *all*?'

'Jesus—I'll put it back,' he said.

'Raymond Donald Gleeson!'

'Bernadette, please.' Her father reached for the Kimberleys and looked hurt to find them empty.

'That's it. You're not going to Caesar's Palace tonight,' her mother said to Ray.

'It's called the Meadowlands?' he said. 'For about twenty years now.'

'And I'll take that car off you too, if you're not careful. Then we'll see what it's called, won't we?'

'Ah, come on!'

'Can't I have anything to myself in this house?' said her mother. 'All I ask, one little thing, is that you don't touch the bridge boards.'

'We'll put them back now—' Her father gestured to Ray, 'Go on.'

'For crying out loud, Francis.' Her mother sighed. 'Is nothing sacred?'

'Don't be fiery.'

Her mother went on about how much trouble it was to align the cards correctly for her classes, but her heart wasn't in it, not really, and Kate knew instinctively that the gymkhana had gone well, that a new rosette would soon be presented at Cranavon. Eventually her mother stopped talking, went to her special press and took out a brand-new box of Kimberleys— chocolate Kimberleys. She left them on the table without a word.

'Lovely,' her father said, taking two. 'Now, are you going to keep us in suspense about today?'

Her mother gave a tight smile, dropped her arms by her side. She had no jewellery on, not even her rings. 'I'll let Elaine tell you yourself. Elaine!' She went to the door and shouted Elaine's name three more times.

Ray covered his ears. Peter cleared the cards, dividing them into quarters for the bridge pouch. Her mother opened the fridge and started to list the contents. Kate hoped Peter had bought his own ingredients for the tamales.

'Kidney beans, cheddar, that bloody pineapple—where's the packet of ham?'

It was not a question, not really.

'Pickled onions, beetroot, brie. Who's been at the brie?'

Elaine came into the kitchen, already changed out of her horse gear. It would be in a heap on the ground between the beds.

'Ta-da!' Elaine did a star shape, her goth band T-shirt riding up above her leggings. 'Here I am, what's the panic?'

'Are you into Slayer now?' said Ray. 'You're so cool.'

Elaine went behind Daddy's chair and gave Ray the finger. Kate didn't know who Slayer was, but she hoped there wasn't a new poster in their room.

Her mother was still in the fridge, at war with a gone-off melon.

'So,' said Ray. 'Where's the trophy?'

Elaine smacked him on the back of the shoulders as she went by. She cocked her head at Kate and pointed to the garden. Kate knew what that meant, though she didn't have them on her. You couldn't hide them in leggings.

'Let's go for a walk, Kate,' she said.

'OK.' Kate looked at the fridge but didn't get up.

'Come on.' Her sister flicked her hair over her shoulder. It was out of the braid and had lovely waves.

'No trophy, then?' her father said. 'Shame.'

Peter echoed the sentiment.

'Tell your father how you got on, Elaine,' said her mother. 'Tell him what happened.' She closed the fridge door.

'Second place,' Elaine said.

'Second?' said her father. 'Hard luck.'

'First loser,' said Ray.

Kate scowled at him.

'I nearly had it, Daddy,' said Elaine, 'but I knocked the top off the redbrick and—'

'It was too high.' Her mother rushed over to the table, 'They put it too high for the final round and they didn't say anything but I saw them lower it after Elaine's go, I swear to God. And Lucy Stevens got it easier than the rest of them.'

'Mammy,' Elaine said. 'Princess just stumbled in the run-up. I felt her hesitate.'

'No, no—no.' Her mother buzzed around the kitchen. 'You had to see it, Francis. It was so unfair. Lucy Stevens who looks like a horse. Who has a face *exactly* like a horse.' She was at the head of the table now, doing an impression of the girl. Everyone was laughing—Peter had tears running down his face. Mammy had brought their boring little kitchen to life. 'That little horse face took home the trophy. But my girl here should have won it. You were wonderful, darling.' She looked in earnest at Elaine, such a look of pride and admiration in her pearly grey eyes.

'Let's go,' said Elaine, pulling the back of Kate's ponytail.

Kate yanked it away from her. 'Guess what?'

'What?'

'We had tamales for lunch.'

'Amazing,' she said. 'Let's go.'

'Where's your rosette, Elaine?' her father asked.

'Bedroom,' Elaine said. 'Come on, come on. Let's go.'

'Where to exactly?' said her mother. 'Dinner will be ready at eight sharp.'

Elaine rolled her eyes at Kate. They both knew that when it came to food, time did not work properly. If dinner was at eight, her mother would start shouting for people to come to the table at ten to, but no food would appear until half past. Peter said she was bad at timings. Ray said she liked to hold the family hostage.

'Oh, sugar!' her mother said now. 'The meats. That damn butcher. The piss—'

'Bernadette,' her father said. He gestured to Peter for the paper.

Her mother rushed to the freezer, started to rifle through the bottom drawer, the ice scraping away and little shards spilling onto the floor. Her father took up the paper. Kate could no longer see his face.

'What's wrong, Mammy?' said Peter. 'Is everything OK?'

'Let's go,' Elaine hissed.

'Where are you off to?' her mother said. 'Didn't you hear me? Where are you going after our big day out?' There was a panic or petulance to her voice now, it was hard to say which. She banged her head on the fridge handle as she stood. 'That damn fridge,' she shouted. 'My head.'

Ray left the kitchen.

'Poor Mammy,' said Elaine. 'Poor head.' She gave her a hug and went over and kicked Copernicus awake. 'We're just going outside to play with him. Come on, dog, up.' Copernicus stretched his front paws and pushed himself to standing.

Elaine pulled Kate from the chair. As the back door latched, Kate could hear their mother asking Peter for ice. 'Is there a bruise?' she said. 'Please don't let there be a bruise.'

Why her father had chosen November, of all months, to bring up the sport of tennis, it was impossible to say. Kate was sitting on the carpet in the good room, her back against the bureau, waiting for the right time to escape upstairs. Her parents had been shouting at each other for an hour, back and forth like a tennis ball themselves, ever since her father had brought up *the waste*: the cost of the rackets and of the snow-white outfit that was *still* snow-white in the built-in wardrobes above, and that would remain snow-white forever. Kate kept having flashes of the fairy-tale princess dead in her glass coffin. Ray was in town, at least, and Elaine had legged it out into the cold the moment her mother had said, *how dare you*. Kate wished now she'd gone with her, jacket or no jacket.

'Mr Moneybags,' her mother shouted. 'Mr Miser Moneybags.'

'Don't you—'

It was harder to hear Daddy, his low, angry growl.

Kate snuck her head around the door and looked into the hallway, hoping for Copernicus. At such moments, he would often know to find her, climb on her lap, his warm weight like an anchor to the world. Sometimes she would cry so much his fur would get wet.

'I'll play when I want to,' her mother said. 'You won't tell me what to do. You don't control me!'

'Just listen to yourself Bernadette. Just look at yourself.'

'Look at *me*?'

Her mother shouted a litany of curse words, with the ease and rhythm of a poet. Piss and fuck and shit and bollocks and—prick, prick, prick.

'Listen to yourself, woman,' her father said again.

'Listen to *me*?' she shouted now. 'Says the mute old man who no one would go near if it wasn't for me.'

Oh, that was a low blow. Kate could feel her father's sorrow through the walls. For it was true, that Mammy was the best, the shiniest of all of them in public. She was the one you wanted to be near. She loved to watch her parents when the family was out together. Her mother, so able for anything. Her father, so bashful and proud.

'Muto,' her mother shouted. 'Big old muto!'

Kate put her hands over her ears and squeezed into the corner beside the bureau. She was too big for it now, the sharp turn cutting her back. Why didn't she leave? Why didn't she go upstairs? They would not hear her.

'I play! I beat Marise Murphy last summer.' Something loud clattered to the kitchen tiles. 'I'm a good player.'

But this was the real problem, her mother only liked to do things she was good at, and she gave up immediately when they got hard, or when she got injured, or when an injury was done to her by some other injurious party. There were many examples: Nanny Gleeson's recipe for coq au vin, the Toastmaster county final, the horse riding or, worst of all, her singing, which she'd been so good at, but was no longer to be spoken of in the house after Marise Murphy (again!) was given the solo soprano in the church choir last Christmas. Mammy had dropped out in a spectacular Christmas Eve showdown right in front of the life-sized crib. Elaine was in full agreement—pathetic to settle for the chorus.

When Kate tuned back into her surroundings, she heard her father's voice. *All we have is ourselves. All we have is family.* Then there was a curious silence. Her ears pricked. A muffling, no, a murmuring, a whimpering even. Her mother was crying, but no, she was laughing now, a shriek of laughter that blasted through the house like light. Kate knew what was going on. Daddy was lifting her up in his big arms, spinning her round the red and white tiles. Smooching, Peter called it. She used to hear it as a child, down the landing at night. She used to listen for it. Sometimes she'd had to wake Elaine to distract herself. The slap of skin on

94

skin. Another blast of laughter came from the kitchen. Kate pulled herself free of the corner and got off the ground. It was safe for her to go.

She went through the good room, avoiding the kitchen, and ducked down the little hallway to the piano room. She pushed against the closed door and jumped when she saw that Peter was inside. He was much too big for the space. 'Sssh,' he said. The lid of her piano was down. Peter was sitting on her stool, hunched, writing something. It looked like a comprehension test, lots of lines and spaces. 'Kate,' he said, covering it. 'Close the door.' She kicked a leg behind her, refusing to take her eyes off him. 'What are you doing?' she said. 'None of your business,' said Peter. 'Ah, come on. I won't tell. I promise.' He straightened up and grinned. 'Swear on your life.' Kate swore on her own life and on Elaine's life too. Peter rose from the stool and let her sit. He stuck his head out the door, then gently closed it. He had the look of a boy about him, which was funny because he'd never looked like one, not even when he was younger. 'Can you keep a secret?' She nodded solemnly. There was an air of mystery in the room, of polished wood and vinegar. 'I'm going back to America, Katie,' he said. 'I got the Green Card! Can you believe it? It was only my second time applying. I won the lotto.' He was beaming. 'How much?' she said, incredulous. And why was he only telling her? She'd be shouting it from the roof. 'Not that Lotto,' he said. 'But the odds are almost the same. It's a dream come true. A green card. It means,' he said. 'It means so much. It means that I'm—an American.' She stared at him in wonder. It was true, he looked exactly like one.

Barely a week had passed before her mother had another of her tempers. It was Ray's fault this time. He'd been skipping applied maths classes, hiding out at the Murphys. There had been war

95

since dinner time and the twins were collateral. Elaine had been sent to her room for dripping spaghetti hoops on the table, Kate banished to the shed for being stupid enough to follow her brother outside.

It was nearly eight o'clock on a December evening, and the shed was cold and dark. Beyond in the garden, she could hear her mother lambasting Ray.

'How dare you, Raymond. When I think of what I'd to do to get you into those classes. You big lummox! You don't know you were born.'

'You're nuts,' Ray said. 'A loony.'

'Wait till your father hears this.'

'Daddy won't care,' said Ray. 'He only cares about Peter and Kate.'

'Don't you talk about your father like that—'

'Like what?' Ray said. 'Leave me alone.'

'Hanging out like a layabout at the Murphy's. As if I wouldn't find out.'

'At least Marise is normal. At least you can have a conversation with her like a normal person.'

Her mother let out a forceful, strangled sound. 'I wish you were dead! I wish all of you were dead.'

'You're mental.'

'I wish *I* was dead!' her mother cried. 'Free of you all—oh, never have children!—they ruin you.'

'A mental case. A loony! Look at you.'

'You won't lock me up in St Dympna's,' her mother said. 'You won't put me in the nuthouse!'

'This *house* is a nuthouse.'

'Why don't you go live with the Murphys so?' Her mother's voice floated off somewhere and Kate imagined her lunging at him, swiping the wet tea towel across his face. The pain of it when the seam caught the corner of the eye. It went right through you.

'You're mental,' Ray said. 'I'd love to live with the Murphys.'

There followed some violent sounds, though it was unclear which of them was winning. Kate wished her father would come home from the mart. It was hours after he was supposed to be back. But, she reassured herself, at least he was home tonight. It wouldn't be like last time, when he'd gone for three nights to Roscommon, when Elaine had been dragged by her hair up the stairs, and Kate had been made to sleep in the shed for the whole night. Though there had been no sleep. The pitch-dark shed, the sound of every movement a thousand spiders or rats. And the warning her mother had hissed through the door hours after Kate was sure she'd gone away. The memory of it was enough to make her sick.

'I wish you were all dead!' her mother said again.

Well, the feeling was mutual. Kate wished her mother would go away and die, and not just continuously threaten to kill herself, and then Daddy might marry a nice, quiet woman who you didn't have to watch out for 24-7.

But later that night, Kate lay wide awake in bed, wishing she could undo her mean thoughts. After the fight with Ray, her mother had driven off in the Jeep, hysterical, and no one had heard from her since. Kate's ears strained for the sound of a car. There had only been five since her father had turned out the lights. Elaine was doing a soft, whistling snore across the way, though earlier she'd sat up in bed and shouted, as if she was awake, *No—I won't*, into their glowing solar system before lying back down and turning into the wall.

Kate wished the cattle grid would rattle.

It had been hours since Mammy had left in the Jeep, hours spent lying here in the soundless dark regretting her thoughts from earlier. It was silly, so silly, but what if her mother died tonight? What if she was in an accident? What if she drove up on the big roundabout on the outskirts of town and smashed into the 'Welcome to Carlow' sign? What if Kate had some unknown power that meant her mother would never come home again? Her Mammy that did everything for her. The tears sprang hot and salty down her face, her nose already raw. She wished the cattle grid would go.

The following afternoon, Kate raced her sister off the bus, winning for once as she legged it up the driveway. Mammy had finally come home at half two the previous night. Kate had snuck onto the landing to make sure it was her, and she'd seen her parents in a long, fierce hug, no smooching, just holding each other.

Now her mother was in a brilliant mood, singing songs from *Annie* in the kitchen. They both sang 'You're Never Fully Dressed Without a Smile' twice over, and afterwards Kate was allowed to help with dinner. She was not a nuisance and she did not make a mess. She cut the carrots exactly like her mother wanted, into dozens of perfect batons. They were much tastier when they were neat.

Elaine traipsed in with her headphones on.

'Come and help us, darling,' her mother said.

'Sorry?' Elaine shouted.

Laughing, her mother reached across and yanked the headphones off her ears.

Elaine scowled. 'Seriously—you expect me to listen to musicals?'

'What's wrong with musicals?' said Kate.

'Urgh,' said Elaine. 'You're so lame.' She stomped out of the kitchen in her black Doc Martens before Kate had a chance to reply.

'Leave her off,' her mother said, straining the celery. 'We're having a wonderful time. Aren't we? I didn't mean any of it yesterday. You know that.'

'I know, Mammy.'

They didn't look at each other, but there was love, right there in the warm kitchen.

'I get myself into tempers, and I don't know how to stop them. I know it's wrong. It's just so hard sometimes. No one tells you how much work it is to be a mother. Men have it easy. Your father has it easy.'

'I know, Mammy,' Kate said, even though her mother had spoken the last few sentences at the extractor fan. 'I know.'

And she did know, too. Her mother wasn't always angry. She had good moods that could last for days, weeks if they were away somewhere, especially if it was on the Continent. (Kate had been to France and Spain, when lots of the girls in her class didn't even have a passport.) In good humour, Mammy was the best. Singing, or dressing up, or showing Kate smart tricks to win the rummy. Sometimes they would even read books out loud to each other.

'Curiouser and curiouser,' Kate said now. 'Goodbye, feet!'

'That's my girl.' Her mother took the batons and fried them in butter.

Ray came in and went to the fridge without a word.

'Well, aren't you going to say hello—Doctor Raymond?'

Kate could feel her brother's anger spread across the tiles.

'And will the good doctor be joining us for dinner?' Her mother winked at Kate.

'Do you hear me, Raymond?' her mother said.

Ray muttered something under his breath and then burst out the utility door.

'Teenage boys and their hormones,' her mother said, sagely. 'If you learn one thing from me, Kate, it's this—let them stew.'

'OK, Mammy. I will.'

Her mother took out the pounder for the mash and the two of them started up a fine rendition of 'It's the Hard Knock Life'.

There followed a time of ease and happiness at Cranavon, which was usually how things went after a meltdown. The pressure was off. It was like the hiss of the hydraulic machines releasing. Kate was learning about them in science, her favourite subject. She'd impressed Daddy and Peter no end by interrupting them at breakfast one morning, and saying, *but isn't that just Pascal's Law?* It was a clever law that turned up in lots of things: any pressure applied to a fluid in a closed system transmits that pressure equally everywhere and in all directions.

With both her parents in good moods, the house itself seemed to grow bigger, more free. It was a place you wanted to be. Ray was staying late for after-school study these days, Peter would go off about the farm with his new mobile phone in the evenings (Kate had heard him whispering *tea-care-ah-mooch-o* over and over again into the darkness of the back garden), and Mammy had ramped up her bridge nights in preparation for the big Kilkenny congress in the middle of December. The house felt like it belonged to Kate and Elaine. They did their homework quickly and early, and sometimes very poorly, and spent the rest of the time eating Monster Munch, watching *Friends* and making prank calls on the upstairs phone. Elaine had a treacherous new scheme where you'd search for a couple listing in the phonebook and then ring poor Mary or Barbara or Cynthia and ask if you could speak to Robert, or John, or William. *Who is this?* the women would ask in various degrees of friendliness. 'Oh,' Elaine would say. 'Oh, is that Cynthia? Oh, I'm sorry. I didn't mean. I didn't think—it doesn't matter.' Then she'd hang up and the pair of them would die laughing on their parents' bed. But, it was awful, truly awful, and Kate had decided they would stop doing it once and for all in January, in the brand-new millennium.

The town was all abuzz about the big countdown and the firework celebrations, though Peter said it didn't matter what the council put on, it would be nothing compared to the fireball that had passed over Leighlinbridge last Friday, whose explosions had been heard all around the county. Lucy Stevens' mother had been on the nine o'clock news and Kate was raging that none of her own family had seen it. A blazing hot fireball detonating right on their doorstep, and not one of them had witnessed it.

On the Sunday evening of the bridge congress, they waited up with Daddy and the boys after *Glenroe* to see how Mammy had done. The television room was warm and sleepy, the earthy outside smell strong off the turf. They knew already that Mammy had come second in the mixed pairs on the Friday night, and third in the Inter As on the Saturday. It was her new Polish Club system. She'd learnt it herself from a book and then taught her partners the rules.

As they were watching the highlights of the football, the cattle grid rattled to the heavens.

It nearly woke Peter in the armchair.

'She's won.' Ray stretched his legs on the couch. His foot touched Elaine's knee.

'Go way,' said Elaine. 'You lummox.'

It served her right. She hadn't moved over earlier, and Kate had carpet sores on her elbows from lying on the rug in front of the fire. She shifted onto her side. The last of the briquettes was turning white.

'I'd say you're right, son.' Daddy turned down the volume on *The Sunday Game*.

The Jeep door banged, the crush of the stones, the rush of footfall on the hall floor. Mammy burst into the room. They looked at her expectantly.

'Well, Bern?' said her father.

She flung her good red coat down on a chair. 'Why are you two still up?' she snapped at Kate.

'We wanted to…'

'Get to bed—now.' She looked hot and bothered, even her eyes.

'But Mammy,' said Elaine, 'it's only half nine. We're fourteen next month.'

It was true. They were practically adults.

'Get. To. Bed!'

Peter woke up, looked shocked to see them all.

'What did I miss?'

'She didn't win,' said Ray, getting up. He jumped over Kate and left the room.

'I did win, actually,' her mother said. 'But who cares?'

Who *cares*, thought Kate.

'Who *cares*?' said Elaine.

'Well done, Bern,' said her father. 'Great news.'

The fire hissed and crackled, a bright red ember shooting out near the rug. Kate squashed it with her book.

'Put up the fireguard,' said Peter.

'Oh, aren't you very sensible, Peter?' said her mother.

'What?' Peter frowned.

Even he hadn't been able to miss that level of sarcasm. Elaine sat forward on the couch, zipped up her black velvet hoodie.

'Tell your father, Peter. Confess. Tell *everyone* here your dirty little secret.'

Peter opened and closed his mouth.

'Go on,' her mother said. 'Tell them. I heard. I found out. I'm no fool, Peter Gleeson.'

Her father stayed silent.

'Mammy,' said Peter.

'Tell them,' she said.

'I,' Peter said. 'I-I-I.'

'Oh, aye, aye, aye.' Her mother turned to Daddy. 'Do you know what your son is up to?'

'Take it easy, Bern. Sit down there.'

'Your son.'

'Mammy,' said Peter. 'I'm sorry, Mammy.'

'*Your* son, Francis, is moving to San Diego—forever, apparently. He's all ready to go. The sneaky snake applied for the Green Card without telling anyone.'

'Daddy knows,' Peter said.

Her father gave him a dangerous look.

'He—what?'

'I had to tell him with the farm, Mammy.'

'And *me*,' her mother screeched. 'Like the village idiot? Finding out from Marise Murphy of all people!'

Elaine shot off the couch and ran from the room.

'You too, Katie,' her father said.

Kate pretended to look for an imaginary bookmark.

'Quickly, Kate.' Her father nodded at the door.

'He can't go,' said her mother. 'You can't go, Peter.'

'It's his life, Bern.'

'But the farm!'

'I've plenty of men.'

'But Hilary Clerkin will be devastated.'

'Mammy,' said Peter. 'I told you a hundred times, we're not getting back together.'

'But the… millennium, Francis. He'll miss the millennium! He can't miss the new millennium.'

Peter went to speak again but her father tapped loudly on the wooden armrest. 'Don't test my patience, Kate,' he said.

She got up quickly, closed the door behind her and ran after her sister. As she flew up the stairs, she heard her mother shout, *over my dead body*.

The next few weeks were like living in a place that was 6 per cent ground, 94 per cent landmine. Elaine retreated to her bunker, where there was, once again, no room for Kate. She didn't understand it. Growing up, they'd gone about Cranavon as one. *Look at them*, their mother would say, *they don't even know I'm here*. It was kind of true. They were a unit. Colouring books shared, dolls beheaded with mutual consent, jigsaws completed in double-quick time. They'd gotten so good at doing them, they used to turn the pieces over and do them backwards.

But since secondary school, the whole world seemed to want in on the action. Their mother, for one, was far more involved in their lives, and in the private bond between them that, really, had nothing to do with her. In particular she hated the way they could pass messages to each other with their eyes. She'd asked Principal Clerkin to put them in different home classes on purpose, claiming it was for their own good, *to mould unique identities*, but Kate felt there was another reason, some unspeakable thing to do with belonging. *I know what you two are plotting*, their mother would often say, when they'd only be deciding what to watch on TV.

The never-ending suspicions would be worth it, at least, if herself and her sister still had their bond, but Elaine had moved away from her, from them, and Kate resented it. Why should she get to decide on her own? There'd been no big fight, no silences—that wasn't possible when you shared a room—just what felt like a thousand nicks that could rupture at any time. The goddamn, event-traipsing horse riding was a problem, yes, but the distance was there even when they were together. They could both be sitting beside each other on the old plaid couch in the television room and still not have their connection. This connection that had started at fourteen weeks, before they were even born, when they'd reached out to each other in their mother's womb. *Hi! Hello! It's me, it's you.* They were the one person in two separate bodies and every time Elaine hid herself away, she killed a bit of both of them.

Peter left in the middle of January. The night before he was due to go, he knocked on their bedroom and asked to speak to Kate alone. In her dressing gown and wet-hair turban, Elaine refused to leave so Kate went to Peter's room. He'd sat her on his bed—so strange his room, the bare green walls and suitcase bulky in the corner—and told her to look out for Mammy when he was gone. When she got up to leave, he'd hugged her tight and slipped a packet of Jelly Bellies into her hoodie pocket. 'Sssh,' he'd said. 'Tell no one.'

Now he was gone in the Jeep with Daddy to Dublin Airport, Elaine and Ray with them, but Kate had stayed behind in case Mammy needed anything. Her mother had taken to the bed after the new millennium and you'd only catch glimpses of her about the house these days. She'd even missed their birthday, which was most unlike her. Aunt Helen had brought them both to Captain America's in Dublin city. It had been an OK day. The humongous burgers, the coldness of the milkshakes sliding down, the empty fourth seat.

'Mammy,' Kate said, rapping on her door. 'Can I get you anything?'

There was silence and Kate eventually left her alone. She went down to the kitchen and took a box of Lucky Charms from the press, poured herself a bowl. It was all plain old oats, not a pastel-coloured marshmallow in sight. Elaine the cereal miner had gotten there first.

The rest of the month dragged worse than any other January Kate could remember. No more Christmas, no more millennium, no more birthday, no more Peter. Life itself seemed to be disintegrating.

Easter came early that year, and with it the hope that things might improve. It had been a long winter, full of dark, brittle days. Their father had spent more time than usual on the farm, making up for Peter's absence. Their mother was largely the same—silences or tantrums, little in between. The mood about the house was at once lonely and suffocating. Late at night, if you paid attention, you could hear the walls pulsing with the weight of it all.

But on Holy Thursday they came downstairs to find their mother frying eggs in the kitchen. Fully dressed, smelling of lilies and humming a song from *Carousel*. On Good Friday, she filled a Trócaire box with coins and told them to pretend they'd been doing it for the whole of Lent. Yesterday she took the twins to town and bought them magazines and Icebergers, and this morning, she burst into their bedroom in a swishing pale-yellow dress that Kate hadn't seen in years. On their way to mass, Daddy said she looked like Easter itself and they'd all packed into the Jeep, laughing at their mother's impression of a chicken.

Things had gone even better from there: mass with the quick priest, Creme Eggs outside the church, lunch in the hotel and free chocolate bunnies from the basket by reception as they left. Now they were in the car park of the hotel, waiting for Mammy to finish her endless woman conversation with Marise Murphy, so they could go home and open their big eggs, which were stacked on top of each other on the mantelpiece in the television room.

The wind was up, and the men were already in the car. Kate and Elaine were leaping about the tarmac, trying to steal each other's bunnies. In front of the car park, the long manicured lawn looked soft and inviting, the tall pine trees in serious green columns at either side. Just as Kate was about to make a break for it, their mother called them to the car. There wasn't a hint of Easter in her tone.

As Kate opened the door of the Jeep, she heard Marise say to her mother, *I believe the police were involved, Bernadette.* Less than a minute later, their mother was climbing into the passenger seat in a ruckus of yellow, banging the door shut.

'How are the births, deaths and marriages?' Daddy made his old joke.

'Drive, Francis,' her mother said, staring out the window. 'Just drive.'

They set off on the bendy road in silence, the bunny melting in Kate's hands. When they got home, her parents went straight to the television room, closed the door and the shouting began. Not even Elaine was brave enough to go in and ask for the eggs.

It was late now, past midnight, the trio of love songs on Atlantic 252 long over. Kate was still awake, staring at the neon constellations on her ceiling. The shouting had stopped only an hour ago when their mother had left the house in a rage, tearing down the gravel in the Jeep, thundering over the cattle grid. Shortly afterwards there'd been the rev of another engine. Kate had bolted out of bed and gone to the window—Daddy's van skidding down the driveway almost as fast as Mammy.

In the creaky quietness of the house, Kate was still trying to piece things together from the snippets she'd overheard. In conclusion: Peter had gone off the rails in America, and it was all Daddy's fault for letting him go. It was a proper scandal, Kate understood that much, something to do with Peter and a Mexican girl—an illegal immigrant, *a fucking refugee.* There was a child involved too but it was not Peter's, at least Kate didn't think so. *Your stupid son is being taken for a ride all over Mexico town!*

Though she tried to stay awake, Kate kept drifting off. She woke with a start to the sound of voices and didn't know how long she'd been out. For a moment she was sure that something bad had happened, but it was OK, there was no shouting downstairs, just the murmuring that was always so comforting to hear after the storm.

Elaine coughed in her sleep, raspy and short like a sick old man. She'd been at it throughout the night. That's what happened when you didn't brush your teeth after four eggs. Looking at her shuddering beneath the covers, Kate wanted to pat her on the back. She turned over herself instead and tried to count the stars and planets but gave up at thirty-nine. It was no use. She was wide awake. The moaning downstairs had gotten louder and it sounded like more people than her parents. Maybe Ray was with them, maybe he'd been the saviour of the night. Imagine that. Kate giggled and switched on the reading lamp. Elaine gave another cough but didn't wake.

On the locker Kate's copy of *The Catcher in the Rye* was ready to go, but it was the kind of book you had to concentrate on and she didn't think she'd be able in the middle of the night. What time was it, anyway? She turned the digital radio to face her. 4.47! It was the latest they'd ever been up. Kate rooted in the locker for her *Sweet Valley High*, an old favourite, the one where Jessica dyed her hair black to become a model.

But no, the pages were all blurry and boring, and she decided to get up. It was only an hour before Daddy would usually wake so she couldn't be in that much trouble. She borrowed Elaine's velvet hoodie and closed their door softly behind her. On the landing, it felt like Christmas morning, that nervous anticipation as she put her foot on the first step, testing. She wished Copernicus would appear with the bright red bow on his collar.

At the end of the stairs she could clearly hear convulsions coming from the kitchen. She switched on the lamp beside the telephone table and the hallway walls lit up around her, white as clay.

The fight was not over.

She would be better going back to bed. And yet her hand gripped the shiny polished ball at the end of the banister and spun herself down the hallway. Her feet prickled with the cold floor, and every budge she made towards the kitchen seemed to make the crying louder. Her poor Mammy was very upset. Kate would hurl herself towards her when she got into the kitchen. She would ignore Daddy and go straight for her mother and hug her about the middle, just the way she liked.

'They didn't,' her mother cried out. 'They wouldn't.'

'It's OK,' she heard a stranger's voice say. 'Sit up here.' They said something else then but the cries drowned it out.

Kate was trying desperately to tune in to the voices, to pick out her father's even tones through the crisis. She nearly jumped out of her skin when she felt the icy hand on her shoulder.

'What's going on?' said Elaine. 'It's five o'clock in the morning.' Her hair was like a nest on her head and she had nothing on over her nightie.

'I don't know,' said Kate. 'Something bad.'

Elaine crossed her arms over the Garfield picture and rubbed away the cold.

'Drink this,' the stranger's voice said. 'Come on, now, Bernadette.'

The cries broke off.

'Good girl.' It was another voice now, recognizable and strange all at the same time, like when you hear a movie star doing a cartoon. 'That's it,' the voice said. 'Good girl.'

'What the hell?' Elaine pushed past Kate and flung open the kitchen door.

Mammy was bent over the table, the bottle of Daddy's good whiskey in front of her.

Kate tried to run towards her but something prevented it, physically held her back. She stopped in the middle of the kitchen and couldn't move. She could barely draw breath. It wasn't Mammy's red face or the stranger woman that did it either. It was the sight of Granny, right there behind Mammy at the table, rubbing her hair.

Elaine screeched into the dimly lit kitchen, a horrible animal sound.

'It's OK,' Granny ran towards her and brought her to the table. 'It's OK.' She was in the floral housecoat that Mammy hated.

The stranger woman, who was not a stranger at all, Kate could see now, but Conor Doyle's mother Brenda with the ginger curls, also went to Elaine. She said the same thing as Granny. 'It's OK. It's OK.'

'It's OK,' said Kate, still stuck to the spot. 'It's OK?'

No one answered her.

Her mother flung herself forward on the table, pounding her fists off the wood before giving up and slumping against it.

'Come over here, Kate,' her Granny said. 'Good girl.'

Kate didn't move an inch. 'Where's Daddy?'

'Come over to me.'

'Where is he? Where's my Daddy?'

'No!' her mother cried. 'I can't.'

'Granny,' Kate pleaded. 'Where is he?'

Brenda Doyle shook her curls and blessed herself.

Tears were falling down Elaine's face, and still Kate didn't get it, not really.

'He's gone, my love—' Granny squeezed Elaine's shoulder, 'my little loves, he's gone.'

Without seeing her move, the Brenda woman was suddenly up close against Kate, drawing her into a milky-smelling cardigan, the wool rough against Kate's face.

Kate couldn't breathe. She pushed her away. 'No,' she said. 'No. My Daddy!'

Elaine was bawling, clinging to Granny.

'Please,' her mother said to no one. 'Please.'

Elaine started to shout their father's name into the night. Copernicus began to bark. Granny turned on the lights over the table and the kitchen was suddenly alive.

'I can't,' her mother sobbed. 'I can't. Get them—please.'

Then they were both being taken by the hands, pulled out of the kitchen, back into the blue darkness of the once familiar hall.

CARLOW

September 2006

B Y THE TIME they got going, it was late afternoon and the sky was heavy and dull. In the passenger seat of the Opel, Kate looked over her shoulder and saw her mother standing in the doorway of Cranavon, framed by the jasmine climber, its small white stars blurry at a distance. She had not come down to say goodbye when they were leaving. Kate waved back at her now but her mother's hand didn't move. Perhaps they were already too far down the driveway and Mammy could no longer see into the car. In her royal blue dressing gown, she looked like a lonely monarch. For a few seconds, before they reached the rusty cast-iron gates, Kate wanted to tell her brother to stop, to reverse, to crunch over the gravel once more and allow her the chance to say a proper goodbye before they hit the road to Dublin.

'Mammy's there at the door,' she said.

Ray turned onto the boreen. He was bringing her back to college, to Trinity Hall in Dartry, which was so popular it had taken until third year to get a room.

'Bit late for that now,' Ray said. 'I've enough of The Noise to do me till Christmas.'

As they went through the crossroads, Kate checked her Nokia just in case but there were no little handsets or envelopes on the screen. 'I didn't mean to set her off earlier.' She tugged at the seat belt, tight across her new red cardigan. No matter what way she fixed the strap, it dug into her. Even now, years later—a reminder. *No belt*, a neighbour had said in the queue at her father's wake. *Straight through the windscreen.*

'I wish Daddy—' Kate said, swallowing hard.

Ray jolted the gearstick and the engine moaned. He turned on the radio to her favourite Killers song. She looked out the window, her eyes flitting over her reflection in the wing mirror.

'Daddy was very good to you,' Ray said eventually. 'But don't be maudlin, Katie. It's a brand-new year. And don't worry about herself either, she'll be grand. Doesn't she have Peter? You just get yourself sorted for college. In your swanky new digs.'

Kate smiled. 'You're right,' she said. 'I can't wait to be back in Dublin.' She considered her outfit, wondering if it was suitable for halls. They were her best pair of bootcut jeans—no scraggly bits from capillary action—but not everyone was wearing bootcut these days. On the back seat, her favourite black coat, a cape of sorts, which her mother said looked like a shroud. Well, her mother was wrong: it was, in fact, a cocoon.

'Do you know who you're sharing with?' said Ray.

'I'm not in the sharey ones. Cunningham Hall only has single rooms.'

'Better off,' he said. 'Remember my hovel in UL?'

'Watch the road,' said Kate, as he swerved around a bend.

'I am.'

'Sorry.' She hated her nervousness in cars, which was so like her mother.

'You're as bad as Mammy,' said Ray.

'I am not!'

Their mother no longer drove, and bringing her anywhere was like having a time bomb in the passenger seat.

Ray said, 'Single rooms. Like, is it a bedsit? What about cooking?'

'Fourteen of us to a kitchen. You can come in, see for yourself.'

'I'm going to have to leg it,' he said. 'You don't have much stuff.'

It was true, she seemed to need less as she got older. She glanced at her brother: clean-shaven and the fringe spiked to heaven. 'Are you off somewhere with Liz?'

'Yeah.'

Of course it was Liz. He'd enough aftershave on to spice Christmas. They'd been going out all summer and it was cute, the way he was still trying to impress her.

'Where are you off to?'

'Just plans,' he said. 'Things to do.' He hit the top of the steering wheel. 'Getting rid of this old banger for one.'

Her brother was all business since he got the job in the rehab centre in Dún Laoghaire. *Raymond is helping cripples*, their mother liked to say.

'Well for some,' said Kate.

'Are you nervous? Is that it?'

'No.' She looked out the passenger window.

'You're full of secrets these days,' Ray said.

The greenery of the back roads, thick and stooping, chinks of light in the gaps.

Ray said, 'I'm only joking.'

'I know.'

'It's all right to be nervous.'

'None of the girls got into halls.' She meant her friend Jenny, really. The rest of them didn't bother with her so much. 'But I don't care. It's a hundred times better than Mrs Collins and her digs.' For the first two years of college, she'd lived in Rathgar, in a dusty old-person room with a spongy mattress and no hanging space.

'Mammy liked that she was from Borris,' said Ray. 'And at least she fed you. You'll miss that.' He looked sideways at her with his hooded eyes.

'I won't miss the damn curfew.' If you weren't back by eleven, you had to sleep elsewhere. Kate had kissed at least three boys she'd no interest in just to get a bed.

'Ha,' said Ray. 'Like prison.'

'Or an asylum,' said Kate.

'Stop your messin. We've no time for messers here.' Ray did an impression of Peter, the face that was so like a guard's when he was mad.

'Ah, he's all excited these days,' Kate said. 'The ploughing championships at the end of the month. Carlow's on the map!'

'What if Peter meets someone at it,' said Ray. 'An actual female. A lady farmer.' He listed the essential qualities of the imaginary woman.

'Don't forget acreage,' said Kate.

'And a creamery,' said Ray.

'Maybe some sheep?'

'And a few chickens to keep her busy in the mornings.'

They were having so much fun they nearly missed the exit for the motorway. Ray squeezed in behind a Micra and all of a sudden, the smooth, slick tarmac seemed to swallow them up like a dark river and carry them away from Carlow.

As they passed the sign for the toll bridge, Ray switched to the hurling. The jaunty voices of the commentators made her feel sick but she said nothing. She looked at the lush autumn colours of the trees that lined the motorway and wondered who had thought to plant them. Closing her eyes, she said a silent goodbye to her home town, to the torquing path of the Barrow and the spire of Myshall Church, to the patchwork fields and the cows, and to the people, too, who only knew her for her loss. First her father and then her sister—two deaths in one family in a matter of years. You didn't come back from that. Hereabouts they were no longer the Gleesons, but the poor Gleesons. This was never going to change, and some people in the family seemed perfectly happy with that.

Though her room was on the ground floor of Cunningham Hall, Ray insisted on helping with the suitcase. Her new key jammed in the lock when she tried to open the bright orange door at the end of the corridor. Ray took off his sunglasses. 'Give it here,' he said. 'You have to pull and twist.' The door sprang back but he closed it again before she'd a chance to see anything. He tapped the shiny number six in the centre of the door. 'Now, you try,' he said.

Inside, the room felt small with the pair of them and her father's maroon leather suitcase flat on the carpet. It was nearly five and the sun had already passed. Kate hit the switch by the door—a too-bright, flickering light. She was glad she'd taken Elaine's polka-dot lamp from home.

'It's cosy,' said Ray. 'Definitely meant for one.'

Elaine and herself would fit fine, she thought. They'd manage.

'What's wrong?' Ray unzipped his jacket.

'Nothing,' she said. 'It's lovely. I can see the old house out the window.'

And it was lovely, her own space, the pleasure of that. She was being foolish. She'd managed two years already at college without Elaine. Why would she go backwards now?

'Will I help you dress the bed?' Ray looked at his watch.

'Nah, don't worry. I'll unpack first. Drown the place in perfume.'

Ray sniffed. 'It's a bit musty all right.' He went to the window and opened the small rectangle on top. 'That's as far as it goes.'

They had a quick, awkward hug goodbye. The door caught on the woolly carpet as she tried to close it—a heavy old beast that needed a fine push. She sat on the bare mattress and surveyed the room. It was perfect, everything you could want or need: the brick walls painted a fresh white, a chair and a stumpy brown desk, the shelves and wardrobe in the same unvarnished wood. There was a large sink at the foot of her bed and a square sheet of mirror pinned to the wall above it. She looked all right, actually—her long, centre-parted hair was in fashion these days and she'd lost weight over the summer, had cheekbones for the first time in her life. They made her dark eyes bigger, more interesting. Today they seemed strangely glittering. But she could not take it for long. This mirror, the oval mirror at Cranavon, the wing mirror of the Opel, any scrap of mirror at all, even her reflection in a window, it was always the same: behind her own face, the shadow of her sister, a permanent reminder of what was lost.

She leaned against the wall and tried to stop the familiar feeling of upset. All weekend she'd been dying to leave home, to get away from the farm—and from Tullow, after her summer working in the pottery shop. The owner was good fun but notoriously stingy. Kate had only made half what she'd made the summer of first year working for Peter. And no sign of a tan at all. She looked down at her pale chest and decided to wear a necklace if there were drinks about the place this evening. She hoped something would be going on. Aside from her family, the only person she'd seen all summer was Conor Doyle. He'd come into the shop one day looking for a teacup, but she hadn't been able to close the sale in the end. Somehow they'd arranged to meet outside the blue door of the cinema in Carlow Shopping Centre to see the remake of *The Omen*. It had been a disappointment, actually, but they ended up going to another film the following Saturday, and another one the week after that, until it turned into a regular activity that she looked forward to. To be clear: he was not her boyfriend, they hadn't even kissed. All the same she missed him, and hoped that he might make good on his promise to visit her in Dublin. Their summer friendship had been well timed in a way, coinciding with another of her mother's depressions and the bitter freedom that came with them. But there had been war earlier today when Conor rang the house instead of Kate's mobile. Her mother had accused her of being dishonest, of being a sly snake who'd end up pregnant with a commoner's child if she didn't watch herself. Kate had been so mad she'd almost choked on Peter's roast chicken. She'd wanted to say that Conor Doyle hadn't put a finger on her, but she knew if she said that, they'd all see how much she wanted him to, so she'd excused herself and run to the bathroom and spat the woolly chicken that was still in her mouth straight into the toilet. (And how did her mother know, how *could* she know, that after *Children of Men* last weekend, Conor and Kate had walked up to the fountain, joking about baby names, settling on Jack and Elaine, and Sheila if they had a third.)

All weekend dying to be back in Dublin, to get started again, to get going, and yet now that she was here, the thrill of it had left her. It felt wrong that Mammy and Peter would watch *You're a Star* without her tonight. Maybe she should run after Ray, ask him if she could come over to their new place in Blackrock, a huge apartment that Liz had found through work, in a lemon-painted complex overlooking the sea. It seemed, right now, to be the very opposite of here. That feeling that she'd had for most of secondary school, of not being safe no matter where she was, came over her. The older she got, the younger she felt. She fought the urge to cry. 'Grow up,' she said out loud.

She got off the bed and opened the suitcase. She just needed to unpack, to make the room her own. She arranged her things in neat piles on the mattress. First the clothes, the tops, jeans, hoodies, her winter coats in black and navy, three pairs of Converse and the kitten heels her mother had given her as a surprise. Textbooks and folders were next. She sorted them in alternate pink and blue stacks, propping them up on the shelves in between the letter bookmarks K and E. She gave one corner of the desk to her Discman and CDs, assembled her make-up in the rickety holder by the sink, hung all her clothes and then finally arranged her photos on the windowsill, keeping the one of Daddy and Elaine and herself for her locker. Her mother would be hurt she wasn't in it, but it was Kate's favourite picture, the three of them happy on the farm the summer of sixth class. She tilted the sparkly glass photo frame towards her. It was a beautiful photo but sometimes it was hard to look at.

When she'd her new purple duvet on the bed, she switched on Elaine's lamp and lay down for a rest. She looked at the ceiling, so white and boring. She thought to text her friend Jenny just in case she'd gotten an earlier flight from Norwich, but no, best not to seem needy. She would meet her outside the coffee dock before Economics tomorrow. It would be an easy enough week: six hours of Economics, but only two History lectures and no dreaded tutorials. She reached over to the windowsill for the photo of herself and Elaine at their sixteenth birthday party. Matching baby blue flares and belly tops. It had been the best of nights.

Someone knocked on her door.

'Hello?' Kate said.

'Hi, oh, hi!' said a voice outside.

She smoothed her cardigan and went to the door.

'Hi there!' The girl was wearing a dark slip dress over a long-sleeved white top. 'I'm George.' She had a southside Dublin accent. 'Your neighbour?' She pointed to an orange door across the hall. 'We're having drinks in the kitchen. You coming?'

'I'm Kate,' she said, but George was already zigzagging her way down the corridor, knocking on doors.

'Super,' George shouted back. 'It's going to be the best year!' Her short blonde hair looked like a swim cap from a distance.

Kate followed after her, forgetting her keys until the door shut behind her. She ran back, pushed it a few times and then gave up. No doubt someone would have a master key and she could be the idiot who needed it in the first half hour of moving into halls. She followed a smell of melted cheese to the kitchen and was surprised to see at least ten people crowded around a communal table. The look of the room was wrong, full of strange dimensions and duplications. There were four identical cookers, one for each worktop. Already the hobs seemed stained, or in use—a sweaty silver pot boiling on the one nearest her—and she realized she was probably the last to arrive. She smiled at the group and said hello. All of them were women except for a tanned, hulkish guy in a college rugby shirt.

'This is Kate.' George came in behind her, 'I think that's everyone.' She kissed the guy on the lips, a long smacker in front of them all. 'Freddie doesn't live here by the way,' she said. 'Well, not officially, anyway.'

A girl in a sheer blouse wolf-whistled. Someone offered Kate a crisp. The pot on the hob started to boil over and two of her new flatmates rushed to contain it.

The second week of October, the city centre sun the hottest it had been since the start of term at Trinity. Three-quarters of the cricket pitch was a bright lime green, the last bit in the shadow of the austere sciences institute. Kate saw Jenny stand and wave from the far side of the Pav. They were on the softer grass near the cricket pitch but not close enough to the lawn to get kicked off. A big group, she could see, some of them lying down. She wondered who else was with them. It could be anyone—Jenny and the girls had skipped Investment Analysis and gone drinking after lunch. A lazy afternoon at the Pav was a good place for making new friends. All around her people were chatting; a loud, discordant noise without music to absorb it. She felt happy and full of energy. It had been like this for weeks, something inside her spinning faster and faster. There was barely a need for sleep. She put her bag of cans on the grass while she took off her wind-breaker and tied it around her waist, regretting the beaded necklace she'd decided to wear last minute over a perfectly innocent white T-shirt. Jewellery didn't suit her, it was always too dangly or too much. Nail polish was the same—insipid or vampish, it was off again by the end of the day.

Kate pushed her way through the crowds, past a group of engineers that were in the same year as George. They were playing a drinking game with a dirty funnel and a bottle of rum. She said a quick hello to the guy nearest her then moved on. Her cans of Bud Light were already losing their coolness. She avoided the steps in front of the Pav and went wide onto the pitch to get to her friends. The lawn had a chemical smell, not like the grass at Cranavon. Sizing up the group on her approach, she could see that the three girls were spread out: Jenny at the edge of the circle, talking to strangers, her high ponytail moving from side to side; Aoife pink-faced and uncomfortable in one of her cheesecloth dresses; Miranda lying down with her head on Bill's stomach.

'Look who it is,' said Miranda, who liked to announce things. She was the class rep for Economics, famous around college for chaining herself to a tree outside the Provost's house in nothing but a bin bag.

'Hey, Kate,' Bill said sleepily.

She vaguely recognized the guys behind him, his mates from English. One of them shielded his eyes from the sun and nodded.

'Hey,' she said.

'How was IA?' said Aoife.

'Thrilling. He did systematic pricing failures.'

'Were we missed?'

'Nah.' Kate sat on the grass near Jenny, hoping she'd turn around soon.

'On the hard stuff already?' Miranda pointed at Kate's cans. She was always making jokes.

'Don't encourage her,' said Aoife. 'Or we'll have Rag Doll before you know it.'

Kate laughed, but she was mortified that they were using her nickname in front of strangers.

'Who's Rag Doll?' said a guy with ginger hair.

'You know Superman,' Miranda said. 'Right? Like Clark Kent. Telephone box?'

'Yeah.'

'Well, Rag Doll is Kate's alter ego.'

'Her superhero,' Aoife laughed.

'Serious student by day, absolute mentalist by night.' Miranda held up her Smirnoff Ice. 'Cheers to that.'

The whole group did a 'cheers' and Kate felt herself relax. Good old Rag Doll.

'It's true,' she said, opening a can. 'I don't know how it happens. But it's a blast.'

Jenny hugged the guys goodbye and moved in beside her.

'Do you've a match?' said Kate, pointing at her green-and-black hockey kit.

Her friend held up a naggin. 'It's only training.'

Kate laughed.

A topless guy ran onto the cricket pitch and did two and a half cartwheels as his friends cheered.

'Look at that tosser,' said Miranda. 'He'll ruin it for everyone.'

But she was wrong. Moments later a wiry-looking security guard raced after him, and the whole place seemed to rise and follow the chase, lifting the afternoon to another level entirely, spinning them all into an early evening and night and the blue-lit morning hours that would follow. It was clear to everyone, as the guy made it right to the end of the pitch before the guard got his hands on him, that the time had come to party. The hooting and cheering grew louder. She joined in, wanting so much for the guy to escape. His courage astounded her. Beneath the glass windows of the Ussher Library, he was dragged away with his arms behind his back.

All the time she'd been in college, one thing loomed over the first month back, and each year when it arrived it was almost a relief—Halloween. Tomorrow Kate would go home to Cranavon for the anniversary, her sister's fourth anniversary, but right now she was under her purple duvet wishing herself to sleep. She'd drunk a bottle of Calpol after her lectures and her mind was in and out of consciousness, full of moving images: Elaine the human haystack jumping out at Peter in the field. Elaine smoking a cigar on the roof of the extension. Elaine locked inside their mother's wardrobe. Elaine crying over sludgy Weetabix, like liquid clay it was, plopping off the spoon. Kate couldn't tell reality from nightmare. Her head was so heavy and the rest of her barely there.

'You missed dinner.'

Kate thought she was definitely dreaming now, until she felt the sag at the end of her bed. She sat up with a jolt. It was only George. The light from the hallway shone dusty on her bookshelves.

'You left your door on the latch,' George said. 'I robbed you blind.'

Kate gave a faint laugh. She switched on the polka-dot lamp, blinked against its brightness.

'There's shepherd's pie left over. Will I bring you in some?'

'I ate already,' said Kate.

'Yeah?'

'In the Buttery.'

George looked around the room. She pointed to the cough bottle on the locker. 'Are you sick?' Her narrow blue eyes were full of concern.

Kate burst into tears.

'Oh, God,' said George. 'What's wrong?'

This was so embarrassing. They'd only known each other six weeks, and Kate hadn't told her yet. She hadn't told any of her new halls friends. It was such an impossible thing to tell these people you met in college, wondering if you knew them well enough to confide in, wondering whether they'd be gone again in a few months and you'd have been better off not telling them at all. Death depressed people, and it changed their opinion of you. Kate had seen that with her Economics crew, even though they'd been lovely to her about it—the news had brought them down. She took the photo of their sixteenth birthday from the locker and passed it to George.

'Wow,' said her friend, not getting it at all. 'You're a twin! Where—'

Kate made a sharp gulping noise. The words were stuck inside her.

'Oh,' said George. 'Oh. I'm so sorry.'

Kate nodded. George squeezed tighter on her calf, tight enough to bruise.

'It's her fourth anniversary tomorrow,' said Kate. 'My brother's picking me up at lunchtime.'

'And tonight?'

Kate shrugged, unsure if she could deal with more kindness.

'Tonight,' George passed her a tissue from the box by her CDs, 'I'm looking after you. And it starts with shepherd's pie.'

It was nice of her, Kate knew, but there was no way she was having dinner this evening. Hunger was the only thing keeping her going.

'Maybe a drink,' she said, trying to smile. 'I've a bottle of vodka under the bed.'

A little tiny stress fracture in the second week of November, a bad month for a bone break, the piercing cold weather still new and so unfriendly. Kate's foot throbbed as she sat at a table near the coffee dock, waiting for Jenny. It was early, the Arts Block quiet, the shutters still down on the soft drinks and juices in the café. The teller was busy setting up the chrome canisters. Tall and shiny, they reflected the shapes and sizes of the people in the queue.

The tables around Kate were empty, except for the far corner one where an ageless man was stacking newspapers in front of him like a fort. Everyone said he was Japanese but no one knew for sure. Maybe he was from Korea, or from Cobh. A few students trailed by on their way to the photocopier machines. Headphones and woolly scarves and long quilted jackets. Kate rubbed the arms of her black coat and went to put her bobble hat back on. Her crutches slipped as she reached for it, clattering against the small square tiles. The old man looked at her in alarm and then went back to his fort.

She retrieved the crutches and leaned them against a chair. Horrid things, so cumbersome. Ray had made her go for the X-ray, had driven her to Vincent's last weekend and waited with her in A&E for four and a half hours. Her foot had been sore since Halloween but it wasn't that bad before the diagnosis, not really. *Bone pain*, everyone kept saying now, *there's nothing like it*. She couldn't understand what had happened. All she had done was take up exercise, trying to be healthy like Jenny. She'd done barely anything in comparison with her friend, who trained three days a week with her hockey crew and then did a 10k at weekends up and down the canal.

Historically, Kate was not a runner, had never done athletics or camogie in the Community. So she'd started small, safe, just like Jenny suggested, a few minutes' run built into her Dodder walk. The first time she'd only managed thirty seconds before her lungs nearly exploded. And yes, things had improved the more she'd practised, but her running was certainly not at the level that caused fractures. That's what the world's most unhelpful doctor had told her at half two in the morning, shortly after a man with a gouged eye had vomited over Ray's runners.

How she had gotten to be here, with her foot in a fibreglass cast, had not been explained at all. (And Kate didn't think to mention the anniversary, or the bottle of vodka she'd consumed with George on Halloween eve before getting up for a run.)

The queue for the coffee dock was growing. She longed to shout at someone to bring her a tea but she would wait for Jenny or one of the others to arrive. They had Less Developed Countries at nine and someone she knew would be along soon. It was not so urgent, anyway. She'd had two coffees with a still drunk George in the kitchen earlier that morning. They'd almost had a fight when George opened Kate's locker by mistake. *Where's your cereal, Kate?* she'd said, banging the door of locker six. *Why don't you have cornflakes? Why don't you ever do any shopping?* Well. George clearly didn't know what they put in cornflakes, how they were full of sugar and awful for gut health. And she didn't know that Kate actually spent hours in supermarkets since coming to college, overwhelmed by the rows and rows of products, that she always seemed to be at her most tired and hungry when she did the shop, and deciding on what was fattening, filling, healthy, healing was too much for her brain. The problem was, she didn't trust her own appetite. It was easier to eliminate things, and it was addictive too. First red meat, then non-organic white meat, then farmed fish, then egg yolks, then eggs. No white carbs, pasta, rice, certainly no bread. No potatoes, sweet potatoes—no carbs. No dairy either, no dairy substitutes, nothing creamy, nothing thick, no smoothies. No rich soups, no blended soups, she had narrowed it down to soups of boiled water and chunky vegetables and a scattering of chilli flakes. Easy. Safe. But Kate couldn't share this information with her friend. She knew how strange it sounded. Was it possible to be a bit mad in one small aspect of life and still be normal? It was not a question you could ask someone as cool and together as George. Instead she had to agree with her: the locker was empty. Then she'd left her coffee, hobbled to the bus stop and spent twenty-five minutes waiting for the 14A. And everything was OK now. She was here, early for lectures, watching the random people come and go. She was OK. A little tiny stress fracture was only three weeks in a cast. It could have been worse.

The queue at the dock kept growing. Kate watched the lady in the hairnet frown as a girl ordered four hot chocolates. She seemed to have no one with her but then she gestured at the slanted glass windows behind her head and mimed smoking a cigarette. The smell of melting sugar wafted towards the tables. Suddenly, the morning's efforts of getting to the campus hit her like a dirty wave—all the ordinary things so painful, even rolling in bed or leaning across the sink to get her toothbrush—and she closed her eyes to stop the tears. The smell was stronger with her eyes shut, the brutal sweetness of melting sugar. Like candyfloss, the flagrantly bad-for-you top notes. The last time she'd eaten it. Maybe. Not maybe. Who was she fooling? That autumn morning, that beautiful, sunny Halloween morning four years ago.

In the cramped tutorial room, Kate's foot went into spasm. The cast had come off last Friday but the bit near the ankle was still giving her trouble. She dipped her head out of the lecturer's eye-line, hoping he couldn't see her. These spasms were frequent, a burning, burrowing sensation that was definitely worse than bone pain. But they'd go away when she rebuilt the muscle strength in her foot. Ray had given her a rehab plan and she was following it to the letter, doing it twice a day instead of just in the morning, hoping for a double-quick recovery. The Economics Ball, the official end to Michaelmas term, was the weekend after next, and she was determined to be ready for it.

She looked around the sparsely furnished tutorial room, wishing there was a window. A sliver of sky, a seagull or two, any kind of distraction. It was almost an architectural feat that the majority of rooms in the five-storey Arts Block were without natural light.

The guy from Clongowes, who still told everyone he was from Clongowes even though they were in third year, was giving a long-winded answer to a question about CFDs. He was very tall and balding and his right foot kept tapping to some imaginary soundtrack. 'The problem,' he said, summing up, 'is trust.' But then he went off again, talking about hedge funds and regulations and some other things that Kate knew only by name. She hoped they wouldn't be on the exam. She could not, at this very moment, even remember what the acronym stood for. She knew it was about spread betting. *Gambling*, her lecturer kept calling it, in his even, sleep-inducing voice.

She rubbed the patch of rough skin on her hands and looked at the other students, wishing she'd had more time to get to know them before they switched tutorials next term. The girl from Kerry with the dead-eyed stare, or the Erasmus student from Munich with the straight teeth. Kate had only spoken to him a handful of times. She found tutorials hard, preferred the anonymity of lectures. But still, she was pleased with how this year was going. Halls had turned her into someone who was adequately popular, normal even, able to muck in with the rest of them. She no longer felt hollow. Though her marks were suffering—she was still making the grade in everything, but in that murky second-class-honours way that her mother considered a fail.

'So, what do you think?' said the lecturer.

She looked up to see who he'd asked, confident it wasn't her. He was one of the nice ones who didn't put you on the spot.

'Kate,' he said. 'Do you agree?'

Oh dear, she'd no idea what acronym they were onto now. The warmth she'd been chasing all morning finally ran through her body. If she hadn't been semi-paralysed by the fact that everyone was looking at her, she would have loved to take off her coat. The rest of them had done so the moment they came into the room. She was always behind.

'Well, Kate. What are your thoughts?'

She couldn't look him in the eye. She focused on his beige blazer, at a small stain that was almost a shamrock near the rim of the lapel.

'Contracts for difference,' the German guy said.

She flicked her eyes at him. He showed his lovely teeth and nodded encouragement.

'Yes, CFDs,' she said. 'Well, it's gambling, really. Isn't it?'

'Exactly.' The lecturer tilted his chair back, 'But why?'

She felt the heat flood every part of her, running up to her brain like water in a rad. A rush of words came out. They were in English, certainly, but not in any coherent pattern. She had no control over them, could hear them, right now, pop out her mouth while she was thinking other thoughts. So who was in charge of the speaking? Who was at the helm?

'Right, OK,' the lecturer said eventually. 'That's not what we were saying. Not entirely.'

'Kate broke the foot,' the German guy said loudly. The room was so small it sounded like a cheer. He leaned forward in his chair to point at her orange Converse. 'She broke the foot.'

Everyone looked at her shoe.

'Is it broken now?' the lecturer frowned. 'Should you be here?'

'I got the cast off last week. It's all better.' Her voice was thin and squeaky. 'I just haven't been able to do the reading.'

'I see,' said the lecturer. 'I didn't know. Stay back after and we'll have a chat.'

She nodded. The German smiled at her like this was a positive outcome. As Clongowes started again, she sank into the folds of her coat and tried to concentrate herself into being cold.

The air in her room was stale and sweet and the sharp winter light seemed to find the one gap in the purple curtains that led directly into her eyes. Kate had been awake for a few minutes, paralysed by the weight of her head and the siren that went off inside it every time she went to move. She was topless, right at the edge of her bed, one arm hanging limply over the frame. Her fingers wouldn't curl. Elsewhere: flip-flopping stomach, mouth dry and crusty, bladder like a hatching egg. At least she was still in her knickers. But she wondered who was snoring behind her.

Oh, why, why did the tassel of the damn curtain seem so far away? She let her eyes go round the room instead—her folders on the shelf, her photos, the digital radio blinking four red zeroes, her beautiful salmon-pink ball dress reduced to a silky mess on the ground. Behind her, a little snort and then a sound like a cow low-moaning. She could feel the bulk of him, whoever he was, the slick warmth against her back. For a moment she imagined it was an actual cow, and she gave a bright, drunken laugh into the room, using the momentum to lift herself fully onto the mattress, elbowing the cow-man so he moved towards the wall.

Half comfortable now, she looked again at the dress, the debs dress her mother had bought her in a fancy boutique in Donnybrook. It was one of their best ever days, the first time (the only time?) she'd made Mammy happy since Elaine. Her mother had been in her element, dressed in her finery, breezing in and out of the shops. Kate must have tried on a hundred outfits and when they'd found the one, her mother had cried and hugged her, and there was such closeness between them that Kate felt for a small moment as if Elaine was there with them in the fitting room. That day, Kate saw what it was her mother wanted, perhaps what everyone in the family wanted: Elaine had been the outgoing one, the easy one, the brilliant one, and when she died Kate was supposed to just switch over and become her. Well, at least she'd managed it for a single day.

All of a sudden, her arm came back to life, aching from wrist to shoulder. She pulled at the loose skin of her tricep and tried to remember what had happened the previous night. Miranda! Oh no, the poor thing, flat on her face on the stage, a sparkly red starfish.

But then? What then? The rest of the evening was only available in shards, piercing into her as they landed. She remembered standing on a chair in the hotel ballroom and someone lifting her into the air. *Rag Doll*, they'd said, *let's go flying, Raggers*. She stuck her legs out from under the duvet into the damp air of the room. No bruises or gashes. There were usually scars after a memory-less night, but no, her pale skin had nothing but goosebumps.

The guy behind her snorted again, rolled into the middle of the bed and cocked his top leg over her. She peeled back the duvet to inspect the leg. She'd known from the bulk of him that it couldn't have been Jurgen, but still she was disappointed when she saw the pasty, hairy thigh. A ferocious weight, like the trunk of a dead elephant, that seemed, somehow, to smell of garlic-and-cheese chips. At a loud groan from behind, she gave the trunk an almighty heave and dashed to the towel rail. When she had the towel tucked securely under her arms, she glanced at the bed.

'Well, Raggers, how's the form? You look hanging.' Clongowes had rolled onto his back and was smirking at her.

She couldn't do anything except stare at him. He took her purple duvet and snuggled it up to his chin. She wanted to rip it off him. How dare he touch her things.

'Who's that?' He nodded at the photo of herself and Elaine at their sixteenth. 'She your sister? Smoking hot.'

'Get—' Her voice was breathless.

'Relax,' he said. 'You're not so bad yourself.'

Kate clutched her stomach.

'Are you OK? Like, you're green, babe. Your face? Are you going to—'

But she was gone, out of the room, keyless, witless, hopeless, running down the hall to the bathroom cubicles, wishing, just wishing to forget.

When the Michaelmas term ended, Kate took the bus home to Cranavon for the holidays. Seasonal preparations went better than expected and even a small pine tree with shiny needles was cut from the farm, brought to the house on the back of the tractor and placed in the good room.

On Christmas Day, they had made it through dinner. The five of them sat around the solid oak table in the good room. No tears, no outrages, no fights. Her mother had so far resisted going over to the stereo, putting on the dreaded CD, skipping five tracks down to 'Lonely This Christmas' and crying into some otherwise festive dish, as she had done every year since Daddy died.

With burnt brandy still in the air and the big bowl of whipped cream going flat beside the elegant candles, they debated whether to cut the Christmas cake. Kate couldn't believe they were considering more food. Her stomach was bloated and heavy, and now she would have to sit with the cramps, feeling each sprout as if it had been a stone.

'Well, I'm stuffed,' said Liz. 'It was delicious, Mrs Gleeson.' She tossed her long blonde hair over to one side like a pop star.

Their mother smiled. 'You're very welcome, dear.'

She went on to tell Liz yet another story about some woman at bridge. Cancer. Then a death. And another one. And then the cancer was back. Or it was a new cancer, Kate had lost track. Her mother had been talking all morning. Kate had literally heard the revving voice in her sleep and had opened her eyes to find her mother there in the room at the peach wardrobe, which was where she kept her special occasion clothes these days.

'Seriously, Mrs Gleeson,' said Liz, who was pretty good at anticipating the pauses for an amateur. 'This was one of the nicest dinners I've ever had.'

'Oh, it was nothing,' her mother smiled. 'Stop now.'

Poor Peter at the head of the table managed to keep his face neutral, though he had grown, prepared and cooked everything himself from scratch. Kate had helped him arrange the cheesy parcels for the starter, and she'd done the table just like Mammy wanted—gold and white settings, not an inch of gaudy red.

'Elizabeth, I'm so glad you came down for Christmas,' her mother said, her grey eyes flashing.

'*I'm* so glad you invited me.' Liz drained her wine.

Her mother gave a coquettish laugh. 'Stop,' she said.

It was like hanging around with friends who thought they didn't fancy each other.

'Seriously,' said Liz. 'It was better than a hotel.'

Well! That was the clincher—her mother practically leapt across the table in her bid to pat Liz's arm. 'You're a sweetheart,' she said, beaming. 'Raymond has done very well for himself. I hope he knows that.'

Ray grunted, but you could see he was pleased.

'I don't think I could manage cake,' Liz said. 'Not yet.'

The rest of them nodded agreement. It was so nice to have a visitor at the table, they said. This was the way to do Christmas. They should have done it years ago. Aunt Helen's visits didn't count—no one with a blood connection counted. Kate winked at Ray through the candles, good old Ray, who had brought some shadow of ease back to Cranavon.

He misunderstood her meaning and took a cracker, pointing it like a gun. He was wearing the light blue shirt with the little horse on the pocket that Liz had given him that morning, and his face was flushed and happy.

'Go on, so.' Kate leant forward.

Her mother turned sharply. Were these the show crackers, not for pulling? To hell with that. She finished her wine, grabbed the end, gave a fine tug, but the cracker split open without a bang. A miniature scissors fell onto the table. Peter extracted the thin brown strip from the debris and snapped it in his fingers. Under the tree Copernicus woke and yelped.

'You didn't even pull it, Kate.' Her mother snatched the gold hat and rested it on top of her bob. 'She didn't pull it, Liz.'

'No,' said Liz. 'Handed it to him.' She mouthed an apology to Kate as Mammy reached for her water.

Her mother went back to telling them the endless story about her visits to the local hospice and how they weighed on her. She'd started going a few years ago and seemed to have forgotten that it was voluntary.

Eventually, when the story was finished, Ray got the box of Penneys crackers from under the tree, and there was pulling and shouting, the smoky smell of gunpowder, some jokes that Peter mistook for trivia, and then a last-minute turnaround on the cake where they all ganged up against her and decided it wasn't Christmas without a slice.

'You cut away,' said Kate. 'I'll finish the clean-up and have some later with charades.'

'Have some now,' Peter said.

'Charades?' Liz looked at Ray in horror, her Dalkey accent more pronounced. 'Like, really?'

'Oh, yes,' their mother said. 'We love a game of charades in this house.'

'Will you have a small slice, Kate?' Peter cracked the icing with the knife.

'Later,' she said.

'There's nothing like charades at Christmas,' said her mother.

Kate had a sudden pang: Elaine in her candy-cane pyjamas, acting out her favourite film, *The Hand that Rocks the Cradle*, and Kate guessing the answer the moment she held up six fingers.

The sprouts started cramping in her stomach again. She took as many plates as she could carry and headed for the kitchen. Copernicus followed her in his slow, limping way.

As she rinsed the plates, Kate caught snippets of the conversation inside. Her mother talking about the bridge feud, Ray explaining the farm to Liz and then Peter talking over him, explaining it better. They had five men full-time, and the two temps who had come this morning before mass. *Because a farm doesn't stop for Christmas*, she heard Peter say with a tinge of something that wasn't just booze. Her brother oversaw everything at Cranavon but she knew he wasn't happy with his lot, that he still dreamed of going back to San Diego. He'd tried to get that girl, that woman, who-ever she was, to move to Carlow with her son, but she wouldn't, or she couldn't, leave America. And there hadn't been a sniff of anyone else since. Imagine keeping a hope like that alive for seven years. She didn't understand it. What was the point in teasing yourself? It was starting to ruin Peter, this other life he could no longer have, or allow himself to have. His golden blond hair had gone white at the sideburns and he'd become sour in the last year or so, a kind of gradual bitterness that had started with jibing at Ray about coming home more often, and had developed now into a general dissatisfaction with anything either of them did for Mammy. Nothing seemed to be good enough. Perhaps he had just been here too long and was becoming like her.

It was a mean thought, the kind of thought she'd grown accustomed to having the longer she lived in Dublin. Her first year in college hadn't been like that. She'd answered her mother's phone calls every evening, spent hours listening to her, trying to ease her sadness and worries, reassuring her that she'd be home on Friday evening, that she'd get the late bus back on Sunday, or the early one from Carlow town on Monday morning if Peter would drop her. That first year Kate had been happy to come back to Cranavon every weekend. She'd been dreadfully homesick, a word that did not really cover it at all. Twinsick. Kate was still, on her bad days, cripplingly twinsick.

But then second year and friends and going out and alcohol. This last one had been a great discovery—the freedom of it, the blankness. Her relationship with her mother had changed enormously. She was less nervous of her and more exasperated by her, by the fact she'd somehow managed to stay the same even through her grief. How had she not been changed by Daddy? By Elaine? Loss had split Kate open. It had halved her and halved her again. And yet her mother, through all her lamenting, seemed fundamentally the same.

The house, meanwhile, had certainly changed. A grim, airless atmosphere hung about Cranavon, even now, at Christmas.

The kitchen never felt clean, like there was an invisible film on the surfaces. Her bedroom, though larger than the one in halls, seemed darker, more cramped. She was uneasy here and it made her short-tempered—sniping at her mother, impatient with Peter, less willing to laugh at Ray's messing. She tried to keep away as much as possible, claiming all sorts of part-time jobs and study groups and imaginary exams in Dublin. (She always did so well in the imaginary ones.)

The china serving plate slipped from her fingers and clattered on the draining board, a white chip flying onto the tiles. Copernicus went to sniff it and she shooed him away. She dried the plate quickly and put it back in the drawer. She was a lot tipsier than she'd felt at the table. The conversations from inside sounded distant and distorted. She longed for a snooze.

'Can I help?' Liz came into the kitchen just as she was putting the last glass in the dishwasher. 'Your Mum has gotten a bit sad, I'm afraid. I'm not really sure what to do.' She looked forlornly at Kate with her cat-like eyes.

From the good room, they heard the music, the bom-bom-bom-bom of the baritone, the lonely strum of a guitar, and then the first line coming softly into the kitchen. *Try to imagine, a house that's not a home.*

Kate went upstairs to their bedroom and curled on the bed, drawing her knees into the acid hollowness of her stomach. Not eating in Dublin made her feel pleasantly empty. It let her float untouched through the city and its strangers. Nothing and no one could get her. But here at Cranavon, from the moment she was over the cattle grid, the shield disappeared. Even through the fuzz of the wine, or maybe because of it, she felt extraordinarily angry. The more her mother cried these days, the less she cared. That was not a natural way to feel. But still, she would love to break the Christmas CD over her head. The anger had been there for days, ever since she'd found a card from Conor Doyle in the opened pile of Christmas cards on the hall table—a robin redbreast on the front and the rough touch of snow. She was sure the card would have been addressed to her personally and that her mother had opened it anyway. But Kate could never simply ask her mother why she would do something like that. It was not a question that existed. Her mother seemed to resent Kate's presence in the house these days. It was like they were vying with each other for attention or sympathy, and her mother was winning, of course, even though it was she—Kate—who had lost her twin. It was not the same for the rest of them. It was not like normal death. Instantly, she thought of her father. That long blue night into morning, and then the new and certain knowledge, like learning the capital of Ghana or the law of the lever, that she'd never be safe again.

But in the weeks and months after his death, Kate had come to think of herself as lucky. At least the twins had each other, while her mother and brothers had to get through it on their own. The twins had slept in the same bed for months afterwards, so many nights tucked into each other, gripping. Or in the daytime, if some neighbour called and made their mother cry, which, in fairness, wasn't hard to do, the twins would give them the finger in various inventive ways—fixing imaginary glasses, rearranging hairgrips or Elaine's favourite, offering a mug of tea with the middle finger burning tight against the side. They were partners again. They were in cahoots. Kate had never thought, for one second, that her sister might be taken from her too.

Now, although she was still living, the best of her was gone. On bad days, even the most obvious things seemed impossible—how to cross a road, use a phone, how to speak. Elaine's death had left her unable to negotiate the world. No matter where she went, there was always someone missing. There was no one to give the finger to. There was no way to laugh at death.

And the people, the other people who Elaine had left her to deal with. All her friends at the pony club, all the girls in school, all the boys too, even Conor Doyle, all at her with their searching eyes, as if Elaine was still inside her, as if she'd devoured her own sister and was now living as both of them. Teachers, the farmhands, the lady in the newsagents. *You look so like her, love. I'm sorry, it's just you're the image of her.* Kate wanted to scream at them, *of course I am—we're twins!* But that wasn't true any more. They were twins. Now, she was just a lone twin, a twinless twin, a reminder to the world about who had been lost.

To the whole world, yes, and also to her mother, who would sometimes freeze at the dinner table, or on the landing, or once when she went to help her bring in the washing. She would stare longingly at Kate—a toothy, hungry look that was almost like desire—before snapping at her over some inadequacy or made-up slight. Her mother resented her being alive, and resented her claim on Elaine too. *A child's mother misses them most of all.* She had said that to Kate, one Sunday in first year as she was going back to college. Her mother had told her to stop monopolizing the pain.

But a twin can never get over a twin. It was like someone asking you to forget yourself. Just as she could remember herself at five, ten, thirteen, she could see all the different versions of her sister, trailing after her like a paper-doll chain.

Most of all Kate remembered Transition Year, the best time of their life. She'd come through the pain of losing Daddy and she'd started to want a new kind of existence that was not so bound to her parents, dead or alive.

Elaine and herself had become a sort of thing around Tullow the summer after the Junior Cert, the Gleeson twins, the *famous*

Gleeson twins, and although Kate mostly felt the opposite of famous, it had been possible to fake it with Elaine next to her, plotting their way. In January that year, they'd had a big party in the GAA club for their sixteenth where their whole class had paired up to come dressed as twins. Ray had organized a DJ and Peter had managed, somehow, to keep their mother and Aunt Helen and the bridge ladies out in the bar until one in the morning. Elaine had shifted five guys, including the DJ, and Kate, well, all she'd done all night was talk to Conor Doyle, and it felt better than if she'd shifted the whole room.

Kate looked at the photo on the pine dresser, identical to the one in her room in halls: their matching jeans and belly-flashing string tops. They'd done a crazy diet from *Cosmopolitan* the week before the party, nothing but soup, cranberry juice and rice cakes. Their mother had pretended to have a fit but she'd allowed it, had secretly been proud of them in fact. At the party, everyone kept telling them they looked like cover girls. Even now, nearly five years later, she could hear them. *The Gleeson twins. Did you see the Gleeson twins?* It had been the best birthday of their life. Every birthday since was only a reminder, especially the big ones. She was refusing to do anything for her twenty-first next month. She hated the word milestone. It made her think of a grave.

Later that Christmas afternoon, when Kate decided it was safe to leave her bedroom, she came downstairs to an empty kitchen. She looked around for signs of the rest of them. The kitchen was in shadows, an unopened tin of Roses on the table. She could hear Liz's elastic laughter coming from somewhere but it sounded like they weren't to be disturbed. Peter was below at the machines, trying to fix a vacuum pump that one of the men had messed up earlier. Through the kitchen window, the sky was low

143

and almost dark and she hoped he wouldn't be much longer. A farm in winter was no place to be alone.

Taking a caramel barrel from the tin, she went into the good room to check on her mother. She was asleep on the longer couch, her dainty ankles propped on a cushion. The candles on the dining table were smaller now, dripped with grease but still flickering their light.

Pouring a glass of some amber liquid from the crystal decanter on the dining table—sherry? brandy?—she sat down in the armchair near the tree, left her chocolate on the side table and watched her mother's chest rise and fall in an uneven rhythm. She looked thin and beautiful, and older than fifty-three. Kate sipped the drink and felt bad for her earlier thoughts. Grief had changed her mother, of course it had, or if it hadn't changed her, it had certainly made her life harder. There was something wrong with Kate for not having more sympathy. She should be nicer to her mother, more patient, less secretive about her life in Dublin. They all had their own way of dealing with loss.

'*Home Alone 2* is coming on,' Peter said, startling her. He blew out the candles on the dining table. 'It's the one where he goes to New York.'

'I know the storyline, Peter,' she laughed. 'Sounds good, let's watch it.'

Liz and Ray came into the room, all arms and tangled attachments. They practically fell onto the shorter couch. Kate wondered what Daddy would make of the display.

'Get a room,' said Peter.

The pair of them cracked up, as if it wasn't the lamest joke in the world.

'Would you stop?' Still giggling, Liz broke free of Ray. 'Will we watch this movie? I'd love a movie. I'm so sleepy.'

'Sleepy?' said Ray, laughing again.

'What in the name of God?' Peter shook his head and took up the TV guide.

Ray did something to Liz to make her screech. Their mother jerked awake.

'Peter,' she said. 'What's that smell?'

'I'm here, Mammy. It's just the candles.'

They all waited. Her eyes widened in surprise and she sat up on the couch and fixed her dress.

'Will we play charades?' She spoke as if she had been the one waiting on them.

Liz groaned. Kate tried to flash her a look—a visitor pass would only get her so far—but the girl seemed oblivious; no, it was not that, she was dreamy and red-eyed and not focusing on anything. She was not oblivious. She was stoned! Kate looked at Ray, at the glazed eyes of total love he was giving Liz. His mouth was wet and bandy, grinning at nothing.

'Yes, Mammy,' said Peter. 'We'll play charades. If you like.'

'*Home Alone* is starting,' said Ray.

'*Home Alone 2*,' said Peter.

'That little blond child and those two eejits?' Mammy shook her bob. 'Oh, I couldn't take that. A documentary, perhaps. But no,' she said. 'We have guests! It's our duty to keep them entertained.'

Peter stoked the fire and drew the curtains. He spotted the caramel barrel on his way back and had it gone into his mouth before Kate had time to tell him it was hers.

Ray put on disc number two of the Christmas CD, the one without the loneliness. Then he split them into teams, said himself and Liz would take on the family.

'And the world,' said Liz, laughing to herself. She took off her mohair shrug and sat back in a low-cut string top.

Kate saw her mother glance at Liz's cleavage.

'I can be adjudicator if you want even teams,' said Peter. He opened the hidden drawer of the coffee table and took out an egg timer, pencil and notepad.

'Oh, don't worry about us.' Ray put his arm around Liz. 'We'll still beat you. Don't forget Liz teaches English. She knows all the books. *And* the films.'

Kate loved the way he said fil-um.

'I do not.' Liz looked over her shoulder. 'Is there, I mean…?' she said to Ray.

He practically leapt off the couch and ran into the kitchen, returning with a bottle of red wine and four glasses. 'Do you want water, Mammy? Tea?' Their mother no longer drank alcohol, not even at Christmas.

'Can we just start, Raymond?' Their mother pointed at the timer. 'Before Christmas is over.'

They got down to it then, no messing. After twelve rounds, the bottle of wine was long gone, Copernicus was asleep under the tree, and the teams were deadlocked. 'This is the last one,' Ray yawned. 'I'm knackered.' Kate could see what he was up to. They'd the spare room ready for Liz, but she suspected there'd be creeping and creaking across the hallway at all hours. She would wear her headphones to bed tonight.

'Me too,' said Liz. 'I'm spent.'

'Well, this is match point, so,' said Peter. 'If we win this one, we're the champs.'

Liz and Ray conferred for a few moments before Liz pushed him away and clapped her hands. 'I've a great one.' She picked up the notepad and scribbled across a new page. 'I'll give you a hint,' she said rather slyly, before passing the pad to their mother. 'It's a book.'

Ray turned the egg timer.

Her mother's face twisted into a frown the longer she stared at the page. 'I,' she said. 'I don't—'

'Timer's on, Mammy.' Ray sat forward. 'You better go for it.'

'Wait a second—' Peter turned the timer on its side, 'Have you heard of it, Mammy? Because if you haven't heard of it, then you can ask for another.'

'Oh, it's very famous,' said Liz. 'The first ever novel, in fact.'

'Liz!' said Ray. 'Don't give it away.'

Kate scanned her memory but it had powered off for the holidays. Peter was stumped too.

'I know the book,' her mother said icily. 'It's just difficult.'

Liz peeled laughing. 'It's awful, I know. I'm sorry.' She didn't sound a bit sorry.

Her mother perched sideways on the couch and took them through the basics, her body far more rigid than her previous goes. They learnt that the book was two words, one syllable for the first and two for the second. For the first word, her mother got all excited, pointing at the photo on the bureau of her parents getting married. Kate shouted out every word to do with wedding and couple and ancient times that she could think of, but nothing was right. Peter was uselessly frowning at the photo as if one of their dead grandparents might call out the answer. The second word showed a glimmer of hope when Kate got the first syllable—kicks—and a fine thump on her shin in the process. But no, Liz was shaking her head, and the salt was nearly finished, and the second syllable was nowhere to be found by the time the clock ran dry.

'So it's a draw,' said Peter firmly.

'But we've the braggers' rights.' Ray kissed Liz on the cheek. 'My smarty.'

'What was it?' Kate said.

'A mean old charade,' her mother said to Liz. 'That's what it was.' But then she turned her look on Kate. 'Don. How did you not get Don?' She pointed to the photo. 'My poor father?'

'Ah,' said Peter. 'But he was always Donald. Not Don.'

'Still!' Her mother's face reddened. 'Could you not work it out, you eejits? It was Don Quixote.' But she pronounced it Kicks-Oat, and they could all, even Peter, see the problem immediately. There was a second in time where it might have been fine, where they could have ended it there and gone off to bed after a pleasant, easy Christmas.

'It's Quixote,' Liz said, 'as in, key-oh-tay.' She mimed a key turning in a lock as a final insult.

Kate wondered if—

'Who are *you*?' her mother said, half-standing.

Kate stopped wondering.

'You upstart, you little Dublin princess. To come down here to my house, at Christmas, and eat my food, and drink me dry all day, and then shove it back in my face? You upstart, you little piss—'

'Mammy!' Ray was standing now, blocking Kate's view of Liz. 'Mammy, you stop that right now. It was only a game. Say sorry to Liz.'

'Me?' Her mother lunged. '*Me* say sorry?'

Kate couldn't believe what was happening. The visitor pass had been rescinded.

'Me apologize to that little piss artist? I will not.'

'Mammy,' said Peter, trying to take her hand.

Ray rushed to Liz and put his arm around her. The girl's face was ashen, the light gone from her eyes. They looked tiny and colourless, though perhaps that was the marijuana. 'I'm sorry, Mrs Gleeson,' she said. 'I didn't mean to offend you.'

'Well, you did. You *did* offend me.' Her mother was on a roll now and Kate knew she wouldn't be able to back down, apology or not. 'You gave serious offence in my own house. And I think you should leave now, I think you should have the decency to leave.'

'Jesus Christ,' said Ray. 'You lunatic. It's Christmas night.'

'Mammy—' Peter took hold of her. 'Be reasonable. Here, sit down.'

'Get off me, you.' She threw him a wicked look. 'Why don't you go back to America to your refugee crisis?'

Peter let go of her arm and dropped to the couch, as if someone had taken a stick to the back of his knees.

'Leave,' her mother said to Liz. 'Both of you. Leave, Raymond. Get out of my house.'

'It's Christmas,' Kate said. 'Mammy. It's Christmas. There's no buses.'

But her mother wasn't listening, she just kept shouting at them to go.

'Oh, you'd love that.' Ray shot off the couch. 'Wouldn't you? You'd love us to get into the car after drinking all day and go back to Dublin. That would be perfect. Off on the winding roads on Christmas night, taking our lives into our hands. You,' he said, pointing at her, 'you're the angel of death.'

Everyone went silent as the meaning of his words took hold. Kate felt her father and sister enter the room like a physical presence, as if they'd been waiting all along in the hall for a chance to join in. Hours and days and years spent waiting. The fire hissed and crackled and cast shadows on the wall. Copernicus's soft snores seemed the only point of life. Her mother burst into tears and collapsed onto the couch. Peter sat up mechanically, put his arms around her. She buried her head in his chest and all they could see of her was the silver blonde bob moving left and right in turmoil. Liz didn't even glance at Ray before she bolted, her steps light and fast on the stairs. For a moment, Ray stared into space, into whatever vast unknowable horror this family meant for him. It was different for all three of them, Kate saw that now for the very first time.

———

In Trinity Hall, Kate lay on her bed, listening to her flatmates gear up for the night ahead.

'Tuesday pints!' George was shouting in the hallway, banging on doors.

Kate pressed the bag of peas down on her hip to see if it was still as sore. It felt OK now, just a bit throbby, nothing like earlier. She would be fine for pints. For the whole month of February, the Buttery was doing a happy hour from seven to eight on Tuesday nights, and The Kitchen nightclub in Temple Bar was a tenner in, two-for-one vodka and Red Bulls. It was a no-brainer, George kept telling everyone. You basically saved money by going out.

'Kate—' George pounded the door, 'can I borrow your Ramones top?' George was some sort of clothing clairvoyant who somehow knew what Kate wanted to wear before Kate herself knew. And it always looked better on George, her smooth, clear skin and perky no-bra boobs, so that when Kate got back the top, or the dress, or her new leggings, they were somehow less appealing than before.

'One minute,' Kate said. 'I'm coming.'

She left the peas on her locker and got slowly to her feet, hoping she might trick her brain if she was very careful about things. But no, the shooting pain returned the moment her foot touched the ground.

'Hurry up,' George called. 'They've a jug of Baby Guinness in the common room.' She hit the door again. The sound seemed to go right through the bone.

'Coming,' she said weakly, limping to the door.

'How about this?' George waved a fuchsia miniskirt in front of her face. 'Got it in Topshop this morning. It would be fab with your velvet coat.'

Kate grabbed the door frame and tried to smile. In fairness, her friend was more than generous with her own stuff.

'What are you thinking for your hair?' George said. 'It suits you blonde.'

'Tell that to my mother. She saw it at the weekend and said it was like a haystack.' Kate touched the dry ends of it now, wincing as her weight shifted onto her bad side.

'Are you OK?' George did her dimply frown. 'Are you limping?'

'Ah, I'm grand. Just did something running.'

'When did you go running? I thought Tuesday was your full day.'

'I ran home.'

'From college? In this weather? You nutjob.'

An image of the slushy footpath by Ho Ho's in Rathmines, her runners sliding as she tried to bypass a woman with a shopping trolley.

'I should have gone to the sports hall.'

'I wish they'd just give us a proper gym,' said George.

'Totally.' Kate thought she might faint.

Jessica from room eleven appeared at the end of the corridor, holding a jug. 'You're missing the fun.'

Kate hobbled to her desk to get her keys and a packet of painkillers. She let George take her by the arm and the pair of them made their way slowly to the common room.

It was incredible what five shots of Baby Guinness, four Nurofen Plus and a naggin of vodka could do for your health. Kate felt invincible as she rode the bus into town with her flatmates. The journey was a blur of frowning women and people leaving the top deck, and the bus driver coming upstairs to make them stop singing before eventually kicking them out by the National Concert Hall.

Her hip hadn't hurt on the walk down, not even when she ran for the lights with the others at the end of Dawson Street. Now, though, they were in an endless queue for the Buttery, huddled together in the sleety weather, coats over their heads, smoking to keep warm. Kate took another of George's Marlboro Lights, promising she'd buy a box inside, but once they got into the packed cave-like bar, the group splintered off to various arches, and Kate found herself in the back room near the canteen, sitting at a table with Jenny and the girls. They were in a quiet spot near the toilets and were much less drunk than her. She sat at the end of the booth, nodding along to their conversation but unable to follow the thread, the bone ache starting in her hip once more. Only the beer was half price, a watery yellow that was cruelly devoid of anaesthetic. She massaged her hip through the miniskirt and thick black tights, pressing her finger into the joint the way Ray did in physio. Mistake. She yelped and took her hand away.

'Are you OK?' Jenny said.

'I'm fine,' she said. 'Sorry, Miranda, go on with your thing.'

Miranda did her annoying one eyebrow trick. 'My thing?' She narrowed her eyes and then looked at the other two. 'Here—does anyone want chips? I'm starving.'

'Oh, yes, please,' said Jenny.

'Me too.' Aoife put on her glasses and dug a fiver out of her purse.

'I wasn't offering,' said Miranda. 'I'm not your slave. Come with me. Kate, what about you?'

'I ate already,' said Kate. 'In halls.'

'Oh, really?' Miranda sounded angry, though Kate couldn't think why. She'd have to concentrate more on their stories. Miranda hated when people didn't listen to her.

'You keep the table, Kate,' said Jenny, standing up. She hadn't bothered to change out of her hockey skirt and the group of lads at the pool table turned their heads. Her English legs were a thing of wonder for all the boys used to Irish girls with Irish knees.

Kate took another painkiller as she waited. Miranda and Aoife arrived back first, leaving down two plates of chips, wisps of steam rising off the gravy. Kate moved a chair with her good foot to let them in. It screeched off the cement floor. 'My teeth,' said Miranda, ducking her face into her lilac hoodie.

'Are you sure you don't want food?' Aoife hung her tie-dye bag on the chair. 'Queue's not so bad.'

'I've eaten,' said Kate testily. Pain always made her so unreasonable.

'But of course,' Miranda smirked. Her jet-black hair was ironed flat to her head in a brutal zigzag parting. The tip of a loose strand caught the gravy as she leaned across the table for the salt. Herself and Aoife started talking about their summer placements in Merrill Lynch in London, how they would live in Camden and go to the markets on the weekend. Kate tried to think of ways into the conversation that kept coming to her seconds too late.

Jenny came back with a tray of golden chips, a glistening chicken breast and a side of mashed turnips that smelt like compost. 'Gross,' said Miranda. 'Like Sunday lunch at the shelter.' They all laughed, though Kate didn't think it was funny.

With Jenny's return, her cheery, inquisitive manner meant an easier flow came to the group, and soon they were bantering about the day's lectures and the fire in the debating society and the chances of Jenny being able to get into The Kitchen in her hockey gear if they lent her a coat.

All around the room, people were talking in similar animated fashion between bites of food and sloppy pints. At the double doors to the bar, she saw George waving and she eased herself out of the booth and limped over to her friend. There'd been some disagreement with a girl from Galway over a lip gloss in the toilets, and she spent the next while talking George down from a state of hysterical revenge. By the end of it, Kate was horribly sober and in agony with her hip. She had to go home right now. Avoiding the throng at the bar, she went around by the dimly lit outer corridor to collect her bag and say goodbye to the girls. The back room had thinned out and she could hear Miranda's voice clearly before she turned the corner. Her own name was thrown out like a grenade. *Kate the Hummingbird.* She stopped short, ducking in behind the doors. She was only a metre or so away from them, had a full view of the table, and yet she was sure they couldn't see her. It was like she was invisible. The food was gone, replaced by a stack of plastic pint cups. They seemed much drunker than earlier. Miranda had an unlit cigarette in her hand, one of those thin, white French ones, and she was waving it like a baton.

'And then she picks at her food like a hummingbird, or she just sits there and watches us all and it's so awkward,' she said. 'I feel like *we're* the ones being judged for behaving like normal people. It's creepy, the way she stays so still, like she's in a trance, like she's not able to participate in regular conversation. Don't you think it's creepy?'

Kate felt her heart flicker on a half-beat. It was like the time she'd sent the text message about Peter to Peter instead of Ray. It was clear that Miranda was mid-rant, that this story, or whatever it was, had started a while ago. 'Just sits there, barely saying a thing, staring with those blank little eyes of hers.'

Jenny tried to speak but Miranda continued.

'I mean, she makes me feel like a pig for having a plate of chips. I should be allowed to have a plate of chips if I want them. I swam fifty lengths this morning. I could have told her that, but why should I have to justify myself to her? If I want a plate of chips—if I want ten plates of chips with curry sauce *and* gravy—I should be able to have them.'

Jenny uncrossed her legs. 'I don't think she's judging you. Or any of us. It's in your head.'

'In my head?' Miranda scoffed. 'It's horrendous, that's what it is. To see someone do that to themselves. Did you see her limping earlier?'

'Don't be mean,' said Jenny.

'Well, it's tragic too, of course.'

'Tragic,' said Aoife, trying to grab the cigarette off Miranda. 'Stop poking that thing in my face.'

'Maybe we should say something to her,' said Jenny.

'I tried to,' Miranda protested. 'All last term.'

'You kept a list of the meals she wasn't eating and then hounded her about it. That's not helping.'

Miranda stabbed the cigarette across the table at Jenny. 'She doesn't want help. You've tried. I know you have.'

Jenny shrugged. 'I don't know the right thing to say. Or even how to say it. Sometimes she seems so normal. I don't want her to think…'

Kate felt like she might be sick. She put her hand against the cool wall.

Aoife said, 'To think what?'

'I don't know,' Jenny said. 'For her to think we're all talking about her. Like, maybe she's OK. Maybe she's just a really thin person. She has tiny little bones.'

'*I'm* naturally thin,' said Miranda.

'And naturally up yourself,' Aoife said.

'I don't mean I'm a model or whatever but I'm thin, I always have been.'

It was true. Kate looked at Miranda's lithe body, the long limbs and neck, the raptor-like quality to her features. It suited her frame, that's what they said about girls like Miranda. And what kind of bullshit was that, anyway?

'We should just make her eat a burger,' said Miranda. 'Like every day until the end of term.'

'It doesn't work like that,' Aoife said. 'You might as well ask her to drink poison. It's like telling a person with a broken back to get up and walk.'

Kate's hip started to burn and she knew it would go from under her if she didn't leave.

'Oh, you're an expert now?' said Miranda.

Aoife twisted the black string of her Celtic necklace.

'Aoife's right,' said Jenny. 'If she is sick, you can't order her well again. You can't force her.'

'I'm not a bully!' Miranda sat back, scowling.

None of them said anything for a moment. As she leaned against the door, Kate felt her life narrowing before her.

'Is it my round?' Jenny asked.

Using all the energy she had in her body, Kate managed to slip back up the corridor. She waited near the bar queue for Jenny, gave her a quick hug and told her she'd see her tomorrow. When she went to get her bag, the others were talking to the pool guys and barely noticed her leaving.

She'd used the emergency passcard to get a taxi home, stopping for a bottle of Huzzar in the Centra in Rathmines. She was safe now, sitting on her bed in her blue pyjamas and puppy-dog slippers, on her second mug of vodka and stolen orange juice. She'd grabbed the first carton in the fridge, which unfortunately had bits in it, and her stomach turned every time she felt them catch on her lips. She tilted the drink quickly down her mouth to get away from the sensation. Her wet shower towel had fallen while she was out and she watched the damp patch on the carpet for something to do.

No matter how quickly she drank, she kept remembering parts of their conversation. These girls she'd thought were her friends

156

who spoke of her as some sort of invalid, pitiful and grotesque, like a disease they weren't fully inoculated against themselves. They didn't want to be around her, not even cheerful, kind-hearted Jenny with her drunken wishes to help. *Help what?* Kate shouted out loud, and then clapped a hand over her big mouth. She didn't need help. She didn't need them. She didn't know what they were talking about, not really. She didn't see what they saw. Mostly she felt that despite all her effort, she would never be small enough. The others were wrong, or they were jealous, or they just didn't get it.

Her phone buzzed—Peter again. She'd had to text him for the pin code and now he was hounding her, which wasn't at all fair. This was her first time in three years at college that she'd had to use the card. Could he not be gracious about it? Her family didn't know the meaning of the word. She'd sent him two texts saying she was back in halls, that everything was fine now.

The phone rang again and she tossed it up towards the pillow. She drained her mug and filled it halfway with vodka, knocked it straight back this time. It was warm and rancid and kind of wonderful. Feeling brave, she filled it higher the next time and did another straight. Her brain felt like it was lit up from inside. She put her phone in the locker, then turned on her Discman, sang and drank and laughed and drank and felt herself go, until she wasn't laughing any more. Her tears tasted of salty vodka, like a blunt-edged tequila slammer. She found herself standing in front of the sink in the small space at the end of her bed. Her hands gripped the ceramic basin as she stared at her reflection, which was shadowy in the lamplight and hard to make out. It seemed confused to see her. Neither of them knew what the other needed. She had a memory of Elaine, standing behind her at the oval mirror in the bathroom at Cranavon, pinning Kate's hair in coloured butterfly clips as she talked about the great freedom they would have in college. But it was not great, this freedom, that was the thing. There was, in fact, surprisingly little freedom in freedom.

Hours went by, people coming and going, slamming doors and giggling and shushing and on and on until there was silence, and the bottle was nearly finished and then completely finished, but it didn't matter if there was another one and another one after that, she knew now—her hip would still be sore. Finally, at some light-dark hour, she puked into the sink, smashed the orange solids down the plughole with the end of her toothbrush, wiped her face with the mouldy towel and lay down in the bed to rest. Inside her head the screaming was loud and unyielding, the pain, and the panic, and the yearning for time to go backwards. If only she'd seen the ice. If only she hadn't run home. If only her mother hadn't visited last weekend. If only Ray and Liz had been around and not off skiing in Austria. But this burrowing backwards through her regret eventually exhausted her. She needed to face it. The bones in some part of her leg, or her hip, or maybe in both, were no longer fused. She burst into tears again. It was the loneliest she'd felt in a very long time. Four and a half years of trying to pretend she was OK. She squeezed her eyes shut as the memories unloaded. The white oak coffin, how her mother had screamed the house down when it arrived with the wrong type of handles. The busyness of Cranavon, so much busier than her father's funeral, as if there was a rule: the younger the person, the bigger the crowd. Everyone had kept saying that Elaine looked exactly like herself, which wasn't true at all. There was so little of her sister in the waxy face and pale lips, in the slightness of her shape, the way her body seemed to be eaten up by the folds of white satin. There was no trace of Elaine's vivacity. If anything, Kate saw herself in the coffin. And she was not the only one to notice this. One night, not long after the funeral, Kate had woken up to find her mother in Elaine's bed. Barely a metre away, her eyes boring into Kate, pinning her to the mattress. Because it was her fault she was alive. Her mother had never said it, or maybe she had said it once in a fit and then taken it back, but either way, she was right. The wrong twin had died.

*   *   *

That morning, Peter drove them to the gymkhana in the Jeep, dropped them near the horseboxes and said he'd try and make the finals if the cows went early at the mart.

'What if I don't get to the finals?' Elaine jumped out of the back seat onto the scraped earth path. Kate followed after her. It was the mildest Halloween ever, the sky a rippled blue. She was glad she'd worn her denim jacket and not the old fleece.

'Nonsense,' said their mother, still in the passenger seat. 'Of course you'll make the finals.' She turned to Peter, instructing him about her list for town. Peter said he wished she'd given the list to Ray, that he'd enough on his plate today with the gymkhana and the mart.

'Blah, blah, blah,' said Elaine, scuffing her riding boots in the dirt. 'I'm going to find Zoe and see where she's put Slayer.'

Kate laughed out loud.

'Elaine!' Her mother turned in the car. 'Your horse's name is Prince Francis. After your poor departed father.'

'Sure—' Elaine started to walk away, 'whatever you say. Are you coming, Kate?'

'Kate stays here,' her mother said. 'You need to get ready. No distractions.'

Elaine gave a quick curtsy, ducked under the blue rope by the path and headed diagonally across the field to the trailers, her high Sun-In ponytail swinging like a gold pendulum.

'I'll throttle her,' her mother said to Peter.

'Now, now,' he said. 'Don't upset her before the competition.'

As she watched her sister go, Kate hugged her denim jacket to her chest. She wished Peter was staying, that she could read in the Jeep while Elaine and her mother got the horse ready. The show-jumping bit wasn't for hours. They had to get through the prancing one first.

Her mother got out of the passenger seat and waved Peter on, though as he began to reverse down the path, she shouted and rushed after him, gesturing for her list. They began another lengthy discussion. It was lovely to see her back to her old self again, dressing in her good clothes and fizzing with energy. Maybe things had been slowly getting better for a while but it was only since they'd gone into fifth year that you'd notice it. The last few months had been, what was the word she was looking for? They had been normal. It was as if the threat or promise of the Leaving Cert had reminded her mother that the twins were important. In May she'd gone back as the District Commissioner to the Pony Club, and Cranavon was horse mad once again. There seemed to be a competition every weekend—the prancing one, or the cross-country, or the jumps, sometimes all three. It was very familiar to Kate. Except now there was no Daddy to ask about the result.

'Get a move on, Kate.' Her mother came behind her.

'Where?'

'To the horseboxes for God's sake.' Her mother gave her a dig, 'Where else?'

'I might…' Kate looked in the other direction, to the pointed roofs of the tents, the stripy orange and black one in the middle, all set up for tonight. Kate couldn't wait for the fireworks.

'You might what?'

Her mother was so suspicious.

'I might get us a good spot in the stand while you tack up. You know I'm useless with Slay—with Prince Francis. And I hate the prancing round.'

'Dressage,' her mother said. 'It's an art form, Kate? Like ballet for horses.'

'Sure.'

Her mother put her hands on her hips. 'Mind you go straight to the stand, so.' Her knitted skirt was the same colour as Elaine's jodhpurs, and Kate wondered if she'd worn it on purpose. 'Get the front row right by the steps. Stay at the edge and tell anyone who asks you to move that you've an invalid with you and it isn't safe for them to be in a crowd.'

'But, Mammy,' she said. 'They'll know I'm lying.'

'And you'd better not get cold,' her mother said. 'You should have your fleece on. I don't trust that sky.'

'This jacket is fine,' said Kate.

'And get water.' Her mother set off on the path. 'Two bottles of sparkling. And no candyfloss!'

Kate waved goodbye and headed off through the long grass towards the tents. She hadn't even thought about candyfloss. Her mother was a genius.

At the food stalls beside the arena, Kate was halfway through a massive wad of candyfloss when she suddenly felt guilty at the sight of her sticky, glistening fingers. While her sister was out in the fresh air, riding her horse, she was here, stuffing her face and it wasn't even noon. Her mother was right—she was some class of deviant. She gave a soft, sugary burp and tossed the rest of the wad into a rusted cylinder bin.

'Nice shot,' a boy called out.

She turned to see Conor Doyle by the burger van, giving a dig to a shorter boy she didn't recognize.

'Straight in the hole!' The boy clapped.

Conor shook his head and smiled. He threw his hands in the air.

Laughing, Kate was about to walk over when she heard her mother's voice in the ether. The lack of a visual was disconcerting, like a recording inside her head. She stopped, looked all around her, even up at the useless sun. Conor pointed to the fences beyond the ring, where she could see now her mother and Elaine, waving. Or rather her mother was waving two hands for both of them. Kate mouthed a thank you to Conor and walked slowly off in their direction, fighting the urge to run. She was not a dog. She would be seventeen in three months' time and her mother couldn't just call her to heel in front of actual human boys. One of them whistled behind her back and she blushed at what it might mean. She wished she had better legs. Thunder thighs, Ray had called her once in the heat of a fight. He'd never said it again but it had stayed in her head.

It was breezy by the fences, a smell of dry grass and manure.

'Where have you been?' her mother said.

'Nowhere,' said Kate.

'Who's that with Conor?' Elaine pulled at the tie of her helmet. 'This thing is too tight.'

'Leave it alone,' her mother said. 'You'll ruin your hair.'

Her sister's ponytail was no more, replaced by a rigid plait.

Kate and Elaine rolled their eyes at each other at exactly the same time.

'I can barely breathe.' Elaine tugged again.

'Stop your dramatics.' Turning towards the arena, her mother raised her hand to block the sun. 'Oh,' she said, grinning. 'Oh, look, look—the judge from Clonmel is over there. It's the same lady! Isn't it?'

'Mammy,' said Elaine. 'Don't make a fuss. Please.' She reached out but their mother was gone, making spectacular strides across the lumpy ground.

'Oh well,' Elaine said. 'That's it. There goes first.' She leaned against the fence and fixed the collar of her stiff white blouse. 'And if I don't win, she'll be raging. But she can never see herself? She doesn't—'

'I know,' said Kate. 'I know. She's just trying to help.'

'I'd love to leg it,' Elaine said. 'Right now.'

'In the middle of the competition?' Kate was aghast.

'Would you do it?' Elaine said. 'Would you come with me?'

Kate gave a giddy laugh. 'She'd kill us. She'd murder you.'

'We'd be gone,' Elaine said. 'To Dublin. To Galway.'

'No,' said Kate. 'London. We'd have to leave the country to be sure.'

'Cut all family ties?'

'Not if we were together,' said Kate.

They smiled at each other in desperation. Her sister went at the helmet again.

'You're lucky you never got dragged into this lark.' Elaine took off her helmet and left it on the fence post beside her whip. Wisps of hair were loose at the crown of her plait. One of them caught the breeze and shot up like a horn.

'I didn't have a choice,' said Kate.

Elaine narrowed her eyes, two amber slits. 'Do you ever think it's weird?'

'What?'

'That she split us up. Horse riding and piano.'

'Nah,' said Kate, though really, she didn't know. 'I don't think I liked horses. I can't remember. You love it though, always did.'

'I don't,' said Elaine, but she was smiling now.

'All your trophies and rosettes.'

163

'Here,' said Elaine. 'Cover me for a second.' Reversing into Kate, she stuck her hand down the back of her jodhpurs. 'My knickers have been twisted all morning.'

'Stop! We look like we're humping.' Kate laughed and glanced over at the burger van. The boys were gone.

When she was done, Elaine leaned against the fence. 'Who was that with Conor anyway?'

'Didn't get to meet him. I was summoned. You saw.'

'Find out. I'm done with the football lads. They're all the same. Smelly old cars and not one of them understands the clitoris.'

'Jesus!' said Kate. 'Shut up.' There was no one near them but a word like that had the capacity to travel.

Elaine roared laughing, grabbed her whip and poked Kate in the belly. 'You have one too. Down, farther down.'

'Shut up!'

'Just a leeeetle bit lower.' Elaine jabbed her thigh.

Kate gave in to the laughter.

'Uh-oh,' said Elaine, straightening up. 'Watch out. Here she comes.' The blonde, beaming head was bounding towards them.

Elaine buttoned her riding jacket and put on the helmet, tying it at the outside notch. 'Stop the messing now, Kate Gleeson,' she said in their mother's voice. 'People are watching.' She flicked her whip at the empty stand. 'All the imaginary people with their imaginary cares.'

Kate laughed again. Her sister was right, as usual, so many of life's troubles were just entirely made up. 'Good luck in the prancing one,' she said, but her sister was gone, setting off towards their mother in her spirited, defiant way.

In the front row of the stands, the midday sun was hot on Kate's face, her thick cord trousers stuck to the plastic seat. She'd been waiting for nearly an hour, reading snatches of her new book, but mostly just watching people come and go through the dark security of Elaine's Ray-Bans. Below in the arena, the stewards were doing the final checks on the fences. There were eleven in total, which seemed a strange number to her, but she'd stopped looking for logic in equestrian sports long ago. There were more rules to it than bridge. Her favourite fence was the redbrick wall, though she liked the ones with the water too, the splash of the planks and poles when knocked. Earlier they had used a thick hose attached to a truck to fill the ditches and as she began to feel sweaty now, she imagined herself paddling in one of them.

Taking off her jacket, she pulled her T-shirt out of her cords. Well, Ray's T-shirt, to be exact, the Nirvana one with the face, whipped from the ironing pile that morning. Some of the stewards down below were arguing. There seemed to be a problem with the final fence, the tricky double-gated one that Elaine sometimes struggled with. All the official-looking people had gathered around it, taking it apart plank by plank. A woman in dungarees eventually came to help them and they began to restack it under her guidance. It was a lovely thing to watch, calming and interesting, like a giant Jenga game where everyone was on the same team.

The stand had filled up after the dressage round, mostly parents and primary school children, with the odd person of interest dotted about the place. Conor Doyle, for example, huddled with the other boy in the back row, doing a poor job of hiding their cigarettes. She couldn't turn around again without being obvious. Conor and herself were sort of friends now. He often saved her a seat in honours maths. He'd gotten rid of the manky ponytail, and he was actually kind of funny if you gave him time to get going.

'Excuse me,' a woman said, startling her. 'Can you move in please?'

'Oh.' Kate sat up straight. 'I'm keeping this seat and the one next to it. I've been here for over an hour.'

'That's ridiculous,' the woman said. 'You can't reserve seats. Move in.'

Kate recognized her, the long chin and jaw that seemed to suck the rest of her face downwards.

'Mrs Stevens?' she smiled. 'Lucy's mother?'

'Yes.' The woman fixed her khaki linen jacket and squinted suspiciously at Kate.

'I'm Kate Gleeson. Elaine's twin.'

'But of course!' she hooted. 'I just met your mother. She's all business down there.' Mrs Stevens gave a tinkling laugh. 'It's like she's never been away. Your sister's horse is a fine specimen.'

'Prince Francis,' said Kate.

'The farmers always get the best horses. The rest of us don't stand a chance.'

Kate couldn't remember what Lucy Stevens's father did for a living.

'But my Lucy has been riding beautifully all year. I think this will be her big one. We're confident.' Mrs Stevens looked at Kate.

Kate felt like telling her she couldn't give a damn who won, that the only reason she was here was because her mother had said she was a bad, unsupportive sister for not coming to the last one in Tipperary.

'Lucy got top marks in dressage. The same as your sister. They're tied.'

'That's great,' said Kate, feeling hungry all of a sudden.

'Of course it makes the—'

Kate nodded along but really she was finding it hard to keep up with the horsey intrigue. The salty sweetness of the onions from the burger vans was drifting on the wind. She wondered if she could ask Mrs Stevens to mind their seats. She looked up at her mopey, heavily made-up face and decided against it.

'And your sister?' Mrs Stevens took off the jacket to a khaki sleeveless top.

'My sister?'

'You can tell she's been practising. I'd say she's out morning, noon and night.'

Kate couldn't tell if it was a question. She glanced at the vans, where a queue was forming.

'I saw her ride in Thurles last weekend,' said Mrs Stevens. 'Herself and Lucy were robbed by that Lanigan girl. Daylight robbery.'

Not again—Kate had heard it about twenty times over the week. Her mother was convinced the judge from Tipp town was biased. Or to be more specific, that she hadn't gotten off her fat, waddling arse to view the dressage properly.

'Yeah,' said Kate. 'But hopefully they'll win today.'

'There's no *they*, dear.'

And hopefully this conversation would end soon too. Her cords began to itch at the waistband.

'There can only be one first place,' said Mrs Stevens with a tight smile that made her chin seem even longer. 'May the best girl win.'

The commentator's voice came through the speakers and gave a ten-minute warning for the crowd to take their seats. The decibel level immediately rose in the stand. Mrs Stevens told Kate to enjoy the event and moved into the row.

Her mother appeared a minute later, no sign of burgers or chips, even though it was gone one o'clock now.

'Take off those glasses,' she said. 'You're not blind.'

'But Mammy—it's sunny.'

'What did Horse Face Senior want?' her mother said, fixing herself in the seat.

Kate laughed. 'You're so mean.' She gave a quick look down the row, then laughed louder as her mother flared her nostrils and stamped her foot on the ground. 'Mammy!' Kate said. 'She'll hear us.'

'With her big horsey ears?' Her mother went into convulsions, eventually stopping to take Kate's fleece out of her tote. 'Put that on. It's getting cold.'

'It's not cold.' Though actually, it was getting a bit chilly, the sun disappearing for minutes at a time. 'And I have this.' Kate put her jacket back on. There was no way she was wearing the old Musto. *Conor Doyle is here.* The thought was in her head before she knew it. She glanced at the back row but he'd moved.

'Oh, fine.' Her mother put the Musto in the bag. 'If you do up your jacket, I won't tell your brother what happened to his T-shirt.' She winked at Kate and the two of them had another giggle. Kate did a few buttons from the bottom. They stood up to let more people into the row, the seats beside them filling up. She gave a polite smile to her neighbour, an older man with a newspaper under his arm.

'Well,' her mother said. 'What did she want?'

'Who?'

A group of small children passed in front of the railing with candyfloss bigger than their heads.

'Horse Face Stevens.'

'She said Elaine had gotten really good over the summer. She'd seen her in Thurles.'

'Robbed! We were robbed.'

'I know, Mammy.'

A cheer went up from the crowd as the horses appeared in the practice ring beside the arena.

'What else did she say?' Her mother zipped her own fleece. It was light pink and brand new, not a bobble in sight.

'That Elaine got top marks in dressage. That's good, isn't it?'

Her mother told the candyfloss children to move on and stop blocking the view. She reached for a bottle of sparkling water. 'Warm,' she said, frowning.

'I've no fridge in my bag,' said Kate.

'Watch your cheek. What else did that woman say?'

'I don't know, Mammy. I'm hungry. Can I get a burger?'

'What else?'

'That the farmers always get the best horses.'

'As if,' her mother said, with venom. 'That's her excuse.'

'Look, Mammy. There's Elaine.'

'There's your sister!'

Elaine had ridden to the gates and was waving at them. Slayer looked blue-black beside the other horses. The size of him always shocked her, so much bigger than Elaine's old pony.

Her mother stood and started to hoot. 'Good luck, darling,' she called.

Elaine turned Slayer around so that his shiny, muscular behind was facing them. Kate tried not to laugh. Her sister could get away with so much.

A woman from the row behind tapped her mother on the shoulder and the two of them got into a conversation about the Swedish oxer, which Kate gathered was the problematic fence from earlier. She tuned out and watched her sister, trotting majestically around the practice ring, the other riders moving out of her way. Elaine would take on the world one day. She wasn't afraid of anyone. She'd spent the last three years begging to go boarding in the Urselines' but now that they were in fifth year, her focus had shifted to college, to the freedom of the future. It was all decided: Trinity College Dublin, Law for Kate, Drama Studies for Elaine, though Kate reckoned her sister would take any course, even Irish if she had to. All she wanted was to be gone from Cranavon. Kate could understand it but thought it was ungrateful too, that she should try to be less obvious.

Down in the ring now, Slayer looked ready to go. Only six riders had made it through dressage. The judges had been ruthless, her mother said, as the winner of the overall competition would represent the county in the All-Ireland Final.

The running order, names and numbers went up in flickering yellow letters on the black board beside the podium. Lucy Stevens was fourth, Elaine last.

'Damn,' her mother said.

Kate nodded, understanding. Elaine wasn't good at waiting.

'She just needs to keep her nerve,' her mother said, brandishing a fist at the waiting horses. It was meant as encouragement, but from over there, who knew what Elaine would make of it. She saw Slayer rear up on his hind legs, only a few inches, but enough to disturb the dappled grey horse beside him.

'Stevens better control her speckled creature. Look how she's unsettling Francis.'

Kate said nothing. The candyfloss from earlier had left her edgy. She wanted something to fill the sugary hollow inside her. And she was cold. She buttoned up her jacket.

'Mammy,' she said. 'Can I go get a burger? Elaine's not until last.'

'They're starting—' Her mother pointed to the stewards with their clipboards, 'don't upset me.'

The steward closest to the crowd blew her whistle, the count-down timer on the board began, and the first rider trotted up to the fence on a chestnut horse that took the jumps with a kind of slow grace that made the whole thing look easy.

'Watch her sauntering,' said her mother in disgust. 'Watch her slump.'

Kate sat straighter in her chair and watched the girl falter on the water fence, two poles splashing into the ditch. 'See,' said her mother. The crowd oohed, and oohed again at the next fault, and yet another on the redbrick, so that it became painful to watch her complete the round.

There was such an age between scoring that Kate could easily have gone down and gotten a burger, so after the second rider was done, she told her mother she was bursting for the loo.

'Can't sit still,' she heard her mother say to someone as she bolted for the tents. It was too dangerous to stop at the burger vans so she made for the Chinese stall at the end and got herself some chicken noodles, wolfing them down as the crowd cheered for the third rider. She thought about buying a cold sparkling water for her mother but it could go either way, so she decided against it and hurried back to the stand.

'Hey, Kate!' A voice called as she neared the stairs. Over by the Portaloos, Conor Doyle and his friend were standing, looking aimless. Kate wiped her mouth and headed over.

'Hi,' she said. 'Bored?'

'My sister got knocked out in the first round,' Conor said. 'The prancing one?'

They smiled shyly at each other.

'So boring,' said the other lad. 'I'm Gary, Conor's cousin.'

'He's only here for the weekend,' said Conor.

Gary shot him a look.

'That's true,' he said. 'Short and sweet, that's me.'

He was a cocky one, right up Elaine's street, with clever brown eyes and the kind of sharp, furtive look she found attractive. Kate had visions of the four of them on a double date in the new cinema in Kilkenny.

'You're a twin.' Gary pulled on the neckline of his Man City top.

'Gary,' Conor warned.

'The Gleeson twins,' Gary said. 'The *famous* Gleeson twins.'

Her heart expanded at the sound of it.

'Yeah,' she said nonchalantly. 'My sister's riding.'

'The fit one on the massive horse?'

'Gary!' Conor went red in the face.

Kate laughed. 'Don't worry. She'll love hearing that. She'll probably get a tattoo of it.'

The three of them were laughing now. In the background there was more cheering in the stands and she knew she should go back.

'Are you going to the fireworks tonight?' Conor said.

'There'll be a bonfire and all,' said Gary.

'Yeah,' said Kate. 'I'm going. We're both going.'

'What's your costume?' said Gary.

'Dunno,' said Kate, though she knew well—a genie and a cat.

'Yeah.' Gary frowned. 'Costumes are dumb.'

'No, they're not,' said Conor. 'You said earlier that—'

Gary stood on Conor's runner. He took out a crumpled box of Benson and Hedges, offered her one.

'I don't smoke,' she said. He looked disappointed, so she added, 'But Elaine does.'

More clapping from the stands. She moved a few steps back as both of them lit up. While Conor held his cigarette over to the side. Gary made an O with his mouth and puffed a series of thick perfect rings towards her. Why did so many boys think it was a talent? She swiped them away.

The commentator's voice cut through their conversation: two poles down, one refusal, no time faults. Another round of clapping, and then they called Lucy Stevens.

'I better go,' said Kate.

Conor's eyes went round in surprise, and she felt giddy that her leaving was having such an effect. Maybe she could stay for—

'Katherine Maude Gleeson!'

She turned to see her mother at the foot of the stairs, doing her vet-comes-to-visit eyes.

'Get!' her mother said, clutching her big black bag.

Kate froze.

'Move it,' her mother said. 'You're a disgrace.'

'I'm not doing—'

'I know exactly what you're *not* doing.'

Kate couldn't look at Conor. She turned away.

'Call me?' Gary winked, first at her, and then at her mother. What was he thinking?

'Get up into the stand away from those hooligans.'

It was loud enough for everyone to hear. Kate dropped her head and walked past her mother, trying not to touch her.

Back in their seats, her mother nearly had a fit when she saw that Lucy Stevens was finished, that she'd gotten a near-perfect score save for one point deducted for time.

'You little vixen,' she hissed at Kate. 'Smoking!'

'I wasn't.'

'I saw you.'

'It was only the boys.'

'Trying to get my attention. Trying to take away from your sister's big day.'

She gave Kate a shove, sending her into the old man and his paper.

'I'm sorry, sir,' said Kate.

He said he was fine but folded the paper and put it away. Half the row turned to look at them. Her mother gave a dangerous smile and told Kate to face forward and keep her eyes on the horses. She hadn't been violent with them for a long time, but it was latent inside her. Kate only remembered in snapshots: a bare-chested Ray made to stand for the night on the landing, a pillow held over Elaine's face, Kate herself racing up the stairs, a hand through the banister sending her flying back down. Short, barely memorable episodes that lodged like splinters in the mind. It was the story that went with them that Kate remembered, whole passages of dialogue that she knew by heart. *I hate you, I hate you, I hate you.* Or the old favourite, the curtain line: *Never have children—they ruin your life!* They sat and watched the fifth girl go round, two faults leaving her in second place at the end.

'Well,' said her mother, composed again. 'All your sister has to do is a straight round. No faults.'

'So she just has to be perfect,' said Kate.

Her mother turned in the seat.

Kate smiled serenely.

Then there was no more time for fighting because the commentator had called her sister's name and here she was, strutting Slayer into the arena. Her hair was still in the French plait, the cause of much contention earlier that morning. As if reading Kate's mind, her mother said, 'It's neater on her. No wisps.'

Elaine passed the railing and ignored their waving, a wild look in her amber eyes.

Kate didn't envy her the hunt coat and necktie. Her face was pink and she kept pulling at the strap of her helmet.

'Elaine!' her mother shouted. 'Good luck, Elaine!'

Kate said a silent good luck and crossed her fingers. Elaine's name was announced over the tannoy and the bell rung. Her sister took off on the split second of the timer.

'Good girl,' her mother whispered, reaching down for Kate's hand.

They squeezed tight as Elaine approached the vertical. She cleared it and went for the water, kicking Slayer's flank with her boot. The horse went high over the fence, his legs not even close to the poles. The crowd clapped. The redbrick was next, a rock-hard look on her sister's face on the approach, a twist to her mouth as she vaulted over it, not quite as cleanly as before. Kate's heart quickened with each jump that followed, her hand gripping her mother's the closer Elaine got to the finish. She used the whip on Slayer for the water jump and although the horse managed to get over without knocking a pole, Kate thought his foot might have touched water. But her mother was beaming, 'Good girl,' she said. 'That's my girl.' Elaine took the turn for the final oxer with plenty of time left on the clock.

'Come on, darling,' her mother said. 'Come on. Easy does it.' She clamped so hard on Kate's hand that Kate lost sensation in her fingers. Elaine was flying towards the oxer, her face in gritted concentration as she booted towards it and went up, up and over the gate, landing with a flourish on the other side and smiling majestically to the crowd as she trotted past. Kate and her mother stood and cheered. Elaine gave them a huge grin before cantering to the waiting area.

Her mother hugged Kate, pulling her into the strong flowery smell of her fleece. When they broke apart, she began telling total strangers that Elaine was her daughter. Her whole face was lit up, young again. Later there would be sadness—because that was the way of death, that any new good thing was also a reminder that Daddy was no longer with them—but for now it was wonderful to watch her enjoy herself.

'A new horse,' her mother was saying now. 'We only bought him four months ago. My daughter.'

As the handshakes and congratulations continued, Kate could see something happening in the arena. The pair of stewards from earlier were at loggerheads again. The large lady was flapping her board dangerously close to the face of the man in the cap. A third official got involved, shoving another clipboard into the fray. They stopped talking to consider whatever was on it. There was a lowering of noise in the stands until it petered out to a few isolated voices.

'What's going on?' her mother began to move onto the steps. 'What are they at?'

Kate searched for her sister, saw her set apart from the other riders, trying to calm Slayer who was once again on his hind legs. He gave a loud, whinnying snort and then settled. Elaine turned him to face the stand. She fiddled with the tie of her helmet and began to walk the horse in small, slow circles.

When Kate looked back at the steps, her mother was gone, tearing across the arena at impressive speed for someone in wedges. She went straight to the stewards instead of going to Elaine.

'Something's going on,' said the old man beside her.

Kate stood up again, wondering if she'd be allowed down there. People in the row behind were saying all sorts of awful things about her sister.

She sat down as the speakers crackled.

'The ruling is in,' said the commentator, 'that Number Six, Elaine Gleeson is penalized for fence four. The judges rule that the foot was in the water.'

A shocked sound went around the crowd and then a cheering began farther into Kate's row. She looked over and saw Mrs Stevens on her feet, clapping and calling, 'Hear, hear—for justice,' as if this was a public execution. Her horsey face dipped left and right in delight.

Down in the arena, her mother was waving her arms at the officials, loud blasts of her voice rising into the stand. 'Perfect,' she kept saying. 'Faultless!' Kate glanced behind her at the crowd to see whose side they were on. Conor was back in his seat. He waved to her and gave a sympathetic shrug.

Elaine was still on Slayer, riding up and down over the same patch of ground like a vengeful queen. For once, she didn't look embarrassed by their mother, but seemed to will her on from her horseback position. 'Rigged,' their mother shouted at the large lady, whose arse, Kate realized now, may well have been the same waddling one from the Thurles competition. 'Robbed!' her mother said.

The crowd was growing agitated. Some man shouted for the winner to be announced. Her mother left the stewards and ran to Elaine. They went straight into an argument themselves, the solidarity gone the moment they had to talk to each other. Elaine shook her head, tried to move off with Slayer, but her mother stood in front of the horse, put her hand on his nose.

'Make up your minds,' the same man shouted. 'Give us the result!'

A few minutes later, the stewards parted and the speakers crackled again. Her sister's face was bright red. She was crying, or sweating, Kate couldn't make out which. She leaned over the railing to try and get closer.

'After deliberations,' the commentator said, 'Number Six, Elaine Gleeson will repeat her round.'

'A sham,' Mrs Stevens cried out, standing and shaking in a squall of khaki. 'A fix!' She went to leave the row but another woman pulled her back.

The crowd booed—they actually booed her poor sister!—and Kate turned to face them, feeling something close to hysteria. She saw dozens of incensed faces and didn't know what to do. The booing continued until the commentator demanded silence and rang the bell. Her mother took Slayer by the bridle and led him over to the starting point, Elaine floppy on top of him, her posture gone. She gave a brief smile, at least, as she took the

177

reins from their mother and sat up straighter on the horse. Kate let out a huge breath.

The commentator was still asking for silence as her mother sat down. She ignored Kate completely, sat forward in the seat and held the railing. The booing stopped but there was a nasty murmuring in the crowd that refused to dissipate. The bell went irrespective, the timer started, and Elaine, somehow, had the courage to trot to the first fence and land it without a fault. She did the same for the next four fences and the crowd went quiet. Kate had never felt prouder of her sister. On the redbrick, Slayer reared but she brought the whip down and they managed to get over it, so close you could barely see the gap. The next vertical was easier but her sister had started to slump again, her fingers lifting off the reins to tug at the tie of her helmet. She went at it again on the approach to the water fence and Kate heard her mother curse. She closed her eyes, she couldn't bear it, and when she opened them, her sister was clear of the fence, no splashes, no faults, with only the final fence left.

Elaine threw her head back and brought her leg down hard against the horse's flank. Slayer sped up, faster than he'd been all day, and shot off towards the oxer. They looked ready for it, like they'd clear it easier than the last round, but just before the jump he bucked and threw Elaine over the fence, high over the crossed poles, her helmet flying in front of her and the rest of her following after it, landing unnaturally on the arena's earthen floor.

The crowd gasped, a terrible sound that took Kate into its clutches so that all she could do was stand there, watching in amazement as strangers ran towards her sister's twisted torso. 'My daughter!' Her mother's shouts sounded far away, as far as another planet. 'My daughter! My daughter.'

*   *   *

A banging on the door woke her. Pain, her body said immediately, pain. She was lying on top of her purple duvet in her pyjamas. Her head was throbbing, but no, that wasn't it. She moved her feet and a sharp twinge ran the whole way up her right leg. Her hip. Swollen, weighted, as if it was chained to the mattress. She looked at the picture on her locker. What she wouldn't give to disappear into it.

'Kate!' A familiar male voice. 'Let me in.'

It was her daddy, here at Trinity Hall to save her.

'Kate!' More banging. 'Are you in there? The guard will have to let me in if you don't get up.'

Oh, God, the horrible logic of the voice. It was not Daddy. It was Peter.

'One second,' she tried to say, but her throat was caked dry and the words squeaked away to nothing.

Her bedroom stank of wet wool, a large damp patch on the carpet. She tried to sit up but the pain was like a knife across her pelvis. A key scratched at the lock, turning the tarnished clasp on the inside to the left. Peter and the old security guard from the main house pushed into her room.

'Kate!' Peter stopped short when he saw her on the bed, the guard bumping into his back. 'Why didn't you answer?'

'I—'

'Why didn't you answer me all night?'

She tried to clear her throat. Her head felt like it might explode off her body, ping-pong around the room and spray the pair of them with her brains.

'She's OK,' the guard said. 'They're always OK.' He shook Peter's hand and left, talking to himself as he went down the corridor.

'Water,' Kate managed.

Peter ignored her. His fair hair was cocked in all directions and his big duffel coat made her feel cold. She reached for the far side of the duvet. The pain was astounding.

'What's wrong with you?' Peter said. 'And what's the smell?' He went on a hunt around the room until he found the towel.

'Please,' she pointed at the sink. 'Water.'

He took her vodka mug from the locker and filled it from the cold tap. She gulped it back greedily, not caring that it tasted of alcohol.

Peter shut the door and sat on her swivel chair. A Gulliver among her things. 'What's happened? Mammy is beside herself.'

'Jesus, Peter.' Kate tried to sit up. 'Why did you tell her?'

'You know well she's as sharp as a compass. Had it figured out before I got off the phone from you. And she didn't buy your text messages either. What's going on?'

Kate shut her eyes and leaned against the headboard.

'Katie?' he said, softer now. 'You can tell me.'

And just like that, he was Daddy again, and she began to cry.

Peter came to the end of her bed, rubbed her foot. Neither of them spoke for a few minutes, just the sound of her crying and every so often another spasmic pain. She was ashamed of her tears, of making another person endure them. It was a primal shame, innate, though she knew that babies were not born that way, that she'd learnt it from her mother, an early lesson: little girls do not cry. No—little girls are disgusting when they cry. In the corridors and echoey rooms of the farmhouse, only their mother's tears. A line popped into her head, like the start of a nursery rhyme. *There was a little girl who thought she was disgusting.* The world felt like it might be ending, none of the usual sounds around halls, no one else about the place. She looked at her radio and saw that it was half six in the morning. For some reason that made it even sadder and she cried harder.

'Listen, Kate, I don't know what to say here,' said Peter. 'I don't know what you want. Will I go and get Ray?'

'No,' she sobbed. 'Don't wake Ray. Liz would be mad.'

'He's down in the car,' said Peter, pointing out the window. 'Will I get him?'

Kate stared at him in wonder. Her brothers, her lovely brothers. But then—'Mammy?' she said.

'At home.'

Clamping her teeth, she inched herself out of bed and went to the window, pulled back the curtain. Over by the bins, there was the new Golf and her brother waiting in it like the driver in a heist.

'I'm not a heist,' she said, realizing as her words slurred that she was still quite drunk.

She clung to the wall and made it to the desk, one hand at a time. Opening her bag, which was thankfully still intact, she popped the three remaining Nurofen from the packet and swallowed them back with the end of the water. The last one caught in her throat and she doubled over coughing until the pill came up. The pain of the cough whipped around her body.

'Jesus, Kate. You have to tell me what's going on. Now.'

She looked at his chiselled face, the dark blue eyes full of trouble. Her eldest brother. She was a lost, stupid child—and she'd never be anything else.

'I think I need to go to the hospital,' she said.

A strange light broke over his face. 'Thank God. We've been so worried. Myself and Ray. You need help. We'll get you proper help.'

Kate frowned. 'How could you know about my hip?'

'Your hip?'

'I hurt my hip. I slipped on ice.' She bent her head. 'I went running yesterday.'

'After the foot? You can't be—'

'Please, Peter.'

He relented and sat her back against the wall, asked her to show him. After he'd listened to her story, he tried to move her leg from the knee but she howled. 'I can't. It hurts too much.'

'OK,' he said. 'OK.'

'Is it broken, Peter?' she asked desperately.

He shook his head. 'I don't know, Katie.' He took his weight off the bed and even that hurt her. 'Do you want help getting dressed?' He looked at the door. 'I mean, I can get one of your neighbours. Who's the one who sounds like Liz?'

'Just wait outside. I'll only be a few minutes.'

'I'm getting Ray,' Peter said. 'We can carry you out.'

He closed the door gently behind him and his consideration for her sleeping housemates set her crying again. There seemed to be no end to his kindness, to the kindness of both her brothers, and no end to her sadness either, here in this tiny room she'd mistaken for a new home.

DUBLIN

May 2018

I T WAS JUST GONE SEVEN in the morning, and all was right with the world. Life was good, life was great. In the basement room of the laser clinic on Nassau Street, Kate hung her dress on the back of a chair and quickly took off her thong. A fluorescent strip light buzzed above her head. The pale, pitted flesh of her thighs looked alive in the oblong mirror. She got on the bed and covered her nakedness with a hand towel. The machine behind her head purred as it powered up, filling the sterile room with a sort of homeliness. Kate put the special glasses on her face and lay back on the bed.

The girl knocked, entered the room and went straight to the machine. 'High or medium?'

'High, please,' said Kate.

'Good woman,' said the girl.

She seemed too young to be in charge of such a complicated-looking contraption but Kate had been to her enough times to know that she was capable, more than capable—a perfectionist in pubic hair removal.

'What happened to low?' Kate tried to arch a brow. The glasses slipped down her face.

'You're no wuss.'

They smiled at each other. The girl's dark hair was in a sheeny topknot, two strands falling symmetrically at either side of her face.

As the girl leaned over the bed to examine the regrowth, Kate longed to tug a strand. 'Go low and go home,' she said. 'Fire her up to the max.'

The girl twisted the knob to the right and the bleeping began, growing louder and louder, like a truck reversing beside her head.

'Where do you want me to start?'

'Underarms,' Kate said. 'Then bikini and legs.' The legs were like a little holiday after the others.

'Lift up your arms.'

As the girl prepared the laser, they chatted about the heatwave and the craic and the state of the canal every morning.

'You must be mad busy this time of year,' said Kate.

'Everyone coming in with tans and sunburn? We can't let the lasers near them. You're like snow though. Do you never go out in it?'

'Rarely.' Kate shut her eyes. She'd enough of the chats now.

His beautiful snow queen. The first morning they'd woken up together, that's what Liam had called her and she hadn't known how to take it so she'd rolled into his armpit and pretended to fall asleep. She still loved the mossy smell of his fancy deodorant, even after she realized he didn't buy it himself. He'd told her they were separated, which turned out to be practically separated, which in Ireland meant not very separated at all. His wife Joanna had dalliances too—a quaint word that seemed easier to rationalize. Kate was fine with it, except when she wasn't. In January they'd spent a fraught night in the family house while Joanna was away skiing with their teenage daughter. When he'd gone to make a phone call after dinner, Kate had put on a childlike amount of lipstick, taken an Avoca alphabet mug from the cupboard—the J mug—and marked the rim with a coral-coloured kiss. She'd wiped it clean seconds later, had washed and dried it, but still, the impulse disgusted her. What kind of person was she at all? Liam had come in just as the press door banged and Kate thought he'd seen, but no, his arms came from behind, arching her back towards him, kissing butterflies on her neck.

Now it was May, and they hadn't seen each other in nearly a month. Liam had been in New York since Easter, and aside from his text messages, which were always short and lacking in humour (lacking in *him*, the real him), all she'd had to sustain her was one lean transatlantic voice call that had taken place when she was half asleep. In the last few weeks, her life seemed to be thinning out. There was no dimension to the days.

The girl began stinging Kate's left underarm, no longer attempting conversation. Kate liked that she knew when to leave her be. She found it impossible to talk and take pain at the same time. The best way to deal with it was to lie back and pretend she was somewhere else.

A clip-on polished silver watch hung upside down on the girl's uniform, reading lunchtime to Kate, though it was half seven really. How was it only half seven? Adrenalin rushed through her as she thought of where she'd be tonight, eleven hours from now, sitting in the plush chairs of the Garden Room restaurant in the Merrion Hotel. A vodka soda for her, or maybe a martini. She liked the look of the olives on the skewer, the way they nestled into each other. Glenfiddich for Liam, double measure, a jug of water on the side. She imagined the pair of them on the high stools at the mirror bar. All she wanted was for time to hurry up.

Kate took the ice packs from the girl and placed them under her arms, clamping onto the cool. She wished they'd just invent a booth where you could go in and have five minutes of unadulterated torture and walk out the other side, smooth and virginal. She'd never been lasered before meeting Liam, but now, even when they couldn't see each other, she felt compelled to keep these appointments. It was a problem she'd never noticed until he'd pointed it out.

'Let your knees flop a bit more.' The girl drew a white grid over Kate's pubic hair, the piece of chalk tickling the skin. 'Are you cold?'

'I'm grand,' said Kate.

'You've goosebumps. Go floppier.' The girl frowned, as she always did when it came to Kate's inflexibility.

'Sorry,' said Kate. 'That's as floppy as they go.'

Kate looked at her thighs. Through the tinted lens of the glasses, they were pale pink, the colour of rashers peeled from the pack. They were flabbier than the last time she'd had this done, or maybe she hadn't noticed the last time. As the stinging began, Kate took a deep breath—the acrid smell of the singed hair. She lifted slightly off the bed as the laser hit the thin, sinewy bit that joined her thigh to her crotch. It looked so silvery and vulnerable with her knees open. She cast her eyes towards the ceiling, pretending to count the galaxy of tiny holes in the poly-styrene squares.

'Stay still.' The girl stopped the laser. 'If it's too much, I can go easy.'

Kate closed her eyes. She had a longing for a cigarette. She hadn't had one in four months, not since her last trip home when her mother and Liz had teamed up to list the things missing in Kate's life: a husband, a family, a career. Kate had tried to play up her role in work in the hope that they'd let the other two go. Career or motherhood, motherhood or career—that was the rule, wasn't it? The trick was to stop appearing as if she had neither.

And they were, finally, starting to take notice of her in the office. All that Keynesian theory learnt by rote might actually come in useful one day. If she got the business development job, she could get away from the reception desk with its plastic plants that looked *so real* to every single person that ever stopped by. In the beginning Kate had been glad of the conversation starter but three years on, the desk was a glossy, public prison of faux botanical hell. Although her boss Anthony loved to drum the marble counter when he came out to meet clients, to Kate it was just a cold, expensive piece of rock with the ghost of a thousand fingertips. And the stains! The cappuccino froth and ink marks—and once, a baby's vomit—that tarnished the marble so quickly, so permanently if you didn't catch them in time, each one noted in the imaginary but extremely real report card that Anthony kept hidden behind his eyes.

'Flip over and I'll do the backs.' The girl smiled and handed Kate a tissue smeared with bright green gel. 'Give yourself a wipe first.'

Kate rubbed the gel in circular motion over her crotch, like the girl had done in the initial appointments, back when Kate was still mortified by the whole thing. She handed the napkin to the girl, whose foot was already on the pedal, the lid of the bin open.

There was a rap on the door. Kate clutched the paper sheet beneath her. A girl with tattooed eyebrows stuck her head around the door and said there was an issue in the facial room. Kate heard a woman crying in the distance, someone shouting for ice packs. The girls vanished through the door. Kate hoped it wouldn't take long, then felt bad for thinking about herself when some other poor woman was dealing with a burnt face.

She sat up in the bed and looked down. The paper had stuck to the aloe vera and she peeled it off, inspecting the girl's work. The skin was red and slick with the gel, dotted with the dead follicles that took ages to fall out if the girl didn't get them. As Kate looked at the angry skin around the lips, she felt impotent.

She tried to push the thought away. It was counterproductive to worry about sex. The tightening happened the moment she thought about it. Right now, it was happening right now—there was no way to stop it—the memory of the last few times with Liam flooding her brain, making it tighter still. The pathetic dryness and the burn as he'd tried to find a way in. There was no give to the tissue around the opening any more. It was too thin and parched and wouldn't yield, not even to a finger unless it was lubricated. And then some unknowable part of her brain did the rest, clamping the pelvic muscles once they felt anything inside her. It was like sandpaper on the thrusts. There was none of the neat, wet communion of the early days, and the more she told herself to relax, the worse it felt. He'd tried to make a joke of it the last time. He'd said maybe the nuns had been round in the night to sew her up. Then he'd gone down on her for ages and she'd made such authentic coming sounds that she'd almost fooled herself. But really, it had gotten so bad that even a hand on her thigh was enough to set the whole thing off—a faulty alarm that didn't know the difference between a burglar and the wind.

The girl came back into the room, apologizing.

'No worries,' said Kate. 'What happened?'

'Just someone with very sensitive skin.'

'Will she be OK?'

'Oh, she's not blind or anything!'

Kate didn't know what to say.

'Right.' The girl picked up the lead, hovering the laser. 'Flip over and I'll do the backs of the legs.'

Kate attempted to flip over while keeping her bum covered with the towel. She rested her forehead on her interlaced fingers and shuffled her body on the bed, unable to get comfortable at the incline. The girl usually flattened it for the legs but Kate knew she would have to ask her to do it this time, and it seemed easier to lie in mild discomfort for the next thirty minutes.

The machine bleeped to life and the stinging began on her left ankle. Her leg lifted for a second, knocking the towel onto the floor. The girl leaned on the bed as she bent to get it, making the incline worse. Kate imagined rolling naked onto the floor, the whole clinic coming out from behind the velvet curtain to gawk. Imagine she broke her pelvis and couldn't get up. Imagine the ambulance crew arriving in and how awful it would be to have wasted their time with such a brainless, trivial accident brought on by the vanity, by the *necessity* of hair removal.

Kate gripped the sides of the bed with her fingers.

'There you go,' said the girl.

As the towel's softness rested on her cheeks, Kate tried to go back into her head, but it was no good. Each sting was sharper than the one before, eroding any thought, any half-thought, so that all she could do was lie there, anticipating the blasts.

Afterwards Kate walked briskly towards Grand Canal Square. It was a shimmery summer morning, office workers in short sleeves and smiles. In her silk dress and belted jacket, she felt like she fitted in.

When she hit the quays on the far side of the square, she stopped to take out her headphones, automatically looking up at the third floor of her office building. Conville Media had the whole floor to themselves. They published monthly magazines and online articles in a variety of unrelated sectors. Finance, cars, teeth—Anthony didn't care, as long as the publications sold ads. They also did one-off magazine specials for organizations on request, which was how Kate had met Liam.

It was too sunny to see whether the lights were on in Anthony's corner room but she could make out a suit jacket on the coat stand through the long glass windows. She darted across the road in front of a lorry. Forty-five minutes early, and she was still late, no time to stop at the coffee dock for a croissant.

In reception, there was a bouquet of white roses on the marble counter. She stopped and took them in, grinning like an idiot. Liam had never sent her flowers before but these were perfect, so neat and exotic. The phone rang on her desk before she could open the card. Leaving down her handbag, she scooted in behind the counter. Someone had messed up her indexed magazines.

'Morning, morning,' Anthony boomed down the line. 'Don't worry about number three. Done. Number bloody two, however.'

Kate sat down, wiggling her feet into the nude kitten heels she kept under her desk. Beside the keyboard Anthony had left a list of tasks, each with an underline and exclamation mark. She tried to tune into his rant but was distracted by the stain on her dress. When the girl had finished the laser, Kate had found the dress on the floor under the hanger, a tangle of cream silk with the tip of a footprint. As Anthony moved to the next point, she rubbed it with her fingers. She had wanted to look well, to look her best, for this evening. She took her mobile from her handbag, unlocked it in case a message had somehow not registered on the screen. Listening to Antony's excitable staccato, she knew he'd had his coffee already and that was one less thing she'd have to do. She took up his list again. The final two items had multiple exclamation marks, before and after the words, which meant they were more important than the tasks farther up the list. When Anthony was finished, Kate hung up and read the card on the flowers: a short note congratulating Francesca from sales on a recent deal. She berated herself for feeling disappointed. It would be reckless of Liam to send flowers to the office. She had been let down by her own imagination, nothing more.

The rest of the office started to arrive. The shaggy-haired production manager, the designer with the nose piercing, the younger sales guys in their crinkled suits, the editor on her hands-free, pointing at the flowers and winking, and gone again before Kate had time to react. She felt ludicrous blushing over someone else's roses.

When she came back from Francesca's desk, Diya was leaning on the marble in a tight-fitting red skirt that Kate hoped wouldn't mean another caution from HR. Diya, the company events planner, was her best friend in work—though also probably out of work if she was being honest. There was Rory, too, a cheerful accountant from Faranfore who loved to tell people about the airport. The three of them were known as a unit about the office.

'Sup,' said Diya, groaning. 'Why did I go out last night?' She left a greasy deli bag on the counter and coiled her long dark hair into a bun.

Kate placed a magazine under the bag. 'Because you can't resist Thursday pints?'

'I went for one measly drink, and ended up in Coppers.'

'You're ten years too old for that place,' said Kate.

'No one's ever too old for Coppers.'

'You look grand,' Kate lied.

'For a dead version of myself.'

Their laughter had an early morning, berserk quality that threatened to turn hysterical as Rachel from HR rounded the corner into the kitchenette.

The door of Anthony's office opened suddenly and he appeared beside them.

'Morning, Diya. Good to see such spirits for work.'

'Morning, Mr Fitzgerald.'

'What's for breakfast?'

'Sausage rolls.'

He tried to hide a grimace, smoothing his hand through his fringe.

'Need you.' He curled a finger at Kate before striding to his room.

She waved Diya off and trucked in after him.

All summer they'd been taking early lunches outside in the square, leaving the office at noon with Rory's tartan rug. Diya and Rory would go to the deli and get the lunches while Kate went to claim their spot. It was right beside the water, the salty smell of the Liffey that Kate could never get her head around—river or sea?—but far enough away from the shrieking local boys plunging into the dock in their underwear. She would watch them sometimes from reception if Anthony was out, marvelling at the hours of activity their wiry bodies could take, envying the great sleep it must give them come night-time.

She stopped now at the usual place and tested the grass with her foot. It had turned a mustard yellow from the implacable sunshine, no padding remained. While she waited on the scratchy rug for her sandwich, she checked her phone again. She wished Liam would call to check in but knew not to expect it. What did it matter, really? In six hours she'd be with him and the gnawing uncertainty of the last month would be over. It was always the same, she reminded herself, an hour or two in his company and everything settled. His voice had a way of sliding through her. Initially, she hadn't liked him over the phone—it was always *urgent, urgent* when he called for Anthony—but he was much nicer in person. In fact, they'd had a laugh that first time. She'd helped him sneak out the fire exit to avoid the head of sales and in their rush down the stairs, she'd dropped the *Business Weekly*s. The two of them had skitted like schoolchildren, sure they'd be caught. Liam was tall and broad and he'd looked so out of place, in his pale grey suit, hunching down on the steps, the outline of his face inches from her own. He'd held a hand out when they'd finished and almost lifted her off the ground. They'd laughed, both of them surprised by it, and then she'd looked directly at him, brazen as you like. Yellowy-green eyes and a quick smile that released to a slack, half-open mouth.

That was nearly two years ago now, which meant that they— Kate and Liam, Liam and Kate—were nearly—nearly. Nearly nothing. Foolish to have thoughts like that, to curse a thing that way. As more people sat on the grass, the water in front of her seemed to grow smaller somehow, dirtier. Kate pressed her phone again. The screensaver of the cliff walk in Ballycotton mocked her, the grey sky and water, the lighthouse in the distance, the safe landscape shot. He'd been behind her when she took it, cautious as ever, offering to take a photo of her if she liked. (She had not liked—she had instead thought of her sister, how Elaine would have been ashamed of her wussy, plaintive response.) A bitter, tar-like taste was suddenly in her mouth and she longed to go back to the excitement of earlier.

But she was hungry, that was all, wishing the others would suddenly appear with her chicken salad sandwich and can of San Pellegrino. A seagull strutted past and cast his glassy eye over her empty lap. She smiled at him in sympathy. How awful, to be circling the dock all morning, tripping out to the quays—maybe even as far as Sandymount Strand—in search of a crust and to have found nothing by lunchtime. Exhausting. Excruciating, really, trying to shake all the other gulls when you did finally spot some leftover chips and then creeping back to the flock, pretending you were still hungry, so the others wouldn't peck your face off. It was a hard life—to be a seagull.

Tilting her face towards the sun, she felt a moisture come alive under her make-up, the foundation sliding into her brows. She opened her eyes and spotted Rory at the entrance of the deli, talking to his friend from the foreign bank. Diya was on her phone beside them and Kate wanted to text her to hurry up. But that was not the kind of person she was at work. She liked who she was in the office, without really understanding who that person was or how she had become her. Calm, for one. Kate was the go-to for all sorts of crises, from broken water fonts to lost PDFs to the log issue, as they took to calling it, in the female toilets. She knew her colleagues saw her as clear-headed and responsible, easy to approach, maybe even funny? She'd wanted desperately to be liked from the beginning, to shake off the solitude of her college years. That Kate was dead now, buried in Trinity under the cobblestones.

'Sorry, sorry,' said Diya, landing on the rug and kicking off her shoes. A blister on her heel was flapping, half-open, a glimpse of ruby. Diya grimaced. 'Will I yank it off?'

Kate turned her head towards the water. 'Gross.'

'Do you think it looks infected?'

'I'll look at it after lunch,' Kate lied.

'Liar.' Diya tossed Kate the sandwich. 'Rory has your can in his bag. I knew you'd be starving.'

'I'm not too bad,' Kate said. Peeling the sticker, she opened the wrapper and bit into the sandwich. She gave the bread a quick sniff and left the package on her lap.

'Sokay?' Diya wiped a smudge of plum sauce from her chin.

'It's fine. They put too much garlic in the mayonnaise sometimes.'

The creamy spread was oozing out the sides of the bread. These were the kinds of things that she'd trained herself not to see and she knew it was bad she was noticing now. But she didn't have time to think about it today—her head was already too full.

A fountain of water shot into the air near the end of the dock and a man in a suit cursed at the young lads.

'You know,' Diya said. 'I'm so happy you ended things with Liam.'

A piece of chicken lodged in Kate's throat. She coughed, wishing Rory would hurry up with her can.

'He'd never have left her,' Diya said.

'Yeah.'

'You haven't heard anything since?'

Kate shook her head. She hated lying to her friend, though it was easier than telling her she'd bottled the ultimatum. It was not from fear of losing him, not exactly, but a more general, nebulous fear of loss itself.

The afternoon was frantic, Anthony's door opening and shutting every few minutes, as if ordering her about was his own personalized workout. Some client had dropped Conville for a competitor earlier in the day, and everyone in the building was responsible.

And still, the only message to come through to Kate's phone today was from Liz, an email-length rant about Mammy and how she'd *psychotically damaged* Ray to the point that he was unable to act like a human being. Psychologically damaged, surely? Though Kate supposed it could be either. On another day a text like that might have meant a trip to the bathroom, or a walk down the quays until she'd shaken it off, but today she'd too much going on. But then, in that wonderful trick of time when you manage to stop thinking about it, she looked at the bottom corner of her computer screen and saw that it was half four. The noise levels coming from the office reflected it, she realized, the furious typing and urgent demands of the afternoon rush giving way to a hum of conversation, the odd phone ringing in the distance, occasional pitchy laughter. The water cooler in the corner of reception gurgled and Kate began to feel excited.

Twenty minutes later, the editor passed by the marble, still on her headset as she wished Kate a nice weekend. Her friendly, brusque style often reminded Kate of her aunt Helen, who had moved to Australia when Kate was in college. Right before she'd met Liam, Kate had been planning to visit her aunt in Melbourne, maybe take a month or two to do the Gold Coast afterwards. Now, it seemed a trip for a younger person.

The journalists slunk out after the editor, though they were supposed to stay till half five like everyone else. Kate put a hand over her eyes and could hear them laughing as they got in the lift. Sales and marketing left next, the interns badgering her to come to the Ferryman. The production lot weren't too long after them, then finally, Rachel from HR, always at twenty-five to six. Kate stood up to close the blinds nearest the counter, the marble digging into her ribs as she reached across for the string. They fell slanted and she ducked out to fix them, imagining what Anthony would say if she left them askew. Her desk phone rang when she was over at the window. Well, the office was closed for the weekend. The machine would kick in.

She got to it just as it stopped ringing and instead Anthony materialized behind her. Finger crooked.

'Need you, Kate.'

He glanced at the chrome clock above her chair and said nothing.

A heavyset man tipped his hat as she ran up the carpeted steps of the Merrion and she wondered which of them was more roasting on this summery evening, him in the two-tone tails or her after racing from the bottom of Holles Street to the hotel when the taxi driver eventually admitted there were several major gigs around the city that evening. She'd thrown the tenner at him and ignored the fact that it was ten cents more on the meter, jumping out of the car and shutting off his complaints with a bang of the door. A group of women with huge bellies had been sitting on plastic chairs at the side entrance of the maternity hospital, their nighties down off their shoulders as they caught the evening sun. Stepping onto the road to get past them, Kate had almost been knocked over by a bike. They'd squealed laughing and one of them had called her a dolly bird, and she wished she'd been brave enough, or on time enough, to have turned around and told them to be kinder to their own children when they had them, especially if they were girls.

Kate checked her phone as she passed through the hotel's scented lobby. Twenty past seven and Liam still hadn't returned any of her calls. She'd gotten one message—*Can I call you later?*—but she knew it was an automated text, the kind you get your phone to send to people you don't have time for. The hotel was quieter than she'd expected, the cream couches beside the bar mostly empty except for a couple of suits. Three older women were on stools at the bar, so fresh-looking in their candy-coloured dresses and matching boleros. A reedy whistle cut through their chatter as the barman polished glasses. The woman with the fascinator tipped a champagne flute to her mouth. Kate looked all around her but she couldn't see Liam. She wanted to go to the bathrooms downstairs and see what state her hair was in after the trek through the park, but she pressed on to the restaurant, kicking over a briefcase as she hurried through the Garden Room. She apologized to a bald man with a kind face and wished he would look away for a second so she could steal his tumbler and knock back his drink.

Kate stopped by the stand at the double-fronted doors to the restaurant. The long-legged hostess frowned when she said Liam's name, disappearing into the room to solve the mystery. An empty table at the front was immaculately laid out, all gleaming implements and overlapping triangles, waiting for some greedy messer to destroy them. Kate tried to breathe. The mindfulness lark was useless in situations where you actually needed it. Liam hated lateness. So did Kate—no, not lateness, she hated time itself, which was always against her, stopping when she wanted it to go quicker, or speeding up when Anthony had her trapped in his office, telling her in his soul-crunching, digressive way the big plans for the week ahead.

The hostess returned with a ledger-sized menu and Kate felt herself relax. At least he was still here. In a lilting foreign accent, the woman apologized for the delay, holding out a slender arm with a solitary silver bangle. As she walked after her, Kate pulled at the chunky copper cuff that had seemed so bohemian that morning but now only highlighted the marmalade patches of freckles on her forearm. She slipped the bracelet off her clammy wrist, smiling at various diners who seemed to notice her as a kind of tail to the hostess. They got to the far side of the restaurant before Kate realized that there was no sign of Liam at all and that the woman was holding open the door to the corridor, waiting for Kate to go in front. Following dumbly, she wondered if she was being kicked out of the hotel. Somehow, it felt appropriate. The pair of them clacked down the hardwood floors to a staircase with a sign for the gym and the petulant whiff of chlorine, but they went left at the bottom instead of right, and Kate twigged that they were going to the Cellar Restaurant and not the Garden Room at all.

The booth was in one of the arches at the back. Liam's shirt looked a burnt yellow in the low lighting, his frame filling the couch that was meant for two, legs out to the side as he read his phone, one brown loafer flexing in time to the swing music. His hair was shorter than the last time they'd met, shorn higher at the sides. He lifted his head as the hostess approached the table and gave his neat, brilliant smile, looking past her, to Kate. The woman left the menu on the table. Kate sat into the booth opposite him.

'I'm sorry. I'm so sorry.'

He leaned across the table and took her hands, his eyes kind. 'Relax.'

'Billy Joel's in the Aviva and…'

'Kylie's in the Point.'

'It's the Three Arena, old man.'

'There she is.' He tapped her nose. 'You look different, you look good.'

Kate withdrew, leaning back against the hard leather seat.

'I do not. My hair is like a bush. I ran from Holles Street.'

'You're here now, relax. You're here.'

Liam looked away from the table and a second later a waitress appeared. He had some magnetic charge when it came to wait staff, unlike Kate herself who often waited longer in a café for the bill than the time it took her to have coffee.

'Wine?' Liam smiled.

'I'll have a vodka and soda, please.'

'Grey Goose,' Liam said to the waitress. 'And a bottle of the Albariño.'

'Of course.' She beamed at Kate as she left.

'Grey Goose?' Kate felt the back of her dress stick to the booth.

'The States always turn me into a snob. Back to naggins on the next date, I promise.'

It was a rush, usually, any mention of the future but the comment left her oddly deflated this evening. Nearly two years together and they were still talking dates. She tried to smile, fiddling with a heavy fork. There were four settings laid out and it suddenly annoyed her that he hadn't told the waitress to take two of them away. She wanted to knock them on the ground, and she brought her hands under the table just in case. As he scrolled his phone, apologizing, she knew she should ask him about his trip. They'd so much to catch up on, almost a month's worth of news and stories—and feelings, if they got drunk enough.

'Is someone else joining us?' The question came out loud, and he looked behind him to their nearest neighbour, a boisterous group of men crammed into an identical booth.

'Are you joking?' Liam said. 'I can't tell. You're in a strange humour. You know—' He tilted his head, 'you do look different.'

'The settings? I meant the settings.' Kate's voice was like glass.

'Right, right,' he laughed. 'The girl can clear them. You hungry? You must be starving.' He went back to his phone. Kate wished the girl would hurry with her drink. She reached across the table suddenly and took his glass, threw down the end of the whiskey. The glass clinked against the heavy table as she left it back.

'Hey! Thief.' His big hands caught her fingers and he began kneading the centre of her palm with his thumb, sending a tremor up her arm. 'Hey,' he said, looking at her directly this time, his eyes opening with sea-like wonder. 'Tough day?'

'Tough month,' she said, though it wasn't true, not in a general sense.

'Tough life?'

She laughed, twisting her fingers under the cuff of his shirt. 'Maybe,' she said, taking her hands away.

'What's so tough then?' He put the phone down. 'Work? Anthony?'

'Well, yeah, he kept me late this evening. Obviously.'

'I don't mind that you're late. Is that what's eating you?' The eyes were back, and the teeth with their surprising sharpness.

'*I* mind. It's my Friday. And I was in before him this morning. Before the whole office.' She hated when she did this, telling lies that made her job seem urgent, vital, as if she was nipping out to do spine surgery between the cappuccinos and indexing.

'Tony wouldn't have kept you if it wasn't important. He's a chancer sometimes but he is fair, isn't he?'

Using the last of her energy, Kate nodded. It was yet another conflict of interest in their growing list of conflicts where she couldn't speak her mind without endangering one or both of them. Liam was head of the Ireland-American Alliance and got all his diaspora magazines from Conville.

'The magazines were a smash,' he said. 'And the fundraising events.'

'Yeah?'

'We netted at least a million.'

'Wow.' It sounded like a lot for an organization that didn't seem to do anything concrete. 'What is it the alliance does exactly?'

'Seriously?' he said.

Kate's face flushed. 'I mean, I know. I just forget sometimes.'

'We need to get you fed.' Liam went back to his phone.

The girl appeared with a tray, the tall tubular glass with her vodka almost full to the brim with mixer.

'Thank you,' Kate said.

'Are you guys ready to order?'

'I'm starving,' said Liam. 'Any specials?'

The girl didn't miss a beat. 'For starters, there's a lobster gazpacho. It's my favourite, so fab. Or there's duck liver pâté on Melba toast with red onion marmalade and pistachio brittle.'

Kate took a lengthy slug of her drink.

'Then for the mains.' The girl scowled as one of the men in the neighbouring booth started to sing. 'They're so loud, I'm sorry.'

'It's OK,' said Liam. 'It's Friday.'

Kate took another long sip until she heard ice clinking.

'Mains are hake with pumpkin ravioli and—oh my God!—are you guys meat eaters?'

Liam arched a brow. 'Do we not look Irish?'

The girl laughed and Kate joined in, noticing how young the waitress was for the first time, how eager she seemed in her pencil skirt and sing-song voice.

'We love meat,' Liam said.

Kate didn't have it in her to remind him that she only ate white meat and fish these days. Really, it was all she ever ate, but she hadn't wanted to seem particular, to seem fussy on those tentative first few dates so she'd had whatever burger, or duck pancakes, or pork belly was going. It didn't matter this evening. She wasn't hungry anyway, she just wanted to get happy and hammered and forget the stress of the day.

'We have an amazing côte de boeuf to share for the price of—'

Liam held up a hand. 'Superb. I've been waiting so long for my friend here that I could eat the whole damn cow myself.' He winked at the waitress. Everyone laughed. Everything was that bit lighter since the girl had come to the table. Kate wondered if they could ask her to join them.

Liam looked at Kate. 'We'll try the starters as well?'

'Sounds good. And another vodka.' She ran a hand through her hair until it got stuck in a knot. 'Grey Goose.'

'Easiest order ever.' The girl took away the menus and Kate's empty glass. 'I'll be back with the drink in a flash.'

'And the wine, please.' Liam smiled.

'Sorry! It's on the way.' She headed in the direction of the bar, her fishtail plait in chevrons down her back.

'Now,' said Liam. 'Now we're settled. We're hungry, that's all, isn't it? Nothing like hunger to start a war.' He leaned across the table and kissed her. There was a briny residue on his lips that made her own tingle. She traced her tongue over them when he moved away. He started to talk about work again and she didn't interrupt, watching instead the way his nostrils flared when he was excited about something. He had a beautiful nose, the bone straight and slender, his features split evenly on either side. He switched suddenly, in that way he had of jumping from topic to topic when he was enjoying himself, to tell her about an architectural boat tour he'd been on earlier in the week in Chicago. Her mind went blurry and it was impossible to concentrate. The descriptions flowed out of his mouth like some random word generator. Silver kidney bean. Howling wolves. A glass step suspended above absolutely nothing at the top of a skyscraper. Chicago, Chicago, Chicago.

'Nothing!' he said. 'It's like standing on air. Gravity shoots through your body. You can feel it in your organs.'

A different girl came back with the drinks and Liam waved her on to pour the wine, not bothering to try it. Kate's vodka had a twisty green-and-white straw this time and she plucked it from the glass and sucked the end before a drop could fall. The girl went to put the wine in the bucket but Kate smiled at her and she tipped a gorgeous, hay-coloured liquid into her wine glass first.

'It's not a race,' Liam laughed.

'But it might be,' she said, biting the straw.

'That skyscraper was something else. You'd have lost your mind up there, if Ballycotton was anything to go by.' He leaned in again and took her hand, kissing it. 'I've missed you.'

She let her hand go limp and pulled away.

He moved his drink to one side. 'What's wrong?'

'I thought you were in New York, Liam.' She took another sip. The vodka didn't taste of anything this time except cold. That's why people really bought the high-end stuff; they didn't want to know how drunk they were getting.

'Damn,' he said. 'I'm sorry. I thought I told you. Change of itinerary last minute. The Midwest guys had to stay local for quarter end.'

'All this time, I thought you were in New York.'

'I must have said.'

'Three full weeks.'

'New York, Chicago, Timbuktu.' He smiled his be-reasonable smile and took her hand again. 'What matters is we weren't together.'

'You know there's a difference.'

'I'm sorry.'

'What if something had happened to you?'

'Look, Kate. You know she was with me. And when she's with me, I can't.'

Oh, look, Kate! Kate looked, Kate knew. Kate was always looking and knowing.

'When Shauna's gone to college,' he said.

It was like the opening line of a poem that never ended.

'But what if something had happened to you?'

Liam picked up his glass and downed the wine. 'I'm going to the bathroom.'

She felt the tears as she watched him walk away. He ducked his head at the low arch near the bar, before taking a left and then he was gone. The first girl appeared at the table, announcing the starters as she put them down, adding an extra plate in case they wanted to share. She did a double take when she looked at Kate and then moved quickly on. Kate wiped away a fat tear and tried to focus on the food, the pinky-grey wedge of pâté with the clarified butter on top, thick as marzipan. The corners of the toast curled inwards and she picked one up and snapped it in half, bits of cracker splintering the table. She put a piece in her mouth and crunched, tasting nothing. Across the table there was a bowl of lumpy coral-coloured soup with a lobster tail standing in the centre. She finished her vodka, ate another bit of toast, and he still wasn't back. She reached for her wine and drained the contents, the floral taste strange and tangy after the vodka. The girl appeared again, the bottle already out of the bucket, refilling her glass. She left two fresh napkins on the table, glancing at the empty booth. Kate wanted to make a joke about the gazpacho getting cold but she didn't trust herself to get it out. She smiled instead and thanked the girl.

All around the restaurant, in the dimly lit arches, people looked cosy and content. The same man was singing again, the song about 500 miles this time. She sat back against the leather banquette, no longer roasting, a kind of post-sweat chill around her neck and shoulders. What if something had happened to him when he was away? She knew he hated that question but it was one that had plagued her from the beginning, and it seemed more real and pressing the longer they were together. What if something happened to him? How would she find out? From Anthony probably, or one of the sales guys keen to be the first with the gossipy thrill of death. She'd imagined herself countless times at the funeral, hidden at the back in most of the fantasies, though occasionally up near the altar in a side pew, like some sort of grief pervert, watching his wife and children.

The girl passed again and Kate nodded at her.

'Can I get you something?' She looked at the untouched plates. 'More butter?'

'A shot of tequila.'

The girl laughed, her eyes brightening as they rounded. 'Seriously?'

Kate smiled. 'Urgently.'

'Understood.'

Less than a minute later she was back with two shot glasses and a squat-looking bottle of liquor whose brand Kate didn't recognize.

'He won't want one,' Kate said quickly, glancing over at the arch.

'He's not getting any.' The girl poured a gold-flecked liquid into the glasses. 'Top shelf stuff is only for the ladies.' Winking, she gave a glass to Kate, held up the other one and clinked. They looked each other in the eye before they drank and Kate imagined for a second that they were sisters, that at the end of the girl's shift both of them would go home to Kate's flat and thrash out the week.

The singe of the drink as it went through her was magnificent.

'On the house.' The girl turned on her heel. 'Say nothing.'

Kate felt Liam's hulk before she saw him, a hand on her shoulder, then he levered himself into the booth. There was a coolness off his face and she wondered if he'd washed it. She noticed now for the first time the sallow half-moons under his eyes, the way the colour seemed to sink into them like a hammock. She reached across the table and touched his cheek, then half stood to kiss him.

'Hey,' he said, when she broke away. 'Get over here.'

He squashed into the far end of the booth, nearly knocking a painting off the wall. Kate went in beside him, wanting suddenly to sit on his lap, to be hugged until she went numb. She settled for turning sideways, kicking her wedges off and putting her legs over one of his. They drank quickly, swapping stories. When he was here, he really listened to her, in a way that no one else did.

She got happier and hazier as they chatted, not noticing the starters disappearing until the girl arrived with the mains. Somewhere in the background she heard a cork pop and a cheer. The girl left the beef on the table. Kate found it hard to look at.

'We're going to need space for this boyo,' Liam said, taking her legs gently from his own. He was talking to the girl, not to her, and Kate followed his voice. She smiled at the girl, almost giggled really, because everything seemed funny now; the secret she had with her that Liam knew nothing about, the secret she had with Liam that the girl knew nothing about, the secrets, the secrets, it was all hilarious.

'Oi.' Liam straightened her up. 'You'll get us kicked out.' He was laughing too though as he helped her back into the other couch.

'Are you OK?' The note of panic in the girl's voice cut through the haze.

Kate put her elbows on the table and rested her chin in her hands. She couldn't stop blinking. 'I'm fine,' she said.

'Don't worry.' Liam smiled at the girl. 'I'll carve.'

She was gone then and Kate missed her.

'Lightweight. Oi, drunko!' Liam waved his hand in front of her eyes and she sat back, surveying the table. There was a mound of crisp chips in a miniature wine bucket and a hunk of beef that looked like a Sunday roast. She wished she could take a picture for Peter but she remembered how much Liam hated her camera phone. She would never be drunk enough to forget that one again. The shock of it, watching her iPhone soaring through the air into the steely Portrush sea. Then he'd stalked off and left her there on the hard sand, with the dog walkers watching her and the tide coming in out of nowhere, drenching her runners. She'd been raging going back to the hotel—passing all those cheery, red-nosed golfers—stripped she'd felt, naked in front of the world without her phone, or her dignity.

No—no—she wasn't going back to that now, not in the middle of all the fun, the antics, the crowd across the way singing, what was it they were singing? It wasn't as good as the miles, there was no chorus to this one, just a lad belting out the words and the rest of them looking on, waiting, waiting for what? Liam stood to carve the beef, holding his elbows high above his wrists, angling his body away from the table as the juices leaked on the wooden board. An intensely sweet smell passed over the table, caramel or coconut. A spriggy herb was draped artistically over the board.

'How many slices do you want?'

'One. From the end bit, no blood.' She took a chip from the top of the mound, bit into it and dropped it on the plate in shock. Steam rose from the fluffy white middle.

'Roasting!'

'Careful,' he said, laughing.

Once he'd served them both he stopped a waiter and asked boring, endless questions about Châteauneuf-du-Pape. 'Pappy!' she called out suddenly. They did not seem to appreciate the hilariousness of the word. 'Pappy! Pappy!' She tried again but it was no use, they were no fun at all. They went back to talking *varietals*. Kate slipped out of the booth, delightfully unsteady on her feet.

'Easy.' She heard Liam's voice as she set off for the arch. Focus, focus on the point at the tip, whose name she knew but couldn't remember, and soon she was up close to it and then it was gone and she could see the varnished oak of the toilet door, but she was outside, suddenly, leaning on the cast-iron railings at the entrance to the restaurant.

A line of taxis with yellow lights were to her right, a couple of drivers chatting to each other, smoking, eyeing her up. One of them called to her and she shook her head. Across the road, the late evening sun was in pink diagonals on the powdery brick of the Dáil. Shouting, farther up the street, at the Irish bar on the corner of Merrion Row where a group of men lifted a guy in a nurse's outfit on top of their shoulders. All the laughter and the jeering—oh, the night seemed full of promise. She wished she was still a smoker, felt the temptation rip through her, if only to have some excuse to be out here, enjoying the world like she should be, not hidden away downstairs in a dungeon with enough food to keep her in dinners for a week. Dinners and lunches if she rationed it. What was he thinking? That he could make up for three weeks of no contact by giving her all the missed meals in one evening? It was a disgusting thought. A cigarette, she needed one. The taxi men. They looked so lonely in their cars, all lined up. She started crying for no reason. It was as if the tears belonged to someone else.

'Kate!'

She looked up and saw Liam at the railings where she thought she was herself, but he was at least a block away and here she was instead, in front of the park, at the bike stands in fact, the metal docks empty, except for one sad-looking creature with its saddle on backwards like an upside-down triangle.

'What are you doing down here?' Liam looked all around him before he came to her. It didn't matter. The heft of him, there in front of her on a summer's evening in the middle of Dublin city. She pressed herself into him, burying her face in his chest.

'Jesus,' he said. 'You're hammered.'

'The room,' she remembered. 'You got us a room. A suite.'

'Kate.'

'Come on.' She grabbed his hand and set off on her mission to nowhere. He was the size of an oak.

'Kate, sweetheart. We can't go back in there. We need to get you home.'

'My bag!'

'I have it here.' The soft leather clutch was bunched in his hand, the clasp all wrong. She took it from him and studiously fixed the button.

'Kate.'

She tried to walk around him. He put a hand on her arm and she stopped.

'Dinner,' she said irrefutably.

'It's eaten. It's cold. You were gone for ages.'

'I'm starving.'

'For crying out loud,' he laughed. 'Look, we'll get you a chipper in Clontarf.'

'I live in Ra-HEEEE-ny.'

'Jesus. OK, listen, Kate. You need to wise up. Excuse me, mate?' He shouted at the taxi men before taking her by the shoulders. 'Kate.' He propped her gently against the bike. 'Stay there.' The saddle was cool and comfortable through her silk dress and she felt like it was a treat to be sitting once again after such a long journey. She started to hum the 500 miles song, delighted with herself for remembering. It was so easy, so lilting the tune.

He was back on the footpath, the tall trees of the park swaying behind him. She felt the wind for the first time, a cold spreading up her limbs, her chicken-skin legs in the glare of the street lamp.

'OK, Kate, it's sorted. Hey, Kate, look at me.'

With a swoop of her head, she dodged his hand. 'Gonna be the man who's working hard for you!' She missed his chest, nearly poking him in the eye.

'Careful. Kate, come on, stand up.' His voice was serious now, Portrushy.

She sniggered. 'You don't like my singing?'

'You need to sober up. I've promised him you won't puke. They're watching us.' The 'us' was like a sound a snake would make.

'Ussssss,' she said.

'I'm coming home with you. Isn't that what you've wanted? Isn't that what you've been asking me to do for months?'

She leant farther back on the saddle until her shoulders touched the handlebars. It was strangely comfortable. She looked up at him. 'For the whole night?'

'The whole night.'

'Promise?'

She felt mean for doubting him, wanted so much to believe it.

'The whole night,' he said, holding out his hands. 'In Ra-heeee-ny.'

He pulled her from the bike and her lower back twinged.

'But I would walk five hundred miles!'

'Sssh,' he said. 'Be good.'

At the corner of the square, a battalion of foreign teenagers with yellow backpacks were squabbling and eating ice creams. One of them waved and said something in French.

'Ignore them,' Liam said. 'Come on. Let's go.'

'Où est la gare?' she shouted and they cheered.

'Kate, please.'

A light rain began to fall, speckling her arms fresh again. The students put up umbrellas and she could no longer see their faces.

'Les Pussies,' she shouted, but no one cheered now, and the high was starting to leave her, working its way through her, so sweet as it went. Parts of her body felt rent from each other. Her fingers were too heavy for her hands and her clutch fell to the ground, the contents spilling from it. She watched her phone bounce and then land on its back in the slope by the dock. Her coral lipstick made it as far as the bike lane.

'For Christ's sake.' Liam crouched and handed her the bag. Items appeared in front of her and she put each one back in it like a good girl: a miniature hairbrush, her keys, her ATM card, the loyalty card for the laser place, a dirty tenner, a tampon whose bright green wrapper was ripped and faded. She didn't know why she bothered to bring one around with her any more.

'Useless,' she said, taking it from him, pointing to the lipstick.

'*I'm* useless?' He strode off to the bike lane. He had misunderstood her but there was no way to explain. Eleven months and counting without a period. It was like a super-long pregnancy with no big belly and no baby at the end of it.

'No baby,' she said.

213

He'd picked up her phone, was wiping it with a tissue. They stared at each other. The rain fell harder now. There were drops running from his hairline. He didn't seem to notice or to care.

'What are you talking about, Kate?'

She knew she had to get it together, that they were on the brink of something and it would be her own fault if she ruined it. He was coming back to her place—to his place really. To their place? Someday. She steadied herself, holding her hand out for the phone.

'Nothing,' she said. 'Let's go home.'

He took her bag and fastened the clasp. She wrapped her arms around his neck, leaning against him, trying to tuck herself into the earthy smell of him, a trace on his shirt if she concentrated. 'I'm sorry,' she whispered. Her wrist burned suddenly and she went backwards, falling against a bike stand. She caught herself before the slope, looking down at her hands, at the thick band of grease across her palm. The dirt shimmered as if it was alive. A voice came from behind her, high and startling.

'William Carroll.'

A woman in a cocktail dress stood under a clear plastic umbrella, her blonde hair in a waxy, movie star wave. The man beside her had a tux jacket over his head, a gleaming white shirt, a dicky bow. They were tall and tanned and po-faced. They were swaying, dancing, the footpath sliding with them.

'Liam.' The man put out his hand. 'You're getting drenched.'

'I thought you and Joanna were in Chicago.' The woman frowned at Kate. 'Who's your friend?'

'This is one of Conville's lot,' Liam said in a stranger's voice. 'You know Anthony? Tony Fitz?'

'Fitzy!' the man said.

The woman was still staring at her.

'After-work drinks. Some of us had a bit too much.' Liam mimed drinking. 'Thrown out,' he whispered. 'I've spent the last half hour trying to convince one of the drivers to take her.' He pointed over her head.

'Good old Fitzy,' the man laughed. 'Knows how to keep the staff happy.'

'Are you all right, dear?' the woman said to her. 'Give her your coat, Liam. Jesus—it's practically translucent.'

Kate didn't know what she was talking about.

'You're right.' Liam took his coat off. 'We don't know how to handle the young ones when they get like this. I mean, she's not my responsibility. I just felt bad. Look at her. If I thought my Shauna—'

'Here you go, darling.' The woman gave the umbrella to the man and took Liam's coat, wrapping it around Kate. The mossy smell was exquisite. The umbrella was over them both now and Kate could see how wet it was, all the pretty drops thudding on the plastic.

The man laughed. 'Feels like we're back in Belfield, Carroll.'

'It's not funny,' the woman said. 'Get a taxi to come around the corner and I'll move her across.'

Liam vanished.

'I can walk,' Kate said.

'She speaks,' said the man.

'Come on, now, we'll get you dry. Watch the kerb. Watch the puddle!'

Her right ankle was submerged in cold all of a sudden but it didn't seem to matter. She was going home now. They were going home.

'I can walk,' she said.

'Help me,' the woman said.

'I'm trying to keep your hair dry,' the man said. 'Which do you want?'

'Liam Bloody Carroll. I'm telling Joanna.'

'He's only helping a young one home. Look at the state of her. You can't think.'

'She had her arms around him.'

'Still.'

'I've known Joanna since we were kids.'

Kate felt her balance go and suddenly there was sharp, burny pain in her palms and on her knee.

'Nicholas!' The woman's voice rang out. 'Help her—help her.'

Kate was up in the air then, wriggling in someone's wet arms, her knee still stinging. Then she was lying on a plastic bed and a stranger's voice was telling her to sit up, to stay awake.

She came round to a prodding at her shoulder and an old man's face far too close to her own. The sound of a scream went off inside her.

'Get out,' the man said. 'Come on, lass, shift yourself. You're here.'

With enormous effort, she sat up. The dirty cream paint of her apartment block was in front of her, a few metres away. Kate didn't think she could make it inside. She tried to lie down again but the old man was stronger than he looked and he yanked her out of the car, shouldered her to the door, got her into the porch somehow and told her that was all he'd been paid for.

'Look after yourself, lass. Get to bed.'

She eventually found her key and got it in the ludicrously small hole of the front door. In reception she sat on the floor beside the mailboxes and watched him drive away. Her keys were cold in her hands and she clasped her fingers around them, thinking how lucky she was to be inside, to have somewhere to go.

DUBLIN

Halloween 2018

KATE WOKE UP ON THE COUCH with a cotton-wool mouth and muddy fingertips. The room had an alien vitality, the grey walls pulsing, a low hum in the air. She wondered how long she'd been asleep. It could have been hours, days, weeks—time was a tightrope snapped in two. She felt like she'd gone hurtling through the ages. So many forgotten things, and somehow, all at once.

The brownie.

On the coffee table, the paper bag was empty, chocolatey marks across the front. It was a neat trick of this drug that it could make her eat and not remember. And yet, it was such a strange, debilitating kind of trip, unsuited to a woman of thirty-two, to the adult personality she'd woken up with one day that was afraid of everything new. She would murder her brother if it lasted much longer. Moving gingerly towards the window, she opened the curtains to a luminous sky, heavy with weather. Three storeys down, the car park was quiet, the mean light of the street lamps the only semblance of life.

Finding her phone, she went to play a song, something minimalist and repetitive, with notes she could absorb. She longed to call Ray but it was too much of a gamble. What if he showed up with Liz? No—no way. Kate was alone in this, and she would either get through it or die. She lay down on the couch. What did it matter if time was broken? We were all alive somewhere. She remembered Peter explaining this the morning after Elaine's funeral. He'd come into the bedroom to find her in Elaine's bed, under the peach duvet that still smelled of her sister. *It's OK*, he'd said. *You know she's still out there? We are all alive somewhere.* Back then, she'd thought he'd meant in heaven but now she wondered if he meant that all times were simultaneously occurring and the real tragedy was our inability to choose a location. To choose a home. It seemed no less crazy an idea than Catholicism and its incentivized promises of eternity. But this was just the brownie talking. Narcotic time—narcotic thoughts—could not be trusted. Elaine was long dead and the true tragedy of time was that it went on regardless in the one lousy direction.

Rolling off the couch, Kate spread her arms over the soft carpet, waving them up and down. There was a rippling below her waist, not exactly desire, but the memory of it—what it felt like to want. Her mind was a set of Russian dolls, one thought inside the next inside the next. She wanted to escape her brain, she wanted to move. Her body said no—an unfamiliar, frightening sensation. In real life she could always make herself go, even if she was sick. She might be weak and sluggish for the warm-up but once she got going, the ill feelings disappeared. Her local gym was open twenty-four hours. Kate imagined going there now, hopping on the mountain climber in the thin, artificial light, watching her shadow bounce in the window, and beyond it, only the dark. It was like dancing with no one, for an audience that didn't exist. She wondered why she'd spent so many nights there in recent months. It was something to do with restlessness. It was like science, or magic, the way you could convert one feeling into another. Lighter, fitter, happier, that old song, which really meant: less toxic. And there was the nebulous guilt if she didn't go, as if she was betraying some self-inflicted principle. Ridiculous. She remembered a booklet they'd given her in the hospital, all those years ago, which had said that anorexics were bright girls who tried too hard and pushed themselves over the edge. This had made her feel safe, another bit of a fact to add to her armoury: she wasn't one of those bright, try-hard girls like Miranda, or the blonde-ponytailed perfectionists who were always in the front row of lectures and the first in the library in the mornings, claiming the same seats every day, so that even when they were in the toilet or out for a cigarette, you could still see their ghosts in the nut-brown chairs, in the uneaten apples and empty coffee cups on their desks. The booklet had both absolved Kate and enraged her. Was there a similar information pack for all the bright, try-hard boys? She remembered asking Ray this question, in her most obnoxious college voice, in a pub one evening not long after she'd been discharged. They'd had a huge fight about gender politics while he'd stared at a few measly chips on her plate. Kate had clung to her arguments like a raft, desperate to talk about anything but herself.

Well, she was not that person now. But who was she? She'd been keeping secrets for so long, she'd started to keep them from herself. Stretching on the couch, she scoured the living room, trying to find something reassuring. Look—the tasteful paint on the walls, the charcoal carpet, the flat-screen television, the round-cornered coffee table with its smooth walnut finish.

And none of it was hers.

Who was she at all? Just a random woman in her thirties whose fine little life was falling apart. Impossible to isolate the problem. The break-up, which was connected to the apartment, which was connected to her job and her friends and her family, which was connected to the past, to her father, to Elaine, to the shared womb, to the mother they'd been cut out of thirty-six weeks later, to her scarred stomach that had never recovered. And who was so connected to where, all the messy 'W's, really, and the worst one of all: why. Why were any of them here? She was not suicidal—just a healthy appreciation of death. She'd known it from such a young age that it was impossible not to consider it, frequently, deeply. And maybe that was connected to the way she lived now, but on the other hand, she had a talent for hunger.

Yet there were other ways to be, she knew that. There were people like Ray and Liz in their four-bedroom Ranelagh red-brick—the future that everyone seemed to want. Miranda from college, who'd married at twenty-five and had some archaic number of children. Most of the girls that Kate knew wanted this kind of life—Diya, the HR team at work, the girls down the gym too. Single girls in their thirties, who weren't really girls any more. Oh, those tricky thirties. A decade of striving and uncertainty. A decade of want. Kate hoped her forties would be happier, though she knew it was foolish to be wishing her life away. Someday she'd look in the mirror at lines like tiny flesh-coloured tributaries around her eyes, and long to be thirty-two again, but it was impossible to imagine that time now, to try and leverage that future longing and turn it into approval in the present. Well, you couldn't leverage things that didn't exist, could you? She was being absurd. About what? Suddenly there was a blank horror in her head. Something in the ceiling or in the room, or in her own mind if she still had one, had wiped her memory.

When she came to, she was on the floor of the living room, curled into a ball. A weak winter sun was shining across the coffee table. Slowly she unfurled herself, the joints of her wrists cracking as she circled her hands. Her forehead was wet, her hair tight and damp against her head, and itchy at the back of her neck. She let her fingers at it until it hurt, a waxy lump coming away from her scalp, dots of blood along the rip. She put her hair in a topknot and touched the raw skin with her finger. Pulling her dress to her waist, she rolled off her tights. Her stomach was hollow and bloated, like she'd eaten too much of the brownie, but also not

222

enough. The drugs had tuned into some forgotten part of her: a voice, not even, a solitary note trapped silent inside her for years. She picked up a cushion and howled into the suede, the lonely cry of a secret outed.

The first time she'd starved herself—some day of that endless week of Elaine's funeral when the neighbours kept coming with tinfoiled plates, and her mother sat regal in the good room with vacant eyes and the meek, medicated voice of a stranger.

The next time—the day after the burial, disgusted by the food accumulating in the house: vats of lasagnes, quiches with lurid rinds, a cooked ham that was too big for the fridge and sat half-covered in the utility, her brothers hacking away at its globular carcass. She hadn't eaten a bite all day. It had been easy. She remembered Mammy noticing, then unnoticing. Suddenly, her mind started to churn, hundreds of thoughts like bats out of a cave, but as with anything concerning her mother, they were too vast, too dense to filter. Instead: another time and another time and another time—all that year, in fact, rolling up her dinner in kitchen paper, running to the garden and stuffing it through the cypress hedge for the foxes, or the rats.

But there were secrets in the centre of the secrets that were still trying to come out. She was just hoping to keep something for herself. Something to feel good about, something that wasn't tinged. Most of the time, she didn't care how she looked—as long as she looked exactly the same. It was reversion to a smaller version of herself, to childhood, maybe, though why she wanted to go back there was anyone's guess. For a split second, she saw herself: a vigilant, anxious woman who had turned away from life, from the deceptively endless sequence of events that occurred between birth and death.

Her mind cleared a little. She thought of her brothers at the dinner—Peter with his looks and questions, Ray with his godforsaken drugs. It was an intrusion into her life in Dublin. It was like they wanted her to live in chaos. Yet there was evidence, hard evidence that she was a functioning adult—her morning croissants, her chicken sandwiches, the sushi buffet she went to with Diya on Thursdays after work. Yes, there were plenty of days when she gorged herself. The pancakes she'd had with the maple syrup and cocoa nibs on the August bank holiday, the avocado smash she got in her weekend brunch spot and usually with an add-on of poached eggs. Would someone with anorexia ask for an add-on? She was certain they would not.

But—the dinner party.

The solitary note sounded again.

She'd tallied the bites when the others had left, but it was also true that she hadn't been able to eat at all. Still, another voice persisted—a scallop cooked in butter, at least a slice of red meat, some pastry flakes, the salt on the vegetables—didn't it all add up? No. But. Her mind was a saw, over and back, deeper and deeper, counting and countering. She had no sense of herself as an adult, of who she was or what she wanted. How come other people knew? Where did they learn it? She seemed to lack the capacity. It was like this messed-up moment was all she had, a hungry infant, unable to anticipate relief. This very evening she had thrown the Baked Alaska into the bin after hours of preparation, days—weeks—of planning, months and years if she was really getting serious. These were not the actions of a sane person. *The terrible sanity of the insane.* She had read the line somewhere and thought it would make a nice epitaph. At last, the tears fell quietly down her face. There was so much to mourn. All the people lost to her, all the years lost to hunger.

For a long time, she looked at the marks on the paper bag— filthy, liquidy squiggles. At some point, her stomach heaved and she ran to the bathroom. Gripping the bowl, she threw up. She vomited again before she'd time to wipe her face, and again and again, until there was nothing left but the slick bile on her fingers. She flushed the toilet, looked down into the clearing water and realized that her life was full of holes. Collapsing onto the tiles, she tried to find a point of concentration that might still the room. She fixed on the toilet paper holder, on the textured, double-ply roll she'd bought especially for the dinner party. All over her body, her nerves were stop-starting awake. A feeling that the world outside the bathroom was being ripped apart and if she let herself think about it, if she wondered long enough, there it was—the choice to go with it.

On the side of the bath she saw her razor. Then she was in the bath, taps running, her dress floating around her like weeds. Wrong way round, toes at the shampoo bottles, head heavy, the burn of the chrome T on the back of her neck. Underwater was a rainbow, orange and red wisps. The last time she went down, it was so warm and comforting that she felt she would stay there, that she'd found a kind of home, and here all along, hidden within the place she thought had been her home. Sinking into the haziness, she heard a banging in some faraway place. She tried to ignore it, but it grew louder and louder, bringing her back to the surface, horribly alive as a coughing fit sent her body into magnificent spasm. She dragged herself from the bath and lay shivering on the floor. Eventually, she peeled off the dress and crawled to the press beneath the sink. At her ankles, dozens of tiny nicks in the hollow beside the bone, thin lines of blood with dark red bubbles. She took a fresh toilet roll, broke the seal on the tissue and wrapped it around. Freezing, she sat for a moment on the tiles before getting to her feet and from there, into the woolly dressing gown on the back of the bathroom door.

The banging resumed as she walked into the hallway, and then, right out of another dimension, she heard the sound of her own name.

'Kate!' Ray's voice, outside her front door. 'Kate, Kate—let me in!'

She walked in a trance down the hall, opened the door and saw daylight in the corridor.

Her brother was in a Fila hoodie that was years old. 'What happened you?' he said.

'Nothing,' she said. 'I'm grand.'

'It's almost three, Kate. I've been calling since ten.'

'Time,' she said, shrugging.

'Tell that to Mammy.'

'Mammy?'

'I've had four phone calls—on the way over *alone*. She's been ringing all day when she couldn't get you. It's like she has a sixth sense.'

That was not the name for it, but she knew what he meant.

'She has me on tilt now. I left Liz and the girls at the zoo.'

'Oh,' said Kate. 'I'm sorry.'

He looked down at the ground, saw her ankles.

'Jesus, Kate. Let me in. You need—'

'I don't need anything,' she said. Though for the first time in a long time, she knew it wasn't true. She stood back from the door and let him pass. He looked like he might hug her but instead the two of them walked slowly to the living room, which was far messier than she'd realized. She looked briefly at the cushion pile on the ground, at the half-finished bottles of beer that were standing like miniature green sentries in various far-flung places. Ray said, 'Bloody hell.' Then they sat down on the couch and she started to talk.

DUBLIN

Halloween 2019

and the memory of a trauma, apparently. Once the alarm was tripped, it went on ringing. *Approach with caution* was how the therapist had put it. Kate had laughed out loud. She'd spent her life approaching the house with caution. There was no other way to get to Cranavon, or even the vicinity of Cranavon. But she was going there now as a thirty-three-year-old woman who had stopped yearning for a different past. At least that was the plan.

The traffic inched forward. A group of kids in costumes and a wet, harried-looking mother were going between the Georgian houses set back from the canal. Up the slope towards Portobello bridge, she could see the lights changing colours without a car getting through. The horns went off again. An old pop song came on the radio and her mood lifted. There was a lot to be grateful for this past year: her therapy sessions, reconnecting with college friends, the apartment with Diya off Pearse Street, her new job in HR (the surprise pay rise, the even more surprising friendship with Rachel). What else? Well, she drummed the steering wheel in time to the music, there was learning to drive, of course. And, also, slowly, slowly, learning to live. These days she was trying, really trying, and somewhere along the way the world began to try with her. Last week one of those human statues on Grafton Street, a young woman, painted head-to-toe in the colours of a unicorn, had jumped off a silver box to give her a coiled-up piece of paper. Kate had dropped a euro in the basket at her feet and was rewarded with a circus smile and the heavy flutter of the girl's lashes. On the bus home, Kate had read the message, which was written in Spanish and yet somehow understandable. *Si no cambiamos, no crecemos; si no crecemos no estamos vivos.* If we don't change, we don't grow; if we don't grow, we are not alive.

Well, it was a bit too real and timely. But maybe life was like that if you gave it a chance. She'd wanted to shout it on the upper deck of the bus, to the half-dozen passengers that were dotted in a zigzag pattern in the seats in front of her. Hello, sir, she'd wanted to say to the man in the plaid peak cap, are you giving life a chance? Instead she'd smiled at him and swung down the stairs just in time for her stop.

Kate almost caught the lights at the bridge, but the car in front stalled at amber and now its bonnet was poking into the oncoming line of traffic. A concert of horns started as cars tried to get round. Kate could see Ray standing under the awning of the café on the corner. She gave a beep but it got lost in the noise. He looked cold and uncomfortable, his back pressed against the shutters. He was staring at the footbridge, where the swans had come together in a fleecy white mass to shelter from the rain. Kate beeped again. The driver in front turned around and gave her the fingers. She pointed helplessly at her brother.

When she was through the lights, Ray hopped into the car, smelling of rain and cigarettes. 'It's wicked out there,' he said. 'We're going to be dead late.'

'Mind the bag,' she said.

'Fancy.' He put it on the back seat, along with her handbag and his rucksack. 'Were we supposed to bring presents? It's not a birthday party, you know.'

'That's not funny,' she said.

'Sorry,' he said sullenly.

She turned down the radio. 'Will you ring home and tell them we're going to be late?'

'Wait till we're off the canal.'

'Ray—'

'Kate, I'm not in the mood. I've had a rubbish day.'

'OK, OK,' she said.

'Two cancellations—it's like I've brought the curse with me. And everyone else in there is booked out.'

'Can you not take some of their clients?'

'It doesn't work like that,' he said.

They inched on in silence. Ray slumped against the window, half-dozing. When they got to the Red Cow, she gave him a dig and he took out his mobile. She turned down the radio and listened to the rings, picturing the old rotary phone in the hallway, though they had replaced it years ago with a sleek, cordless one with a terrible signal.

'It's me,' Ray said into his handset. 'Traffic is a nightmare. It will be half seven before we're down. The rain.'

Kate waited for the flurry, but it was Peter's voice that came muffled into the car. She made out *no bother* and said a silent thank you for her brother, who was like a human fort down there in Carlow, so solid and steady and able to withhold any weather. She wondered what would have happened if he'd never come back from San Diego. Would they even be here? Would she be here?

Ray hung up. 'No bother,' he said, in Peter's accent.

They both laughed, but she felt mean. 'He's great, you know— Peter,' she said. 'We're lucky to have him.'

Ray played with his seat belt, yanking it from the holder.

'Go gentle,' said Kate.

'Look who's car proud,' he said. 'How's the driving going? Have you figured out the roundabouts yet?'

'Shut up.'

He laughed.

'How are the girls?' she said.

'Ah, they're OK. Lia's been like a detective with the questions, but the other one doesn't give a rats. We've told them I need to be near work. I see them most evenings.'

'And Liz?' Kate switched lanes as they passed the big garden centre. She went to fifth gear and sped after a van.

'A bit better,' Ray said. 'We're going to counselling next week, actually.'

'Oh, yeah? That's great news.'

'Is it?' he said. 'I just want things to go back to normal.'

'Seriously, Ray. It saved me. I can't tell you how much.'

'Yeah, yeah, you're all New Age now.'

'It's not New Age! It's just talking.'

'Slow down,' Ray said, pointing at the left lane. 'Get back in there, boy racer.'

Without realizing it, she was twenty kilometres over the speed limit.

'Whoops.' She put her foot on the brake but stayed in the right lane. It was a release after the gridlock, to be hurtling down the motorway at last, the black road and the black sky and the bushes all black to match.

'The counselling will be good for you,' she said.

'Or it will finish us off. Liz has been trying to get inside my head for years. She thinks I'm messed up.'

'Yeah?' said Kate. 'But isn't everyone.'

Ray took a protein bar out of his pocket. He went to take a bite but she asked him to split it. The pair of them chomped companionably through the cookie dough texture. She didn't believe that protein bars were healthy, no matter what they claimed on the packet, but also she didn't care. She could be dead tomorrow. It was her new motto.

'What did it do for you?' Ray said, after a while.

'What?'

'Counselling.'

'Um,' she said.

'How did it work, like? She helped you with food,' he said. 'Obviously.'

'Yeah. She helped me a lot.'

'You look so much better.'

Kate bristled.

'Well, it's great,' he said. 'About the food.'

'Yeah.'

But it was so much more than that. The weekly sessions had helped to change her outlook on the world. For the longest time she'd thought there were only two kinds of people—the ones who were all dramatic and needy, and the rest, the people who clung on silently. Kate had learnt that it was better to talk about Elaine. And it was OK to be lonely, she didn't owe anyone an explanation for that.

'She taught me I could be someone else,' she said. 'Give up your story if you don't like it.'

'Right,' he said sceptically.

'Seriously. I guess—'

'What?'

She looked left, at his troubled, familiar face, so lovely in the blue dashboard light.

'I guess what I'm trying to say is that you don't have to be the person you were when you were young.'

'Jesus—no,' he said. 'I hope not.'

She laughed. 'Get the money ready for the toll, will you? It's there in the holder.'

When she turned into the driveway at Cranavon, the cattle grid gave a dull rattle. The front of the house was dark except for the light in the good room. It made the place look spooky, like a pumpkin with a half-smile. They parked behind Peter's Jeep and moved quickly across the tarmac in the rain. Neither of them had thought to bring a key. Kate wasn't even sure if she had one. A figure came down the hallway, shadowy in the frosted panels of the porch. Their mother opened the door and looked past them both, as if she was expecting someone else.

'Hello, Mammy,' said Kate.

'Welcome home,' her mother said. She was in her cream two-piece, as expected, though she wore no jewellery or make-up. Her face was pale, her grey eyes sunken.

'Sorry we're late,' said Kate.

Her mother gave a small smile and stood back to let them in. 'You're here now,' she said.

'Hi, Mammy,' said Ray.

'Hello, Raymond.'

In the hallway they all reached for each other at the wrong time, Kate getting her mother's shoulder, Ray taking Kate's elbow and their mother twisting left and right, so bony and frail in the middle.

'Oh,' her mother said, frustrated. 'Would you ever stand still.'

'Thanks for the group hug, folks.' Ray started down the hallway and they followed. Her mother's cream slip-ons made no noise.

In the kitchen, Peter was at the cooker, his broad back so reassuring, the hunch at the shoulders, the bear-like dip to the head. He brought a wooden spoon to his mouth and tasted some sauce. Curry, maybe. The room was warm with spice and onions.

'Ah,' Peter said, turning off the fan. 'Ye made it.'

'Smells delicious,' Kate said. 'I hope we haven't ruined it. The traffic was chronic.'

With the blind down on the big window, the space felt smaller than usual, the roof lower than she remembered, the red and white tiles brighter. She left her bags on the counter. Peter offered the spoon and she took a taste. The sauce had little lumps of meat, soft and fragrant—chilli con carne.

'What is it?' said Ray, sifting through the bowl of fruit on the island.

'Just chilli,' said Peter. 'I didn't have time for fancy.'

'He's barely home from his classes,' said her mother. Somehow, Kate had forgotten she was in the room, hadn't seen her sit down at the old oak table.

'What classes?' said Ray.

'Spanish,' said her mother. 'Again.'

Peter was doing the beginner course in the language centre for the third time. You had to go all the way to Carlow town if you wanted the next level.

'Is there any beer?' said Ray.

'On a Thursday?' her mother said.

'Yes, Mammy, on a Thursday.' Ray picked up an orange and pretended to pitch it at Kate. A speck of meat lodged in one of her back teeth and she pushed her tongue into the crevice to free it.

'Sure, it's Halloween.' Ray put the fruit back in the bowl and went to the fridge. 'And we're over eighteen.'

Her mother didn't laugh. 'It's your sister's anniversary.' She put a hand to her chest. 'My Elaine.'

'I know,' said Ray. 'Isn't that why we're here?'

Kate gave him a look.

'It's not a party,' said her mother. 'That's all I'm saying.'

'You should tell that to Kate. She brought presents.' Ray folded his arms and smirked. Even though he was wearing his physio uniform, the navy V-neck sweater and matching tracksuit bottoms, he looked like a boy again. She imagined his old Nirvana T-shirt under the sweater. And then she imagined giving him a dead arm.

'Presents?' her mother said, her face lighting up.

'It's nothing.' Kate went to the counter for the gift bag and put the truffles on the table. 'Just some chocolates for the chef. And a little something I spotted in town last week. I know you love the colour.' She passed the bag to her mother, unable to look her in the eye.

'Coral!' Her mother took out the cardigan and held it up. 'A beautiful colour. A stunning colour! For me? Aren't you very good? A pet. Thank you. I love it. Thank you. Thank you.' She took off her jacket and draped the cardigan over her silk blouse, fixed it this way and that, all the while thanking Kate. It was such a disproportionate response, it made the cardigan seem trivial and useless. It was only a wool-blend thing from M&S.

Her mother had gone to the utility door and was looking at her reflection in the dark columns of glass. Her delight continued to build, until it peaked, and they heard a soft sob.

'Ah, Mammy,' said Peter. 'What's wrong? It's a lovely cardigan.'

'I know,' her mother said, sitting down. She held the corners like a little girl clutching a pinafore. 'I know, I know. It's beautiful.'

Kate glanced at Ray for help, for distraction—anything. He was staring out the window at the darkness, his arms still folded in their brooding criss-cross.

'Coral was Elaine's colour too,' her mother said now, worrying the material between her fingers. 'Do you remember?' she said.

Kate nodded, though in truth she could only remember her sister in black or grey or army green, was sure she'd never gone near coral. Hadn't she hated the peach walls of their bedroom?

'My Elaine.' Her mother wiped her eyes.

'Our Elaine,' Peter said. 'She'd love the cardigan. And she'd love that we were all here, together, for her.'

Her mother blessed herself. In recent years, she'd become very religious. God was no longer a piss artist who could go piss himself. She'd started to *take mass* every morning since she'd turned sixty-five, or sixty-nine on her passport—Kate remembered the shock of finding it last summer in the bureau, the absurdity of her mother's lifelong lie. She gave an inappropriate giggle and they all turned towards her.

'Everything OK, Katie?' said Peter.

'Beer,' said Ray. 'Where's the beer?'

'It's in the utility room,' said Peter. 'I'll have one too.'

Her mother dropped her head.

'What about you, Kate?' said Ray.

'Oh, no,' she said. 'Not with the car.'

Her mother stood. 'You're not driving back tonight, are you? You'll stay.'

'Work,' said Ray matter-of-factly.

'Really,' her mother said. 'And how is work these days, Raymond?'

Ray ignored her and went out to the utility. Kate took a tea towel from the rad. She picked up the plates heating on the stove. 'I'll bring these in,' she said.

'Muchos gracias,' said Peter.

'No bloody Spanish tonight.' Her mother blessed herself again. 'Excuse my tongue, but he'd wear you out, Kate, with his *muy biens* and *por favors*. As if I have a clue what he's talking about.'

'You're great at languages, Mammy,' said Kate. 'On holidays, you always knew the right things to say.'

'All brains, that was my problem.'

The light in the room dimmed. Kate thought it was a trick of her mind until Peter told Ray to stop messing with the switch. He was over by the utility, fiddling with the dial, a six-pack of Heineken in his other hand, hanging loose, like a gorilla with its prey.

'Let's eat,' said Kate, watching her mother watch the beer.

'Yes,' said her mother. 'Good idea. Let us break bread.' She drew the cardigan towards her neck like a cape and started to glide away. Kate put the serving spoons on top of the plates and followed her saintly walk.

In the good room, the light above the table was at full wattage, shining on the settings—the heavy silver cutlery and linen place mats. There was no tablecloth this evening, just the iridescent turquoise table runner that Liz had brought back from some holiday years earlier, maybe as long ago as their honeymoon in Morocco. Her mother had never liked it. Kate watched Ray pause for a second as he noticed it too. Beneath the runner, the table looked hard and unfriendly, the polished wood unprotected, easy to stain. The rest of the room was in semi-darkness, only the small Lladró lamp in the far corner turned on, its child figurine forever in prayer.

The three of them had just sat down when Peter called from the kitchen to say he'd ruined the rice. It had boiled over and was like a paste. Could they talk amongst themselves? Beside her, Ray sighed at the news, but Kate felt oddly delighted, elated even. Though she'd been hungry on the way down, her appetite had left her. She poked at the gap between her molars. The meat fragment was gone.

Across the table, her mother straightened a fork. 'I'm ravenous,' she said. 'There's nothing worse than waiting for food.'

'Yes,' said Kate.

'So,' her mother said. 'Tell me everything. How's the flat? How's Daya?'

'Diya,' said Ray.

'That's what I said.' Her mother frowned. 'How is she to live with? Is she clean?'

'Oh, very,' said Kate, though this was not true at all. She spent her life picking up foil containers and half-finished bottles of Lucozade.

Her mother squinted at her.

'We get on really well,' said Kate, not wanting to tell another lie. How did her mother just know?

'She's a bit wild.' Ray drained his can. 'Always out, and those skirts.'

Kate kicked him under the table.

Her mother started a story about Marise Murphy's daughter, the one who used to wear nothing as a teenager. At the mention of pregnancy, Kate tuned out. In the kitchen, Peter was singing the very same pop song she'd been listening to earlier in the car. He had a fine melodic voice that she hadn't heard in years.

'Seriously? The big house after Myshal,' Ray was saying now. The conversation had taken a twist, and Kate tried to catch up. There were none of the usual words, no *wantons* or *hussies*, not even a cursory *unmarried*.

'Yes,' her mother said. 'The mansion. Did the whole place up while she was pregnant no less. She'll have five children under the age of ten. Five children. Can you imagine? She deserves a medal.'

Ray tipped Kate's foot, but she didn't engage.

'And to think,' her mother said. 'Marise Murphy's house was always a kip. She never cleaned, never went to mass, smoked and drank like a sailor. And all her children have turned out so well.' Her mother propped her elbows on the table and looked accusingly at Ray. Kate was relieved he was there to take the brunt.

'Oh, yeah?' her brother said. 'You *should* give her a medal so. Organize a ceremony.'

'All of them,' her mother said to Kate. 'Success stories. Even Phillip. Could you credit it?'

'Maybe it's because they were just a regular family who loved each other in their big godless pigsty,' Ray said.

It was a brave, dangerous move, and Kate couldn't help smiling.

Her mother turned sharply, losing one side of the cape. 'There's nothing funny about your brother and his situation,' she said. 'Don't encourage him—you.'

Kate glanced at the door to the kitchen.

'Tell us, please,' said Ray, opening a new can. 'What else has Marise been up to?'

'Oh, she has me withered,' her mother said. 'That woman never shuts up about her grandchildren. Twelve she has, with Phillip's three, and Brendan's. His wife had a new one just last week. Marise always has the phone out, lording her photos over everyone.'

Her mother continued to talk for the next five, ten minutes, maybe longer, time had been leeched out of the room. Kate looked at her animated face across the table and for once she didn't feel like screaming. It was sad that her mother was so afraid of silence, or of the words of her own children, the horror and love that might slip out if she gave them a chance.

'Maybe she's just happy to be a grandmother?' Ray said eventually.

'Maybe, maybe,' said her mother. 'You can stop your maybes. It's all show with Marise Murphy.'

'Can't you show back?' said Ray. 'Send her pictures of the twins. God knows Liz takes enough of them. Lainy is a monkey for the camera.'

'Well, yes,' her mother said. 'She's adorable, Raymond. They both are. But they're six now—it's not the same. It's all about babies these days.'

She looked at Kate and closed her mouth, pressing her lips together so that she suddenly seemed like an older, toothless version of herself. The silence had a heft to it. The light beamed on the table like a message from heaven. What could her mother possibly want her to say? There was no right answer. Perhaps she could just steal a baby before coming down the next time. Perhaps she could ask one of the sales girls if she could borrow one from the photos on their desks, whichever tiny bald creature was the quietest and most pliable. Though any of them would do, really. Her mother wouldn't care.

'I'll go and see if Peter needs help,' said Kate, rising. She'd taken off her blazer in the kitchen but she felt too exposed now in her work dress and its flimsy sleeves.

Ray looked like he might bolt with her. She nodded at the can of beer. If she was the designated driver, he had to pull his weight somehow. He sat back and gave a peaceable smile, asking their mother whether anyone had recently died. As Kate left the room, she caught two bridge deaths and a cousin of the vegetable man.

In the kitchen, Peter was still humming, tapping a yellow desert boot on the tiles. He jumped as she passed. 'I don't know what's wrong with me tonight,' he said. 'I've the willies.'

She put on her blazer and smiled. 'Halloween.'

'I didn't mean,' he said.

'I know.' She approached the cooker. 'Can I help with anything?'

'No,' he said. 'It's all done bar the rice.'

'Are you sure?' She stuck her head in the chilli to see if he'd gone overboard with the beans.

'No help needed,' he said. 'Definitely not with dessert, anyhow. Not after last year.'

She looked at him, offended. It was so unlike him to be mean. But his bright, wide face was as friendly as a cartoon dog, and she realized he was joking, that he didn't realize she'd thrown the Alaska in the bin on purpose. He smoothed his grey-blond fringe over to the side, the way he'd started to wear it to hide the triangles of flesh in his hairline.

'Shut up or I'll take the chocolates back,' Kate said.

'Thanks for those. You know she loves truffles.'

'I do,' she said.

'And you're very good to get her the cardigan. You saw how thrilled she was. She's very grateful these days—for everything. She's changed, you know. Changing.' He leaned against the counter. 'If we could just see you a bit more.'

'I know,' she said. 'I do. OK?'

'You're flying it though,' Peter said. 'Whatever it was last year.' He gave her a lopsided, meaningful look and she thought for one dreadful second that he knew about Liam. 'Whatever it was,' he said. 'You're doing so much better now.' His eyes scanned her like one of those X-ray machines at the airport.

'Yeah,' she said tetchily. 'I'm all good.'

'Just a few times a month,' he said. 'Come down here. Come and visit us. We'd love to see you for a full weekend.'

'OK, Peter. Watch the rice.' She pointed to the bubbling pot. 'I'm going for a wander.'

Up in their old bedroom, Kate left off the light and lay on the springy double bed. Her mother had bought it years ago, for guests she'd said, though Kate couldn't think of one person outside their immediate family who might use it. Still, her mother had done up the room. She'd replaced the peach paint with a striped gold wallpaper and matching cushions. The bedspread was a soft pink, with gold leaves that looked like teardrops from afar. It was a beautiful room now, worthy of a hotel, and it was a shame to think of it vacant. But what did she know, really? Peter was right. She wasn't part of Cranavon any more, didn't know what went on here between her visits.

So Marise Murphy had seven hundred grandchildren—so what. Her mother's response was typical. She was always so competitive about these things. But no, Kate sat forward on the bed. That was a narrow-lens view of things. If she was to survive this evening—this life—she had to go wider. Her mother didn't like

243

to win, she needed to win. It wasn't really a choice. In therapy Kate had talked about her mother's childhood, not the poor-me tale they all knew by heart, but the facts of the situation, which were brutal and difficult to argue with, as facts usually are. There was no need to go into the details. It was a fact: her mother had been afraid for most of her life. And if there was one thing Kate understood, it was fear. For years she'd sought safety in food, in her anorexia, to name it, which had little to do with how she looked. It was an emotional illness, a symptom or rather a solution, a way to deal with all the feelings she wasn't entitled to. Her mother, when it came down to it, was just afraid too. The strangest part of this realization was the rage Kate had suddenly felt at her father, her poor dead father who had married a difficult woman and done so little to help her, a woman whose crime was not being a field, a cow or even a tractor. There had been no manual in the box.

A flat, solid beam of light shone from the landing onto the back wall, almost reaching the window. Outside, the dark sky had pockets of brightness. When she came home, she always noticed the stars, so many more than in Dublin. She knew it was to do with light pollution, but some childish, romantic part of her liked to think of her father and sister, up there, floating in trillions of happy particles across the dark-bright folds. *We are all alive somewhere.*

On the ceiling of the bedroom, the occasional bump of plaster was the only reminder of her glow-in-the-dark planetarium. Kate missed getting lost in the patterns. She missed the posters on the walls too. She tried to remember the room as it had been—a space so familiar to her, so tangible and imprinted in her brain that as a child it seemed impossible she would ever forget. The old furniture was still in her memory—the number of drawers in the pine dresser, the way they split them, every second one, the way Elaine's stuff spilled over into her own. Their two single beds, flush against the walls, the pine locker between them. All gone. Even the wardrobes were different now. She remembered the peach one with the double doors; how they'd written the songs they wanted at their funerals on the back of it, behind their hanging clothes. A secret in a house where secrets were forbidden. Kate hadn't been brave enough to tell Peter or her mother before the funeral. It had been a private game, a dare between twins, not something that was supposed to be aired, or shared, or ever needed in real life. The only song she could remember was 'Everybody Hurts', and she wasn't even sure which of them had picked it. She would love to see their lists again now. But the wardrobe was gone, taken away and dumped, she supposed, along with everything else.

Kate closed her eyes and tried to picture other, smaller details. Smells, feelings, conversations, jokes. It was no good. The room was foreign to her now, like the dimensions themselves had changed along with the furniture. There was nothing for her here, not even a faint memory of her sister, or herself. Suddenly she realized that the only voice from the past left inside this room, this whole house, seemed to belong to her mother. She felt older than she had in years, a good feeling, like she was finally becoming the age she was meant to be. All her life time had played tricks with her, making her grow up too soon, then turning her back into a child when she needed to be an adult. Downstairs, Peter was calling her name. She got off the bed, straightened the covers and went to the landing. Two moths were frantic at the lampshade, batting their wings against the material, a soft thudding noise like an early morning rain. She switched off the light and left them motionless, suspended in the dark air, resting.

In the centre of the table, the rice was in a ceramic bowl with a clear glass lid. Peter lifted it as she ducked in behind his chair and a sweet, doughy smell filled the room. Beside the rice, there was a shallow bowl of spinach in a pool of green juice.

'Where were you?' her mother and Ray said within seconds of each other—a high-pitched fugue.

Ray had taken off his jumper and looked ready for a match in his stripy sports top.

'Upstairs,' said Kate, sitting down beside him.

Across the table, her mother was fidgeting with her hair. Her hand went to her neck, touching the skin around her collarbones. There were more wrinkles than Kate remembered, a diamond pattern criss-crossed in the hollow above the bone.

'Can we start?' Ray trowelled his mince, dropping his head as he took a bite, protective.

Kate peered at her own plate. Peter had served a large portion of chilli, bigger than she would have given herself, but she was hungry again and happy to eat. She turned up the cuffs of her blazer.

'What were you doing upstairs?' her mother said.

'Bathroom,' Kate said instinctively.

'What's wrong with the downstairs bathroom?' That voice again, the blunt insistence.

'Nothing.'

'Humph,' her mother said.

Peter took a seat at the head of the table, to the right of their mother, making an uneven party. Her mother gave a lonely sniff towards the empty chair on her left.

'Can you hold off a second, Ray?' Peter joined hands and rested them on his stomach. The pink shirt she'd gotten him last Christmas was loose at the shoulders. 'We'll just take a second.' He bowed his head. It was a dignified way to acknowledge the occasion, and she followed suit.

'You need to say something, Peter,' her mother broke the silence. 'A prayer.'

'All right, Mammy.' He spoke a few lines about Elaine, and then about Daddy, said he was thankful the family were here together to remember them.

'Amen,' said her mother.

'Amen,' said Ray, the fork already back in the chilli.

'Will I serve you, Mammy?' Kate stuck the silver spoon in the cake of rice.

Her mother nodded. She gave her a careful spoonful without spilling a grain, then went to serve herself.

'That's far too much,' her mother said. Using a fork and her fingers, she put most of the rice back in the bowl. Some of it fell onto the serving spoon. The others were watching, waiting for their turn. Kate put some rice on her plate and nudged the bowl towards Peter. He served himself and Ray, and the pair of them began eating. Kate took a mouthful of mince, washed it down with water. Across the way, her mother was moving the fork through her food in a painfully slow snake. The cardigan, Kate noticed, was no longer around her shoulders. Leaning across the table for the spinach, she saw a coral heap on the carpet beside her mother's chair. Peter was wrong. Her mother was not a grateful person. It was not in her nature to be thankful for the good things in life; rather she seemed only to notice them when they were gone.

'Where's your cardigan, Mammy?' Kate said, sitting back down.

Everyone looked at her in surprise.

'It's…' her mother said, patting her shoulders helplessly, 'it must have fallen. Peter.'

Peter retrieved the cardigan. Her mother made a fuss of fixing it over her shoulders, and Kate was sorry she'd said anything. Why couldn't her mother just wear it like a regular person? Why

247

did she need to act like a superhero in a cape? Perhaps it was too small, Kate realized, but the next size up would have surely caused offence. Oh, it was so hard to get anything right. She took a large helping of spinach and tried to pass the bowl to Ray, who made a face like he was sucking a lemon. She took another bite of her chilli, the meat dry and tangy. It caught in her throat and she coughed.

'More water?' said Peter, holding up the tinted glass jug.

'What about a beer?' Ray said, though it was clear he was not talking to her. He would be raging if she left them stranded here for the evening.

'Go on, so,' said Peter. 'You've twisted my arm.'

Ray reached over the side of his chair and yanked the remainder of the six-pack off the ground. He gave a can to Peter, took one himself and left the spare can with the plastic rings in the middle of the table.

'Could you take that off the table, please?' her mother said.

It was not an unreasonable request. Kate reached for the can, the empty rings jutting from it like tiny plastic nooses.

'Leave it,' said Ray. 'It's doing no harm.'

'It's no centrepiece,' said Peter. 'I should have got the candle out. The fat yellow one. I forgot.'

Her mother's face softened. 'No, Peter,' she said. 'That was my job.'

'Well,' said Ray. 'Now we have the can. It even sounds like candle. Perfect.' He let a crazed laugh loose on the room.

'Put it on the ground,' her mother said.

'Sure, it will be gone in a minute. Relax.'

Her mother's cutlery clattered on her plate.

They waited.

'Are you an alcoholic now, Raymond, as well as everything else?' she said.

248

In the silence, only the sound of Peter chewing. Kate wondered if the old CD player still worked. Even loneliness at Christmas would be better than a fight on the anniversary. She ate more rice without mince and left her fork to the side. She couldn't handle a meltdown. *Approach with caution* wouldn't get her far in a thunderstorm. It wouldn't get you over a puddle, really.

Ray tilted the can to his mouth, smacked his lips.

'Cop on, Ray,' Kate muttered.

'Raymond,' her mother said.

'Yes, Mother? Mother dearest.'

'Are you a drunk? A boozer?'

'Not really,' said Ray. 'I just like to give you something new to complain about each time I come home. I know how much you need that.'

'Do you hear that tone?' Her mother challenged Peter, who in turn eyeballed Kate.

'You're never happy, Mammy,' said Ray. 'It's like you need something to worry about.'

'I *care*,' her mother said. 'All I've ever done was care about my family. And look—'

'He's only having a can or two, Mammy,' Kate smiled. 'That cardi is lovely on you. It's definitely your colour.'

'A can?' said her mother. 'There's five of them gone. I might be old but I'm not blind.'

'Blind? Not you, Mother,' said Ray.

'Peter!' The colour came up on her mother's face.

'Leave off, Ray,' said Peter. 'Do ye not like the chilli, or what?' He pointed to their plates.

Her mother wrinkled her nose. 'It's fine,' she said. 'Perfectly fine.'

Ray left down the can and began to shovel huge forkfuls of mince into his mouth, barely pausing to swallow. 'Delicious,' he said, still chewing. A chunk of meat hit the table runner with an oily orange mark. 'Scrumptious, Peter.'

'Look—' Her mother stood, pointing. 'You've messed on the runner. Liz's runner. The beautiful runner from Africa.' She made it worse with her napkin.

'An antique!' said Ray, still shovelling food.

'Stop it, Ray,' said Kate. 'You're not a child.' She nudged him with her elbow and a grain of rice flew off his fork, high into the air.

'Oh, but it's delicious,' said Ray. 'We're having such a nice meal. Isn't that right, Mother?'

'I don't know what I've done.' Her mother sat weightlessly into her chair. 'For a child of mine to wag his tongue at me this way. I don't know why—'

'You know!' Ray dropped his cutlery. 'You always know exactly what you're doing. With your subtle table decorating and your not-so-subtle accusations. She said—' He turned to Kate, 'when you were gone upstairs, she said—'

'There's no one called *she* in this house,' Peter frowned.

Ray pushed his plate away from him and even Peter downed tools. Nobody was eating their dinner.

'*She*,' said Ray. He was furious now, sparks of spit coming from his mouth. 'She said that I deserved to be on my own.' He shifted forward, pressing his hands on the table. There was an alcoholic heat off him, from his breath or his pores, a staleness that made her think these few cans were merely a continuation of some heavier, earlier session. She didn't know how she'd missed it on the way down.

'I did not say that,' her mother said.

'You did!'

'I said, that you—'

'You used those exact words.' Ray banged his hand on the

table. 'You said I deserved it. When, well you know how much I miss—' His voice went high and crackly.

'What I said, Raymond, is that you only have yourself to blame. There's a difference.' Her mother sat straight in her chair and sniffed the air. She bunched her shoulders in such a way that two coral-coloured horns gathered on the cardigan.

'Well, now,' said Peter.

Kate glared at him. It was not OK that her mother was like this, that she couldn't bear to be near a problem without deciding on a culprit. At Cranavon, bad things did not happen by chance.

'We'll leave it there,' Peter said. 'Can we go back to eating our dinner?'

Kate watched Ray's hands grip the table, his fingertips a waxy white. She was afraid to turn towards him, afraid it might upset him further.

'Mammy, there's not a huge difference between those two things,' she said. 'To be honest.' An image of Elaine flashed in her mind, not Elaine the teenager, but the older, desperate face she'd seen trapped in the television the night of the brownie. 'You're basically saying that Ray deserved it. And he didn't deserve it, Mammy. They're just going through some stuff. And they're sorting it out. Like adults.'

'Like adults?' her mother said. 'Is that it, Kate? Aren't you very grown-up all of a sudden?'

She could sense Peter shaking his head.

Beside her, Ray gave a grunt.

'You two have always been thick as thieves,' her mother said. 'You've always been against me.'

Kate knew she could leave right this instant if she wanted to—she had her own keys of her own car in her own bag—and she had her own flat back in Dublin as well, but she was here now, one foot already in the bog. She could limp away as usual or wade on in.

'For or against,' said Ray to himself. 'Some family.'

'Excuse me, Raymond?' Her mother came forward but the fight was gone from Ray. He sagged in the chair and drank his can.

'Look, Mammy,' said Kate, attempting Peter's calm manner. 'All I'm saying is that nobody deserves to have their family broken up.'

'Don't you think I know that?' her mother cried. 'There's only one thing breaks up a family.' She looked at each of them in turn, her grey eyes shining. 'Death.'

Kate felt a sliver of sympathy. She hadn't thought about it that way.

'Death,' her mother said, again. 'My father. My husband. My child. Don't talk to me about broken families.'

The sympathy disintegrated, which was unfair, really, as unless her mother had drawn her attention to it, she wouldn't have seen it at all—but the woman did not know when to stop. This was the problem. Once she had your ear, she needed to devour every last part of you.

'Raymond is disgracing himself,' said her mother. 'Instead of trying to fix his family, he's taken to the bottle.'

Again, Kate could see some shard of truth in what she was saying, but it was all wrong, the way it came out, and it was never just about the person at hand.

'Would you leave him be?' Kate said. 'He's having a few drinks. He's just trying to—' She searched around for what she wanted to say, could not find it.

'To escape,' said Peter.

He hadn't said anything for a while, and they all cast their eyes towards him, waiting for more. A kidney bean had fallen onto his shirt, was resting on the lip of the pocket. Against the fine pink material, it almost looked like a logo. He stared back at them with deep, sad eyes.

'To escape from what?' her mother said.

Ray was so far back in his chair he seemed to have deflated. 'From life, Mammy,' he said wearily.

Her mother humphed. She finished her water and gave a triumphant, knowing smile. At the sight of her thinning lips, Kate suddenly found what she'd been trying to say.

'It's not from life, Ray.' She turned to her brother, tried to grasp his fingers which refused to come out of their fist. 'You're escaping from this house, from whatever's inside you, that's inside me, that's inside all of us. Even you, Peter.'

She expected Peter to stop her, but his arms were folded and he seemed, from the head of the table, to look down at them from afar, like a judge without a gavel, or a judge who had retired and given back his gavel after seeing too many innocents go down.

Her mother pushed her chair from the table and went to stand.

'You're escaping from her,' Kate said, without even meaning to. But once it was out it had a leaden truth. 'You're escaping, by whatever means necessary, from the way we learned to live.'

Her mother stayed in the chair, trembling now, the coral horns moving too.

'All I ever did,' her mother started. 'I did for this fam—'

Across the table, Kate watched the dry corners of her mother's mouth. It was moving, moving, and she was aware in a general sense of the sounds coming out of it, could probably, if she had to, repeat the lines verbatim, except that right now they didn't seem to land at all. It was as if a magnificent glass sheet had been lowered from the heavens onto the table, splitting her from her mother. Hundreds of thousands of thoughts were rushing through her brain and, as usual, she couldn't decide which of them mattered. She could never seem to pin down in words the

253

angry, hurt atmosphere they had lived with, that was unable to be measured in increments of time, that blended and weaved with periods of happiness, and days and months and years of service that were all bound up in this one formidable woman at the centre of everything. All Kate had ever wanted, she suddenly realized, was to live in a house where a mother might say: I'm struggling, today was a hard day. Instead she lived at Cranavon, whose singular motto was always and would ever be: I'm suffering, look at what's been done to me.

'And *you*—' Her mother was pointing a bony finger across the table at her.

Kate couldn't help smiling. She imagined it going through the glass, could see the tip, the pearly pink varnish on the nail, poking out the other side, while the rest of her mother's hand was trapped behind the pane. She knew then that she didn't need to tell her mother what was in her head. She'd said enough.

'We all know what kind of a life you,' her mother went on.

Blah, blah, blah, thought Kate, who could feel a bubble of a laugh somewhere inside her. She looked at Ray, his face the colour of ash. She smiled at him, wanting him to feel this ease she now felt, wishing she could squeeze it out of her in drops and give it like a tincture to both her brothers, and to her mother too, if there was any left over.

'An affair with a married man!' Her mother stood and threw her napkin at Kate. It didn't reach its target, which was her face, landing instead in the middle of her chilli.

The glass pane shattered. It disintegrated in front of Kate's eyes, in some deft, feverish magic trick. In full focus, her mother was a sight, her face a mottled pink, the white-blonde eyebrows disappearing in the wrinkled fury of her forehead. Her bottom teeth jutted out. She grasped the cardigan, flung it on the ground.

'You,' she said to Kate, slapping the air. '*You're* the real disgrace of this family. The true homewrecker.'

As she went on with her name-calling and insults, Kate tried to hold her gaze. A hot, drumming sound made it hard to follow the sentences. She looked away, down into the room, to the lamplit couches, and beyond them into the darkness where the bureau was just a bulky shape by the window, the photos impossible to make out.

'A married man with *children*,' her mother said now. 'Children! Your father would be ashamed of you.'

Kate felt the tears warm on her face.

Ray moved his chair closer. 'It's over,' he said. 'It's over a long time. Leave Kate alone.'

'Yes, of course,' her mother said. 'Poor Kate. Little Katie. The men are always on your side. So nicey, nicey to the men. Wouldn't say boo to a man.'

Kate knew what was coming next.

'Just like your grandmother!' Her mother guffawed. 'Meek and mild Kate. Wouldn't hurt a fly. Well, I know—I know, we *all* know what you are. And don't you forget it.'

Kate pictured her father looking down on them, shaking his head at his daughter; the slut, the homewrecker, the hussy, and all the other names that were still flying from her mother's mouth. And her mother was right. Daddy would be ashamed of her, and he would be angry—his big hands curling and uncurling, the pulsing vein on his neck—that she had tried to break up that most important and indestructible of units: a family. But unlike her mother, Daddy would blame himself, that he hadn't taught her the right way to live, that he'd let her loose into the world without morals or sense. And he would be sad, too, that his daughter, his little girl, his favourite (it was OK to say it now, years later and no one around to care), that his Kate had chosen such a lonely

255

path in life that a few dates a month with a man she barely knew was enough to constitute love.

'Are you done?' Kate heard a voice say. She moved away from Ray, wincing at a loud bang. But it was not some random object flying through the air and smashing off the wall behind her. Peter had smacked his hand on the varnished wood, his dinner plate still clattering in its wake. He stood, all six foot four of him, and loomed over the table. The triangles at his hairline were shiny with sweat.

Her mother turned to face Peter, placing her hands on her hips.

'It's you who's disgraced yourself tonight, Mammy.' Peter's voice was slow, thick-tongued.

'I have not,' her mother said.

'You've disgraced yourself. And this house. And the memory of Elaine.'

'You're the one who told me, Peter,' her mother said. '*You're* the one who spilled the beans.'

Kate tried to catch her breath. Peter was wringing his hands. 'I only told her so she might understand, Katie,' he said. 'So she would be kinder to—'

'What's kinder got to do with anything?' her mother shouted. 'A married man. With children.'

Ray said, 'You shouldn't have done that, Peter.'

'I thought—'

'You thought you'd wade in as usual.'

'You're the one who told me!' Peter said.

Kate looked at Ray, whose squirmy little face told her it was true. Of course it was. How else would they know?

'But Mammy didn't understand,' said Peter sadly. 'She took up the wrong meaning.'

'Oh, go away, Peter,' said her mother. 'I'm sick of the sight of you.' She put a hand behind her and felt for the chair. How could she do it, Kate wondered, how could she change from a ferocious, ageless creature into a pitiable old woman with one simple gesture of her hand? All of a sudden, Kate wanted to go over and help her.

'Pardon me?' said Peter.

'Do you think I love looking at your big mug every day for the last forty-two years?' Her mother took a seat.

It was strange to hear the number out loud like that—four long decades and already into the fifth. Kate waited for Peter to sit. Her eyes willed him into the chair, to drop onto the crushed velvet cushion and bring stability to the house once more. Across the way, her mother had started to scour the table, picking up anything within range—her fork, a glass, the silver salt cellar.

'Is that right?' Peter said.

Her mother didn't reply. The anger had left her, like a wave rolled to shore, reduced to a crusty foam. Kate saw now, in the relative peace of her movements, how much her mother needed her rage. And it was not just her mother. Kate had a memory of herself and Elaine as children, maybe seven or eight, locked in the upstairs bathroom, bruised and sore from the tea towel, or the wooden spoon, or whatever ordinary household item had been used in that particular instance. Very clearly she could see them both: Elaine roaring her hurt into the world, and herself silent in the corner, watching the door. The people who shouted out in life survived. Her sister should have survived. But for the first time in her life, Kate realized it wasn't her fault. It wasn't anyone's fault. She looked at the bright ceiling light until her eyes started to water. As a hand covered her own, she shivered and came back to the room. The hand was light and dry, the nail polish shimmering as the fingers withdrew. She looked at her mother and something passed between them.

257

'Is that right?' Peter repeated.

'It's OK, Peter,' said Kate. 'Let it go.'

'I will not let it go,' said Peter. 'This day has been coming for a very long time.' He stepped back from the table. 'Mammy—I'm moving out of Cranavon. I'm moving in with Serena.'

'Who?' said Ray.

'Who?' said Kate.

'His Spanish teacher,' her mother said with an eye roll.

'You know?' said Peter.

'Of course I know. You big fool. Who does the same course three times? No child of mine, that's for sure.'

'You *know*?' Peter was even more incredulous this time. He put a hand through his fringe.

'I always know,' her mother said.

In an evening of truths, this was no exception. Kate felt she owed her mother the acknowledgement.

'You do, Mammy,' she said. 'Actually, you always do.'

Her mother gave a stiff nod and tucked her hair behind her ears. When she looked up, their eyes locked and for a moment Kate thought she might smile. It felt as if her mother was noticing her for the very first time, that Kate alone was enough to fill the space.

'Serena who?' said Ray, ruining the moment. 'There's no Serenas in Tullow.'

'She's from Kilkenny,' Peter said.

'Ooh,' said Ray.

Peter glared at him, but you could see it was bravado. He kept glancing at their mother.

'You can move out whenever you want, Peter,' she said, with a majestic wave. 'Or you can move Serena Donnelly in here if you'd prefer. You know the farm belongs to you.'

Kate agreed instantly, Ray murmured his assent a moment later.

Peter started to laugh. 'Are you serious, Mammy?' He rocked on his heels. 'Are you fucken serious?'

Ray was next to go, then Kate and even their mother—all of them laughing, a maniacal, homely laugh that took the evening into its fold.

'Is that the first time you've ever cursed, Peter?' said Ray eventually.

Peter held out a hand, doubled over, gripped his left side. 'Stop,' he gasped. 'Stop it.' He settled into the chair once more and raised his glass. 'To our sister Elaine,' he said. 'For looking down on this house tonight and bringing it more happiness than I ever thought possible.'

'Oh, Peter,' her mother said, with a sob. 'You've got me going again.'

And it was not just Mammy this time. Kate nodded through her tears, smiling in solidarity at the blurry version of her mother across the way.

Ray woke up when they were on the canal. 'What time is it?' he said.

'Twenty to eleven,' said Kate. 'You'll be in bed before you know it. Only a few more bridges to Portobello.' She wondered what his bedroom looked like. She had offered to help him move but he'd said he was only bringing a bag.

Ray yawned and put his hands on the dashboard, stretching. 'Do you think?'

'What?' Her eyes were tired and she blinked at the road. The Luas glided past them in its easy, muted way.

'Ah, nothing.' He tapped on his phone, laughing occasionally. She resisted conversation, knowing how prickly he could be when he had to multitask. She got off the canal at the bridge and pulled in by a bus shelter on Richmond Street.

'You know,' said Ray, pointing to a takeaway with a neon sign, 'I'd murder a kebab.' He undid the seat belt. 'That chilli feels like it was hours ago.'

'Well, it was,' she said.

'And the coffee cake was dry as dust.'

'Mammy's trusted recipe never lets her down,' said Kate.

They laughed.

'Seriously,' said Kate. 'It was like pencil shavings on the outside.'

'Do you fancy?' Ray gave her a bemused look. 'Ah, you've work in the morning. We both do. Well, I hope I do.' He stared out the windscreen at the road, still greasy from the rain.

She reached over and patted his hand. 'You'll get back on track,' she said, trying to quell her eagerness to bolt, to kick her poor brother out of the car and leave him to delight alone upon the many takeaways that all seemed to be empty but open, with glistening hunks of meat rotating in the windows.

'I know,' he said. 'If I can survive a night like that at home, I can survive anything. I was texting Liz to tell her. She—' He looked at the keys in the ignition. 'I better let you go.'

'No, go on,' she said. 'Tell me.'

He leaned in and gave her a kiss on the cheek. 'Next time. Let's catch up soon. OK? Thanks for the lift.' He opened the door and got out. A smoky night chill came into the car.

'Ray!' she said.

'Wha?' He ducked down to her level.

'Get back in,' she said.

'Why?'

'Just get in!'

He sat into the car and shut the door.

'How about we go to my place and order pizza? Have some wine.' She smiled at him and started the engine. 'So I can tell Mammy you're a committed alcoholic and all.'

He grinned at her. 'Seriously?'

'Yeah,' she said. 'Let's do it.'

A double-decker bus loomed in her rear-view mirror—an urban whale with a deep, blasting horn. She put on her flashers and pulled away as quickly as she could.

The apartment was in darkness when they got in. Kate switched on the hall light and held a finger to her lips. It wasn't a hall, really, just a small space for shoes and coats. They snuck into the living room and closed the door. Ray left his rucksack in the corner beside the dead spider plant. The orange security light from the swimming pool building across the street shone in the long rectangular windows, turning the leather couch a strange green until she switched on the reading lamps. Ray moved a couple of Diya's work tops off the cushions and sat down.

Kate drew the roller blind. She gave a quick smile to the statue of the countess in front of the swimming pool. She'd started to think of her as a friend, which almost seemed like a normal thing to do in comparison to some of her past imaginings. She'd even christened the little dog statue at her feet.

'Good old Copernicus,' she said to Ray.

Ducking in behind the dining table, she reached for the shoe-box on top of the cube-of-cubes bookshelf that had taken herself and Diya two weekends to assemble.

'He was a great dog,' her brother smiled. 'The best dog.'

'We all loved him.' She sat at the table, took the lid off the box and rooted through the menus.

'Except Mammy,' said Ray.

'Mammy loved him too. I used to catch her giving him treats when she thought no one was watching. *You hungry, good-for-nothing mutt*, she'd say, and then she'd make him give her the paw.'

'Is that where he learned it?' Ray said.

'It's where he learned everything,' said Kate. 'He'd never do a tap for me.'

'Except lie all over you. You were inseparable about the house. Myself and Peter used to joke that he was your real twin.'

Kate gave a loud, raucous laugh that was not unlike a bark.

'See?' said Ray.

'Poor Elaine,' she said. 'She'd kill you.'

'Seventeen years.' Ray took off his runners. 'Isn't that nuts?'

Kate felt her throat constrict. She nodded, continuing through the menus. There were at least five for Domino's but none for the wood-fire place on Dame Street. She put back the box and reached for her handbag.

'I have it here,' said Ray, bringing over his phone.

'How did you know which place?'

'I know,' he said. 'I *always* know.' He did their mother's squinty eye.

Laughing, Kate took the phone. 'There's a bottle of white in the fridge. You know where the glasses are?'

Ray saluted and headed for the kitchen. She could hear him stomping his way down the corridor and she wondered how someone could make so much so noise in their socks. She hoped he wouldn't wake Diya. It wasn't that her friend would mind—she was great like that, always up for the chats, able to adapt, to bend to the demands of the day—but rather that Kate wanted to have her brother to herself for once. She'd learnt something about family this evening, even if she couldn't name it exactly, just a vague sense that it was important to have Ray here, to talk to him like a human being, to make an effort with him like you would with some stranger at the water cooler in work.

'Ta-da!' He came back with the bottle of white and two mugs. 'No clean glasses,' he said. 'Scummers.'

'Sssh,' she said. 'Diya.'

'I think we're safe. Her door was open.'

Kate remembered then—the Halloween table quiz in the Ferryman. There was a strong chance if they'd won, or if they hadn't won at all, that they'd go to Coppers. She checked Ray's phone. It was gone eleven. 'We better order,' she said. 'What do you want?'

'Pepperoni.'

She scanned the list, though she knew already. 'There's no pepperoni.'

'Meat,' he said. 'Sausage, salami, ham, whatever.'

'They have that exact one.'

As he filled the mugs, she put the order through online: a large spicy chorizo pizza and a starter of chicken wings. Then she went into the kitchen to heat the plates.

When she came back to the living room, Ray made space for her on the couch.

'Did you go medium or large?' he said.

'Large,' she said. 'And wings for the craic.'

'Good woman.' He cupped his chin in his hand and looked at her.

She waited.

'So, what's the latest in work?' he said. 'How's Red Sole Rachel?'

She looked straight at him, into the flecked green of his eyes.

'Thanks, Ray,' she said.

'For what?'

'For not making a big deal out of it. I just want everything to be normal. I want to be normal. And I'm getting there.'

'I know,' he said. 'I *always* know.'

It was less funny this time. She had a flash of her mother saying goodbye after dinner, fumbling for Kate's hand and then bringing her close into a taut, promising embrace.

Ray took another glug of wine and made a face.

'What?' she said.

'It's no Sancerre, I'll tell you that much. You're lucky Liz isn't here.'

He gave a twinkly smile and she knew it was OK to go with it. 'Liz knows her wine,' she said.

'You mean she's a wine snob,' said Ray. 'And she's proud of it too.' He moved over on the couch. 'You know, she went looking for that Sancerre after your dinner party. The very same one. Went to three off-licences and a supermarket before she found it.'

'Why didn't she just call me?' Kate said.

'You weren't—'

'What?'

'You weren't exactly in the best frame of mind.'

'You mean the brownie?'

'I mean the lot of it.'

'Well,' she said. 'I've no idea what wine it was, anyway. I only remember that it was warm.' She checked her phone to make sure it wasn't on silent.

'I can't believe you managed to get a dinner up that night,' he said. 'You looked like you were going to faint from the moment you opened the door.'

The wine went down the wrong way and she coughed.

'Are you OK?' Ray sat forward. 'Do you want a slap on the back? A kick up the arse?'

She laughed, which made it worse. Ray went to his rucksack and took out a plastic gym flask. She sipped at it until she felt better. He poured them both more wine, leaving only an inch in the bottle. She wondered if they were done talking about the dinner party.

'You're all right now,' said Ray. 'I hate when things go down the wrong way.'

Kate left the flask on the table and put on a playlist on her phone. '80s rock anthems—the scratchy, rumbling guitar of 'Welcome to the Jungle'.

'Will you still be able to hear the delivery guy?' Ray frowned.

'You sound like Peter,' she said. 'Stop worrying.'

Ray smacked a hand off his thigh. 'Peter the secret romancer. Did you suspect?'

Kate shook her head.

'And Mammy knowing it all,' said Ray. 'I can just picture her in her blue dressing gown, peeking out the blinds. Can't you see it?'

'I can't believe she managed to keep it to herself. Peter thinks she's changing.'

'A leopard,' said Ray, raising his eyebrows.

'A leopard in a royal blue dressing gown.'

The two of them howled laughing.

'I wonder what she looks like,' said Ray.

'Who?'

'Your one. Serena. It's hard to imagine him with anyone. Except Mammy.'

'Ah, stop, Ray,' said Kate. 'He's only forty-two.' The number had stayed with her. Why had they never done anything for his fortieth, or his thirtieth? For his next birthday, Kate would throw him a party.

'I wonder if they've shagged,' said Ray. 'Can you imagine Peter—'

'Stop it! Come on. He deserves to be happy. Aren't you happy for him?'

'I am,' said Ray, looking towards the curtains. 'Of course I am.'

In the slump of his shoulders, she could see his own losses cloud in around him.

'It's OK, Ray,' she said.

'Wha?'

'I know you're happy for him.' She made a face. 'Ser-eena. I'd say she's a looker.'

'You think?' Ray grinned. 'Like Mammy?'

'No, I'd say she's different. Something else entirely.'

'Hopefully,' said Ray. 'Or he won't live it down.'

She pointed a finger. 'You'll be nice—either way.'

The chorus of 'Another One Bites the Dust' was cut off by her phone ringing.

'Hiya,' she said, picking up. 'No, we're the next block down. No. Opposite the leisure complex.' She listened to the delivery guy list a number of locations that were nothing to do with her. 'Can you see the statue of the woman and the dog?' He gave another rush of detail down the phone. 'Yes, that's the dog I mean. I'll be down in a flash.' She hung up.

'Good old Constance,' said Ray. 'Still helping out Dubliners a century on.'

Kate picked up her handbag and asked him to get the plates from the oven. 'The light will be green,' she said.

Ray rubbed his hands together when she came back into the room. He took the boxes and hunkered on the ground beside the low-slung table. There were newspaper sheets spread out on the clear glass surface. As he went to open the pizza, she noticed the smudged print on his fingers.

'Wash your hands,' she said, tearing off a sheet of kitchen paper from the roll.

'Too hungry.' He gobbled half a slice in one go. 'Hot, hot,' he said.

'You're a pig.' She put the playlist back on, leaving her phone on the armrest.

Kate looked at the pizza, a vast circle of oily white and red, the cheese all melty in pockets. She went for a knife but there was no need. The slices broke away easily. She felt the old resistance as she picked one up, the flour from the dough coating her fingers, but she brought it quickly to her lips and took a bite, another bite and another, until it was gone.

'Sgood,' said Ray.

'Yeah,' said Kate, though she hadn't tasted much at all. She went back for a second slice. Ray was already on his third. She tried to go slower with this one, but it was hard to do. Mindful eating didn't seem to work for Kate. She just needed to eat and not think. If there was a voice inside her head talking to her about food, she knew now to ignore it. This was the task. There was no second guessing or see-sawing allowed—no thinking necessary at all. And distraction worked too.

'When do you think we'll meet her?' Kate wiped her fingers on the kitchen paper and finished her wine.

'Peter's bird?' said Ray.

'Buurd,' she said, wagging a finger.

Ray shrugged. 'Soon, no doubt. Mammy will want a dinner, a fuss.'

'I don't know,' said Kate. 'She seemed to think it was the most natural thing in the world for her to just move into Cranavon. There wasn't a hint of a tantrum.'

'She's afraid she'll be left alone,' said Ray. 'That's what it is. She's old—and getting older.'

It was true. They both stopped eating and looked at each other.

'What if…' said Ray.

'Don't say it.'

'What if Peter moves out?' Ray gnawed on a crust.

'I don't think he will—the farm. Or if he does, it won't be far.'
She pictured her mother sitting at the oak table alone, staring out the window at the fields like she used to do when Daddy was late. What did it mean to have no one to wait for?

'You know,' she said, 'I think Mammy would be OK. Sometimes I think she's better on her own. She only gets in moods with other people.'

Ray tucked into a fresh slice.

'And you know what?' she said. 'I kind of get it. People can be exhausting.' She reached over and turned down the music. 'I'm going to try and visit more.'

'Yeah?' he said. 'Brave.'

'I'll keep it nice and breezy. Go down for a day, maybe a night. But regular, like.'

'Really?' Ray held up the wine bottle, offered her the remainder. She covered her glass and he poured it into his own.

'Well, I'll try,' she said. 'I mean, she's not going to be here forever.'

'Hurrah!' Ray held up his glass.

'Seriously, Ray. One day she'll be gone. And then there's nothing.'

'Then there's peace,' he said. 'Peace and quiet.'

'Or else there's not.' She couldn't explain it to him, not right now, maybe someday. She couldn't really explain it to herself, just had an inkling—some wizened shadow of the future—that there was no ending when it came to family, only beginning, and beginning again.

Instead she said, 'Family is important.'

'Ah,' said Ray, 'I'm almost getting teary.'

She picked up one of Diya's shaggy cushions and tossed it at his face.

'Mammy will outlive us all,' he said. 'She'll hang in there for the sympathy.'

They laughed. Kate left her last slice of pizza in the box. She was full.

'Four children,' she said. 'Imagine. Peter's right—it's some job. I can barely look after myself. You know, a lot of the time, Mammy did OK.'

'Hmm,' said Ray. 'But I will thank her for this evening. I was texting Liz about tonight and she said we'll get back together if only to spite her.' He roared laughing. 'Liz always had her measure.'

'Jesus,' said Kate. 'Remember that Christmas?'

Ray covered his head with the cushion, emerging with a grimace.

'You and Liz will work it out,' said Kate. 'I'm sure of it.'

He nodded and looked away.

She let him be.

'I'm going to go,' he said, already getting up. He wiped crumbs off his tracksuit and took a neon yellow jacket from his rucksack. She walked him to the door, offered to call a taxi.

'Gonna stroll,' he said. 'Get some air.'

He gave her a quick hug and turned to leave.

'Bye,' said Kate.

'Thanks for the pizza,' he said. 'I needed it.'

She closed the door and went back to the living room, surveyed the mess, which was not a mess at all but an empty container of wings and a cardboard box with a slice and a half of pizza leftover. In their poky, windowless kitchen, she put the full slice on a plate, covered it with tinfoil and left a note for Diya.

Eat me, she wrote, and afterwards, a smiley face.

In bed, she left on her old polka-dot reading lamp and began to doze in the easy orange light of the room. She felt the evening sliding inside her, like the disjointed middle of a dream, so many remarkable things she wanted to remember but they were whirling up, getting ready to leave. And they were jumbling, the images, the faces: Peter standing tall with his news of the future, and Ray pulling his chair closer, and then their mother, her mother, the metallic sheen of her eyes and the clawed hands of all that worry and hurt. Kate could see herself too, could see the four of them now sat around the table, existing in the same space together. Surviving. Really, she thought, they were all strange, troubled individuals but beside each other, they were very clearly a family. You could not call it anything else. It was all they had, and it might be enough. This was something she could imagine her father saying. Perhaps he had said it once. As she drifted, she could hear the odd car speed down the street outside. It was half twelve and she'd be tired for work tomorrow, but it would be a rich, comforting kind of tiredness, so unlike the hollowed-out feeling of sleepless, hungry nights. It would be a tiredness in her body rather than her soul. Of all the anniversaries of her sister's death, this was her favourite, which was a weird way to think, perhaps, though she knew Elaine would get it. Her sister, who would always be her sister, wherever she was. She turned in to the wall and pulled the duvet tight around her, her head sinking into the pillow, her breath warm against it, in and out, warm and trickling, and so alive.

TOPICS FOR DISCUSSION

1. '"Everything is ok," she said out loud to no one.' (12) Kate is a character in denial for much of the book. In what ways does this manifest? Is it noticeable in other characters too?

2. The idea of splitting is important in the book, both in terms of the twin relationship, and in Kate's eating disorder, which sees her lead a double life. Is Kate 'living for two' (33), or is she living only half a life?

3. 'It was different for all three of them, Kate saw that now for the very first time.' (149). How are each of the Gleeson siblings affected by their family tragedies? How do they try to distract themselves from their pain?

4. There is plenty of dark humour in *Dinner Party* to offset the tragedies. Who is the funniest character and why? Ultimately, is the book a sad or hopeful story?

5. The messy web of family is at the heart of the book. Did you feel like the siblings have a supportive relationship? Has Bernadette as matriarch helped or hindered these relationships?

6. Much of the drama of the novel revolves around Bernadette and her erratic behaviours. Did you feel sorry for her at all? Is she a victim or a product of the society and age of the times?

7. The book explores mental illness in various guises. Kate sees her eating disorder as a solution, rather than a problem. Why do you think this is? The other characters can be helpless in the face of such certainty and rigidity. In what ways do they try (and sometimes fail) to connect with Kate?

8. 'Oh those tricky thirties. A decade of striving and uncertainty. A decade of want.' (222) What do you think of this characterisation of being in your thirties? Why do you think Kate's struggling came to a head at this point in her life?

9. 'Rag Doll... serious student by day, absolute mentalist by night' (125). Do you feel like Kate becomes a different person when she goes to university? How is leaving home a catalyst for her character to change?

10. The beginning of the book offers a version of an alternate life: the twins running away together from the farm and family. Do you think Kate's life would have turned out differently if Elaine had lived?

Acknowledgements

To my editor Laura Macaulay and all the team at Pushkin, for their enthusiasm and hard work in getting this book out to the world. To my agent Sallyanne Sweeney, who does her job with such skill and grace. To my fellow students of creative writing, and all my teachers on the UCD MFA 2019, particularly Anne Enright and Gavin Corbett, for their help and engagement with early drafts of this book. To Claire Keegan, for her brilliant writing workshops. To Frank McGuinness, Sinéad Gleeson and Lucy Caldwell, for guidance and encouragement along the way.

Thanks to Susie Orbach for her books *Hunger Strike* and *Bodies*, to Laura Freeman for *The Reading Cure*, to Dr Jennifer Gaudiani for *Sick Enough: A Guide to the Medical Complications of Eating Disorders*, all of which helped to inform the novel. To the Arts Council of Ireland, for a literature bursary that gave me time to redraft this book. To Martin Doyle of the *Irish Times* and *The Stinging Fly*'s Declan Meade, for giving me the chance to read so many books and stories. To my teachers over the years who passed on their love of writing.

To friends who have helped me with this book and earlier writing, Fionnuala McInerney, Colin Corrigan, Stuart Cross, Joanne Murphy, Mikey Stafford, Kieran Nolan, Paddy McKenna and Paula McGrath. To Jane Lanigan, for her expertise on the horseriding world. To Henrietta McKervey, for her considered feedback and good humour. To Sheila Purdy, who is one in a million as a reader and a friend. To my two families, the Gilmartins and the Bavalias, for all the support and generosity down through the years. Lastly to Sunil, for living with a writer, and for the free hugs.